↑

NAOMI

A Novel by
JUNICHIRŌ TANIZAKI

Translated and with an
Introduction by Anthony H. Chambers

NORTH POINT PRESS
Farrar, Straus and Giroux
New York

This translation is based on the ChuoKoran-Sha, Inc.
edition of *Chijin No Ai*, published in 1985. *Chijin
No Ai* was serialized in issues of the *Osaka Asahi*
and *Josei* in 1924.
Published by arrangement with Alfred A. Knopf, Inc.
Cover design by David Bullen
Cover painting courtesy of a private collection
Library of Congress catalog card number: 90-52851

North Point Press
A division of Farrar, Straus and Giroux
New York

Sixth printing, 1999

The earthquake that devastated Tokyo and Yokohama in 1923 was a dramatic turning point in Tanizaki Jun'ichirō's career. For almost a year, he had been living a fast life on the Bluff, the home of most of the Westerners who gave Yokohama its cosmopolitan reputation. The earthquake forced him to evacuate to Osaka, where he settled down to wait for Tokyo and Yokohama to rebuild; but, unlike most of the other refugees, he stayed on in western Japan. Though he visited Tokyo from time to time, he would never again live there.

Thirty-seven years old at the time of the earthquake, Tanizaki had made a name for himself as a writer of audacious, sometimes shocking, stories, plays, and motion-picture scenarios. But it was only after the earthquake that he wrote his first important novel, *Naomi*. (The original title, *Chijin no Ai*, has often been translated as *A Fool's Love*.) The move and the novel pulled him out of a slump and initiated the long succession of masterpieces that continued until his death in 1965. Today, *Naomi* is one of the two or three works for which Tanizaki is best remembered in Japan.

The novel is, among other things, a vivid evocation of popular culture in Tokyo between World War I and the earthquake: the "operas," reviews, and movie theaters of Asakusa; sea bathing at Kamakura; and, above all, the cafés of Asakusa and dance halls of Ginza. Though Tanizaki was sometimes regarded in the 1930s and '40s as a conservative in cultural and aesthetic matters, he had embraced the popular culture of the early twenties with real enthusiasm. He was so convinced of the importance of movies that he devoted most of 1920 and 1921 to writing scenarios for a Yokohama studio. He also approved of social dancing and ridiculed conservatives who considered it degenerate. Here is what he wrote on the subject in 1922:

> My [wife's] younger sister learned to dance from a Western friend and got the rest of the family interested. Her first pupil was my daughter, who's seven this year. I began by cheering her on from the sidelines.
>
> When I stayed for about a week at the Kagetsuen Hotel in Tsurumi [Yokohama] to do some writing, I found that there was always a dance going on in a hall next to the dining room where I ate dinner every night. It looked interesting, and I went in to watch. Finally, the hostess, Madame Hiraoka, said, "Why don't you give it a try, Mr. Tanizaki?" She introduced me to the basics. I've always been clumsy, though. I didn't learn much, and before long I checked out of the hotel; but it seemed a pity to give it up once I'd started, so I began to take lessons from a real teacher, a Russian named Vasily Krupin, who lives in Yokohama and gives lessons twice a week on the second floor of a certain café. Besides my wife and me, the pupils are two foreign married women and the daughter of a physician on the Bluff. Social dancing is more difficult for men than for women. It took the women about a month to learn the one-step, the fox trot and

the waltz, in that order; but after a month I was just getting started on the fox trot. Then summer came, it got too hot to practice, and I stopped going to the lessons; but I still go shamelessly to dance at the Kagetsuen now and then. I don't have the courage to dance with anyone I don't know, because, from what I've seen, I'm the worst dancer there. Kume [Masao, the novelist; 1891–1952], on the other hand, is rather daring. He says that he's never taken proper lessons; the best way to learn is to be brave and dance with a variety of partners. The younger you are, the quicker you learn. Everyone says that my daughter is much better than I.

The evils of dancing? Perhaps there are some, but nothing is without its evils. In my case, anyway, it's entirely wholesome, because I go with my family—wife, sister, and daughter. It's preposterous for men who spend their time in teahouses to say that dancing is unwholesome. Dancing makes a person feel young, cheerful, and lively, which alone is enough to make it far better than a teahouse party. Besides, it's economical. Young and old alike should plunge into it. Whether people think dancing is good or bad, there's no going against the trend of the times. No doubt dancing will grow more and more popular. I very much hope so.

The character of Naomi is often said to have been inspired in part by the sister-in-law who sparked Tanizaki's interest in dancing.

Tanizaki was less enthusiastic about cafés, and his comments give us a clear idea of the sort of place Naomi worked in:

... I have a strange aversion to cafés. The reason is that they appear to be places for eating and drinking, whereas in reality eating and drinking are secondary to having a good time with women, and yet the women aren't always at your side to wait on you. Such a shady, ambiguous setup is distasteful to me. I'm not sure how cafés are now [in 1929], but that's what they were like when I knew them. A café was a place where you went to run after women, not to have a good time with them. I have no use for a mean, sordid, craven pastime like that. . . .

The few times that I've been taken to cafés, there was hardly anything to drink. If you order tea, the smell of rust clings to it; the brandy and whiskey are usually diluted. I don't know why their customers put up with it. . . .

Another phenomenon of the early twenties was the "modern girl" who, in defiance of Japanese convention, cut her hair short and wore high heels, went to movies, danced, played sports, and was open, frank, and hedonistic. Naomi was one of the archetypes of the "modern girl," so much so that her name and "Naomi-ism" became household words. Tanizaki's own thoughts on the Westernization of Japanese women are suggested in a 1931 essay entitled "Love and Lust":

The influence that Western literature has exerted on us has taken many forms, without any question. One of the most important, in my view, has been "the emancipation of love," or, to take it one step further, "the emancipation of sexual desire." The literature of the Friends of the Inkstone group, flourishing in the 1890s, is reminiscent of the *gesaku* writings of the Tokugawa Period; but with the *World of Literature* and *Myōjō* movements and the popularity of Naturalism, we forgot the circumspection of our ancestors, who held that love and sexual desire were utterly base, and abandoned the proprieties of the old society. . . .

While literature reflects its age, there are times when it moves one step ahead and points the way for the will of the age. The heroines of *Sanshirō* and *Gubijinsō* [1908 and 1907, by Natsume Sōseki] are not descended from the women of old Japan, who, according to the ideal, were to be gentle and demure; somehow they are like characters in a Western novel. While in reality there may not have been many women like them in Japan at the time, society hoped for—

dreamed of—the appearance, sooner or later, of the "awak-ened, self-aware" woman. In greater or lesser degree, all of my contemporaries who aspired to literature had this dream in their youth.

Yet dreams and reality rarely coincide. The elevation of Japanese women, encumbered by centuries of tradition, to the position of Western women would require many generations of spiritual and physical cultivation. It could not be accomplished in our generation. . . . I will confess now that, in my youth, I was one of those who embraced this preposterous dream and felt a terrible loneliness at the realization that my dream was not about to become a reality.

Serialization of *Naomi* began in March 1924, in the *Osaka Asahi* newspaper. Just before publication commenced, Tani-zaki wrote:

. . . For someone who writes as slowly as I do, each install-ment is a full day's work. Newspaper novels are painful. . . . Whether I like what I'm writing or not, whether I'm feeling inspired or not, I have to write an installment every day.

I always begin the first installment with the intention of writing something good; but the newspaper novels that I've written in the past have generally begun well and ended poorly, because I forced myself to write willy-nilly. This time, however, I'm prepared. I don't want to let the same thing happen again. I expect to maintain my inspiration and enthusiasm to the end.

The novel was received enthusiastically by the young, progressive readers who coined "Naomi-ism"; but government censors were less pleased, and their warnings were reinforced by objections from conservative readers, perhaps the same sort who found dancing to be unwholesome. Bowing to pressure, the newspaper ceased serialization in June 1924, after eighty-seven installments had brought the novel to the middle of chapter 16. Tanizaki wrote at the time:

For reasons of its own, the newspaper company has asked me to forgo serialization of my novel *Naomi*. Recognizing that there is no alternative under the circumstances, I have complied with their request.

Nevertheless, this novel is my favorite of recent years, and my inspiration is at its peak. As soon as I can, I shall find another magazine or newspaper in which to publish the remainder. . . . This I promise my readers.

Serialization was in fact resumed five months later, in the magazine *Josei*, and proceeded without incident until the novel was completed.

It can be deduced from topical references in the novel that Naomi was born in 1904 and Jōji in 1891. The action begins in 1918 and ends in 1926. Since the last installment was published in July 1925, Tanizaki was projecting the last part of the story about one year into the future.

In the translation, personal names and ages are given in the Japanese style: family name precedes given name; and the calendar years in which one has lived are counted, rather than the number of full years elapsed since the day of birth.

To approximate Japanese pronunciation, pronounce the consonants as in English and the vowels as in Italian or Spanish.

Friends have helped at each stage of the translation. In particular, the first draft benefited from the scrutiny of Robert Campbell and of my parents, Pauline and Curtis Chambers. It happens that my parents are precisely of Naomi's generation (though not of her temperament); their recollections of the twenties and their reactions to the novel have enhanced my own enjoyment and understanding. The translation is dedicated to them.

ANTHONY H. CHAMBERS

NAOMI

I

I'M GOING to try to relate the facts of our relationship as man and wife just as they happened, as honestly and frankly as I can. It's probably a relationship without precedent. My account of it will provide me with a precious record of something I never want to forget. At the same time, I'm sure my readers will find it instructive, too. As Japan grows increasingly cosmopolitan, Japanese and foreigners are eagerly mingling with one another; all sorts of new doctrines and philosophies are being introduced; and both men and women are adopting up-to-date Western fashions. No doubt, the times being what they are, the sort of marital relationship that we've had, unheard of until now, will begin to turn up on all sides.

In retrospect, I can see that we were a strange couple from the start. It was about seven years ago that I first met the woman who is now my wife, though I don't remember the exact date. At the time, she was a hostess at a place called the Café Diamond, near the Kaminari Gate of the

Asakusa Kannon Temple. She was only in her fifteenth year and had just started working when I met her. She was a beginner—an apprentice, a budding hostess, so to speak, and not yet a full-fledged employee.

Why I, a man of twenty-eight, had my eye on a child like that, I don't understand, but at first I was probably attracted by her name. Everyone called her "Nao-chan." When I asked about it one day, I learned that her real name was *Naomi*, written with three Chinese characters. The name excited my curiosity. A splendid name, I thought; written in Roman letters, it could be a Western name. I began to pay special attention to her. Strangely enough, once I knew that she had such a sophisticated name, she began to take on an intelligent, Western look. I started to think what a shame it would be to let her go on as a hostess in a place like that.

In fact, Naomi resembled the motion-picture actress Mary Pickford: there was definitely something Western about her appearance. This isn't just my biased view; many others say so, even now that she's my wife. It must be true. And it's not only her face—even her body has a distinctly Western look when she's naked. I didn't learn this until later, of course. At the time, I could only imagine the beauty of her limbs from the stylish way she wore her kimono.

I can't speak with any assurance about her disposition in the days when she was working in the café; only a parent or a sister can understand the feelings of a fifteen- or sixteen-year-old girl. If asked today, Naomi herself would probably say that she simply went about everything impassively. To an outsider, though, she seemed a quiet, gloomy child. Her face had an unhealthy look. It was as pale and dull as a thick pane of colorless, transparent glass—having just begun work there, she hadn't yet started to wear the white make-up the other hostesses used, and she hadn't gotten to know her customers or her fellow workers. She tended to hide in a corner as she did her work silently and nervously. This may also be why she looked intelligent.

Now I must explain my own background. At the time, I was an engineer with a certain electrical firm, earning a monthly salary of one hundred and fifty yen. I was born in Utsunomiya, Tochigi Prefecture. After finishing middle school I came to Tokyo, where I enrolled in the higher technical school at Kuramae. I became an engineer shortly after graduation and every day except Sunday commuted from my rooming house in Shibaguchi to the office in Ōimachi.

Living alone in a boardinghouse and earning one hundred and fifty yen a month, I had a rather easy life. Though I was the eldest son, I was under no obligation to send money to my parents or siblings. My family was engaged in farming on a large scale; as my father was dead, my elderly mother and a loyal aunt and uncle managed everything for me. I was completely free. This doesn't mean that I led a fast life, though. I was an exemplary office worker: frugal, earnest, conventional to a fault, even colorless, I did my work every day without the slightest complaint or discontent. In the office, "Kawai Jōji" was known as a "gentleman."

For recreation, I'd go in the evening to a movie, take a stroll on the Ginza, or, once in a great while, treat myself to an outing at the Imperial Theater. That's the most I ever did. Of course, being a young bachelor, I had nothing against the company of young women. Still a country bumpkin at heart, I was awkward with people and had no friends of the opposite sex, which no doubt is what made me a "gentleman." Yet I was a gentleman only on the surface. Each morning, as I rode the streetcar, and whenever I walked in town, I secretly used every opportunity to observe women closely. Once in a while, Naomi would appear before my eyes.

But I hadn't concluded that Naomi was the most beautiful woman in the world. In fact, there were many women more beautiful than she among the young ladies I passed on the streetcar, in the corridors of the Imperial Theater, and on the Ginza. Whether Naomi's appearance would improve was something only time would tell; she was only fifteen then, and I viewed her future with both anticipation and concern. My original plan, then, was simply to take charge of the child and look after her. On the one hand, I was motivated by sympathy for her. On the other, I wanted to introduce some variety into my humdrum, monotonous daily existence. I was weary from years of living in a boarding-house; I longed for a little color and warmth in my life. Indeed, why not build a house, I thought, even a small one? I'd decorate the rooms, plant flowers, hang out a birdcage on the sunny veranda, and hire a maid to do the cooking and scrubbing. And if Naomi agreed to come, she'd take the place of both the maid and the bird. . . . This is roughly what I had in mind.

In that case, why didn't I find a bride from a respectable family and set up a proper household? The answer is that I simply lacked the courage to marry. This requires a detailed explanation. I was a commonsensical person who didn't like to act recklessly—indeed, was incapable of doing so; and yet I held rather advanced, sophisticated opinions about marriage. People tend to get all stiff and ceremonious when someone mentions "marriage." First, there has to be a "bridge-maker," who tries in roundabout ways to learn what the two sides are thinking. Next, a *miai* is arranged—a formal meeting of the two parties. If neither side has any objections, an official intermediary is chosen, engagement gifts are exchanged, and the trousseau is carried to the groom's house. Then there is the bridal procession, the honeymoon trip, and the bride's ceremonial visit to her parents—a very tiresome set of formalities, which I thoroughly disliked. If I'm going to marry, I thought, I'd like to do it in a simpler, freer manner.

At the time, there would have been any number of candidates had I wanted to marry. It's true that I was from the countryside, but I had a strong constitution, irreproachable conduct, and, if I may say so myself, at least average good looks, and the trust of my company. Anyone would have been glad to help me. The fact is, though, that I didn't want to be "helped." Even if a woman is a great beauty, one or two *miai* are not enough for prospective partners to get to know each other's temperament and character. The idea of choosing my companion for life on the basis of a casual impression—"Well, I could live with that," or, "She's not bad-looking"—is too foolish. I couldn't do it. The best approach would be to bring a girl like Naomi into my home and patiently watch her grow. Later, if I liked what I saw, I could take her for my wife. This would be quite enough; I wasn't interested in marrying a rich man's daughter or a fine, educated sort of woman.

Moreover, to make friends with a young girl and observe her development, day by day while we lived a cheerful, playful life in our own house—that, it seemed to me, would have a special appeal, quite different from that of setting up a proper household. In short, Naomi and I would play house, like children. It would be a relaxed, simple life, not the tiresome existence associated with "maintaining a household." This was my desire. The "household" in modern Japan requires that every cabinet, brazier, and cushion be in its proper place; the chores of husband, wife, and maid are fastidiously distinguished; hard-to-please neighbors and relatives must be humored. None of this is pleasant or beneficial to a young office worker, as it requires a good deal of money and makes complicated and rigid what should be simple. In this respect, then, I considered my plan an inspiration of sorts.

I first spoke of it to Naomi after I'd known her for about two months. During that time, I'd gone to the Café Diamond whenever I was free and contrived as many opportunities as possible to talk to her. Naomi was fond of the movies, and would go with me on holidays to a theater in the park. Afterwards we'd stop for a bite of Western food or some noodles. Even on these occasions, she hardly said a word; she usually had such a sullen look that I couldn't tell whether she was happy or bored. Yet she never said no when I invited her. "All right, sure," she'd reply docilely, and follow me anywhere.

I didn't know what sort of person she thought I was or why she came with me, but I supposed she was still a child who regarded men without suspicion, and that her feelings were uncomplicated and innocent. My assumption was that she came with me because I took her to the shows she liked and treated her to dinner. For my part, I was a baby-sitter, a gentle, kindly uncle; I never behaved in any other way, nor did I expect anything more from her than that sort of relationship. When I recall them now, those fleeting, dream-like days seem like a fairy tale, and I can't help wishing that we could be again the guileless couple we once were.

"Can you see, Naomi?" When there was no place to sit, we'd stand at the rear of the movie theater.

"I can't see a thing," she'd reply, straining to stand on tiptoe, trying to see between the heads of the people in front.

"You won't be able to see that way. Get up on this rail and hold my shoulder." I'd give her a boost up and seat her on a high handrail. Legs dangling and one hand on my shoulder, she seemed to be satisfied as she gazed intently at the picture.

When I asked, "Are you having a good time?" she would only say "Yes." She never clapped her hands or bounced with joy; but I could tell how much she liked the movies from her face as she watched in silence, her intelligent eyes wide open like those of an alert dog listening to a distant sound.

"Naomi, are you hungry?"

Sometimes she'd say, "No, I don't want anything." But more often, when she was hungry, she'd say "Yes," without the slightest reserve. Then, when I asked, she'd tell me whether she wanted to eat Western food or noodles.

2

" N A O M I , you look like Mary Pickford." This came up one evening at a Western-style restaurant in which we'd stopped after seeing a Mary Pickford movie.

"Oh?" She didn't seem particularly pleased. She looked at me quizzically, as if to ask why I should say such a thing out of the blue.

"Don't you think so?" I persisted.

"I don't know if I look like her or not, but everybody says I look Eurasian," she said nonchalantly.

"I'm not surprised. To begin with, you have an unusual name. Who gave you a sophisticated name like 'Naomi'?"

"I don't know."

"Your father, maybe, or your mother?"

"I'm not sure . . ."

"Well, what does your father do for a living?"

"I don't have a father."

"And your mother?"

"I have a mother . . ."

"How about brothers and sisters?"

"Oh, I have lots—a big brother, a big sister, a little sister . . ."

These subjects came up again from time to time, but whenever I asked about her family, she'd look annoyed and give evasive answers.

When we went someplace together, we usually arranged to meet at a certain time at a bench in the park or in front of the Kannon Temple. She was always on time and never broke an appointment. Sometimes I was late for one reason or another, and would worry that she might have gone home; but she was always right there waiting for me.

"I'm sorry, Naomi. Have you been waiting long?"

"Yes, I have." She didn't seem to be particularly resentful or angry. Once we were to meet at a certain bench, when it suddenly began to rain. I wondered what she'd do. When I got there, I was touched to find her crouching under the eaves of a little shrine by the pond, waiting for me.

On these occasions she wore a well-used silk kimono— probably a hand-me-down from her sister—with a colorful muslin sash. Her hair was done in a traditional style appropriate for her age, and her face was lightly powdered with white. On her little feet she wore tight-fitting, white Japanese socks, patched but nonetheless smart. When I asked why she did her hair in the Japanese style on holidays, she just said, "Because they tell me to at home." As usual, she didn't offer a full explanation.

"It's late. I'll walk you home." I made this suggestion a number of times, but she always said, "That's all right. I can go by myself. It's not far." When we reached the corner by the Hanayashiki Amusement Park, she'd say good-bye over her shoulder and run off toward the alleys of Senzoku.

—I almost forgot. There's no need to dwell too much on the events of those days, but we did have one rather intimate, leisurely talk.

It was a warm evening at the end of April; a gentle rain was falling. Business was slow in the café, and it was very quiet. I sat for a long time at my table, sipping a drink. That makes me sound like a great drinker, but in fact I hardly drink at all. To pass the time, I'd asked for a sweet cocktail of the sort that women drink, and was nursing it slowly, one sip at a time.

When Naomi brought my food, I asked, "Won't you sit down here for a minute?" I was somewhat emboldened by my drink.

"What is it?" She sat down obediently beside me and struck a match when I took out a Shikishima cigarette.

"You can talk for a few minutes, can't you? You don't seem to be very busy tonight."

"It's hardly ever like this."

"Are you always busy?"

"Morning to night. I don't have any time to read."

"Do you like to read, then, Naomi?"

"Yes, I do."

"What do you read?"

"I look at all kinds of magazines. I'll read anything."

"I'm impressed. If you enjoy reading so much, you ought to go to girls' school." I said this deliberately and looked into her face. Perhaps she was offended; she turned up her nose and stared off into space, but the sad, helpless look in her eyes was unmistakable.

"Naomi, would you really like to study? If so, I can help you." She still said nothing, and so I added in a more cheerful tone, "Speak up, now. What do you want to do? What would you like to study?"

"I want to study English."

"English and . . . anything else?"

"Music."

"Well, then, you ought to go to school. I'll pay your tuition."

"But it's too late to go to girls' school. I'm already fifteen."

"Fifteen isn't too late for girls, only for boys. And if you just want to study English and music, you don't need to go to school. We could hire a tutor. How about it, Naomi—do you feel like going into this seriously?"

"Well, yes. . . . Would you really do that for me?"

"Yes, indeed. But you couldn't go on working here. Would that be all right with you? If you're willing to quit this job, I wouldn't mind looking after you. I'll take full responsibility and bring you up as a splendid young woman."

"Yes, that would be fine," she said without the slightest hesitation. Her prompt, definite answer startled me.

"Do you mean that you'll quit your job?"

"Yes."

"That might be all right for you, Naomi, but you ought to ask your mother and brother what they think."

"I don't need to ask them. They won't say anything." So she said, but I was certain that she was more concerned than she appeared to be. Unwilling to give me a glimpse of the inner workings of her family, she was pretending there was nothing to worry about. I didn't want to pry when she was so reluctant; but to fulfill her desires I'd have to call at her home and discuss things thoroughly with her mother and brother. As our plans progressed, I asked her repeatedly to introduce me to her family, but she was strangely unenthusiastic. Invariably she'd say, "You don't need to meet them. I'll talk to them."

There's no reason to make Naomi angry by airing all her family linen; she's my wife now, and for her sake, for the sake of "Mrs. Kawai's" good name, I'll dwell as little as possible on the subject. It'll all come out someday; and even if it doesn't, anyone will be able to guess what sort of family hers was, if he considers that her home was in Senzoku, that she was sent out to be a café hostess at the age of fifteen, and that she didn't want anyone to see where she lived. Not only that: when I finally prevailed and met her mother and brother, they weren't at all concerned about their girl's chastity. I told them I thought it would be a pity to leave her at the café when she'd expressed an interest in studying, and I asked if they'd consider entrusting her to me. There wasn't much I could do for her, but I was in need of a maid, and if she'd do the cooking and scrubbing, I'd see that she got an acceptable education in her spare time. Of course I told them frankly about my circumstances and that I was still single. When I'd made my appeal, they responded with something anticlimactic, like, "That'd be wonderful for her." It was just as she had said. There was no point in meeting them.

The world has its share of irresponsible parents, I thought; but to me that made Naomi's case all the more touching and pitiable. From what her mother said, I gathered that Naomi was a bit more than the family could handle. "We were going to make the child a geisha," the mother told me, "but she wasn't interested, and so we were obliged to send her to the café. We couldn't let her just go on playing." The fact was that it would be a relief for them if someone else took charge of Naomi and brought her up. After talking with the family, I finally understood why she always went to the show on holidays. She hated to be at home.

Nevertheless, it was fortunate for both Naomi and me that she came from such a household. As soon as I reached an understanding with her family, she gave notice at the café and joined me every day to look for a suitable house to rent. We wanted a place as convenient as possible to my office in Ōimachi. Sundays we met early in the morning at Shimbashi Station—weekdays, in Ōimachi, right after my office closed—to explore the Kamata, Ōmori, Shinagawa, and Meguro suburbs and, in the city, the area around Takanawa, Tamachi, and Mita. On the way home we dined together and saw a movie or strolled along the Ginza, if time allowed. Then she went home to Senzoku, and I returned to my rooming house at Shibaguchi. We went on this way for about two weeks. Rental houses were scarce at the time, and we had trouble finding what we wanted.

If anyone took notice of us—an office worker and a poorly dressed girl with a Japanese coiffure, walking side by side through the verdant suburbs of Ōmori on a bright Sunday morning in May—what might he have thought? I called her "Naomi," and she called me "Mr. Kawai." We couldn't have been mistaken for master and servant or brother and sister, man and wife, or friends. We must have made an unlikely couple as, a little shy with each other, we walked about happily on a long, late-spring day, hunted out addresses, gazed at the view, and turned to look at blossoms in a hedge, in a garden, or at the side of the road. The blossoms remind me that she loved Western flowers and knew the names—troublesome English names—of many flowers that I was unfamiliar with. Apparently she'd learned them at the café, where she was in charge of the vases. Sometimes we saw a greenhouse beyond a gate as we passed. Always alert, she'd stop and cry happily, "Oh, what beautiful flowers!"

"Which flower do you like best, Naomi?"

"I like tulips best."

Her longing for spacious gardens and fields, and her love of flowers, may have been in reaction to the squalid alleyways of Senzoku where she had grown up. Whenever we saw violets, dandelions, lotus grass, or primroses growing on a levee or by a country road, she would hurry over to pick them. By the end of the day, she'd have a great many flowers grouped in any number of bouquets. And she would still be holding them carefully on the way back.

"They're all wilted now. Why don't you throw them away?"

"Oh, they'll come right back if you put them in water. You ought to keep them on your desk, Mr. Kawai." She always gave the bouquets to me when we parted for the day.

Search as we might, a good house wasn't easy to find. Eventually we rented a shoddy Western-style house near the tracks of the National Electric Line, twelve or thirteen blocks from Ōmori Station. Modern and simple, it was, I suppose, what people would nowadays call a "Culture Home," though the term was not yet in vogue then. More than half of it consisted of a steep roof covered with red slate. The white exterior walls made it look like a matchbox; rectangular glass windows had been cut into them here and there. In front of the entrance porch was a small yard. The house looked as though it would be more fun to sketch than to live in, which isn't surprising, as it was built by an artist who had married one of his models. The rooms were laid out in the most inconvenient way. On the ground floor were an absurdly large atelier, a tiny entryway, and a kitchen—nothing else. Upstairs there were two small, Japanese-style rooms, six feet by nine feet, and nine-by-nine, respectively. Hardly more than attic storerooms, they were really quite useless. This attic was reached by a stairway in the atelier. Climbing the stairs one came to a landing enclosed by a handrail, just like a box at the theater, from which one could look down into the atelier.

Naomi was delighted with the house from the first time she saw it. "Oh, it's ever so modern! This is the kind of house I want." Seeing that it pleased her so, I immediately agreed to rent it.

No doubt the odd design—it was like an illustration for a fairy tale—appealed to Naomi's childlike curiosity, despite the impractical arrangement of the rooms. To be sure, it was just right for an easygoing young couple who wanted to live playfully and avoid the trappings of a conventional household. No doubt this is the sort of life the artist and his model had in mind when they occupied the house. In fact, the atelier by itself was large enough to satisfy the needs of two people.

3

I T   M U S T   have been late in May that I finally
took full charge of Naomi and moved into the "fairy-tale
house." Once there, I realized that it wasn't as inconvenient
as I'd thought. The attic rooms were sunny and had a view
of the sea; the yard in front had a southern exposure and was
the perfect place to plant a bed of flowers. The trains that
passed from time to time on the National Line were a draw-
back, but a small rice paddy between the house and the
tracks kept the noise down. I decided that it was a perfectly
acceptable place to live. What's more, in view of the house's
unsuitability for most people, the rent was surprisingly low.
Even in those days of low prices, twenty yen a month, with
no deposit, was very appealing to me.

"Naomi, from now on, call me 'Jōji,' not 'Mr. Kawai,'"
I said the day we moved in. "And let's live like friends, all
right?" Naturally, I informed my family that I'd moved
from the rooming house to a house of my own, and that I'd
hired a fifteen-year-old girl to serve as a maid; but I did not

tell them we were going to live "like friends." My relatives hardly ever came from the country to visit, and if someday there was a need to tell them, I would.

We spent many busy, happy days buying furniture appropriate to our strange new home and arranging it in the various rooms. To help cultivate her taste, I asked Naomi's opinion on almost everything we bought. I used her ideas whenever I could. There was no place to put the usual household items like cabinets and braziers in a house like this, so we were free to choose our pieces and carry out whatever design we liked. We bought some inexpensive India prints, which Naomi, with her uncertain fingers, sewed into curtains. At a Shibaguchi shop that specialized in Western furniture, we found an old rattan chair, a sofa, an easy chair, and a table, all of which we set out in the atelier. On the walls we hung photographs of Mary Pickford and several other American movie actresses. I also wanted Western-style bedding, but I gave up that idea because two beds would have been expensive, and I could have Japanese bedding sent from my home in the country.

When the bedding arrived, Naomi's turned out to be the kind a maid uses: a stiff cotton quilt as thin and hard as a cracker, adorned with the usual arabesque pattern. I felt sorry for her. "This won't do, Naomi. Let's exchange it for one of mine."

"No, it's fine," she said, pulling it over her as she lay down alone in the six-by-nine attic room.

I slept in the room next to hers—the nine-by-nine room in the attic—but every morning we'd call to each other, from room to room, without getting up.

"Naomi, are you awake?"

"Yes. What time is it?"

"Six-thirty. Shall I boil the rice for you this morning?"

"Would you? I did it yesterday, so you can do it today."

"All right. But it's a lot of trouble. Shall we make do with bread?"

"We can. But you're sneaky, Jōji."

When we wanted rice we cooked it in an earthen pot, which we put directly on the table without bothering to empty it into a wooden tub. With it we'd eat something out of a can. When that was too much trouble, we got by with bread, milk and jam, or a piece of Western pastry. For dinner we had noodles or went to a Western-style restaurant in the neighborhood, if we wanted something fancier.

"Jōji," she'd often say, "order me a steak today."

After breakfast, I left Naomi alone and went to work. She spent the morning puttering in the flowerbed. In the afternoon she locked up the house and went to her English and music lessons. Every other day, she went to Meguro to practice English conversation and reading with an American woman named Miss Harrison—we thought it best that she start right out with a Westerner—and at home I helped her review her weak points. I had no idea what to do about music lessons, but then we heard of a woman, a recent graduate of the music school at Ueno, who gave instruction in piano and voice in her home at Isarago in Shiba Ward, and so Naomi went every day for an hour's lesson. Wearing a dark blue cashmere formal skirt over a silk kimono, black socks, and charming little shoes, she looked every inch the pupil. Bursting with excitement at having realized her dream, she went off to her lessons diligently. Now and then I ran into her on my way home, and I could hardly believe that she had grown up in Senzoku and worked as a hostess. She never did her hair in Japanese style any more; she wore it in braids, tied with a ribbon.

I think I said earlier that I would "keep her like a little bird." Since coming under my charge, her color had improved and her disposition had gradually changed, so that now she'd become a truly radiant, vivacious little bird, and the enormous atelier was her cage. May came to a close and bright, early-summer weather set in. The flowers in the garden grew taller and more colorful day by day. In the evening, when I returned home from work and she from her lessons, sunlight streamed through the India-print curtains and played on the white walls as though it were still the middle of the day. Wearing slippers on her bare feet and an unlined flannel summer kimono, Naomi would stamp time as she sang the songs she'd learned. Sometimes she'd play tag or blindman's buff with me. Racing around the atelier, she jumped over the table, crawled under the sofa, and knocked over the chairs. And when that wasn't enough, she ran up the stairs and scurried back and forth like a mouse on our theater box of a landing. Once I played horse and crawled around the room with her on my back.

"Giddap, giddap!" she cried. For reins, she made me hold a towel in my mouth.

It must have been one day when we were playing that Naomi, squealing with laughter, ran up the stairs too fast, lost her footing, tumbled all the way down from the top, and burst into tears.

"Where does it hurt? Show me." As I picked her up, she went on sniffling and drew up her sleeve for me to see. She must have scratched herself against a nail or something as she fell; the skin was broken at her right elbow and a little blood was oozing out. "Here, this isn't worth crying over. I'll put a bandage on it for you."

I applied some ointment and tore up a towel to use as a bandage. She sobbed all the while like a small child, her eyes full of tears, her nose dribbling. Unfortunately, the scratch became infected and took five or six days to heal. I changed the dressing every day, and she cried each time.

Was I already in love with Naomi? I'm not certain. I suppose that I was; yet it was my intention and delight to bring her up as a fine young woman, and I believed that I'd find satisfaction simply in doing that and nothing more. But that summer, when, as every year, I went home to the country for my two-week vacation, leaving Naomi with her family in Asakusa and closing up the Ōmori house, I found my days in the country to be unbearably monotonous and lonely. Can it be, I wondered, that life without her is so dull as this? It occurred to me for the first time that I might be experiencing the beginnings of love. Making excuses to my mother, I returned to Tokyo ahead of schedule. I arrived after ten o'clock at night and, despite the late hour, rushed by taxi from Ueno Station to Naomi's house.

"Naomi, I'm back. I have a car waiting at the corner. Let's go to Ōmori."

"Oh? I'll be right there." Keeping me waiting outside the sliding lattice door, she finally emerged carrying a small bundle. It was a hot, humid night; Naomi had changed into a thin, unlined, white muslin kimono with a grape design in pale lavender, and had tied her hair with a wide, bright, pink ribbon. I'd bought the muslin for her during the recent Bon Festival, and during my absence she'd asked someone at home to make it up into a kimono.

"What did you do every day, Naomi?" Sitting beside her as the car moved off toward the bustling thoroughfare, I brought my face a little closer to hers.

"I went to the show every day."

"I don't suppose you were lonely, then, were you?"

"Not particularly. . . ." She thought for a moment. "You came back early, didn't you, Jōji?"

"I was bored in the country, so I cut it short and came back. There's no place like Tokyo." Heaving a sigh of relief,

I gazed through the window at the gay, flickering lights of the city at night.

"But I think it'd be nice to go to the country in the summer."

"That depends on the place. My family lives in an out-of-the-way farmhouse. The landscape is dull, there are no historic sites, flies and mosquitoes buzz around in broad daylight, and it's unbearably hot."

"Oh, dear. Is it that kind of place?"

"That's right."

"I want to go to the beach," she said abruptly. Her tone was very appealing, like that of a willful child.

"All right. One day soon I'll take you someplace to cool off. How about Kamakura? Or Hakone?"

"I'd like the ocean better than a hot spring. Oh, I *do* want to go."

The ingenuous voice sounded like the same Naomi as before, but somehow, in the ten days that I hadn't seen her, her limbs seemed to have stretched and grown perceptibly. I couldn't resist stealing a glance at the contours of her full shoulders, moving under the unlined muslin kimono as she breathed, and at her chest.

"You look nice in that kimono," I said after a pause. "Who made it for you?"

"Mother did."

"What did she say about me? That I made a good choice of material?"

"Yes, she said it wasn't bad, but it's far too modern and stylish."

"Your mother said that?"

"Yes. She doesn't understand anything." With a far-off look she added, "Everybody says I've changed."

"Changed in what way?"

"They say I've gotten terribly modern."

"I'm sure they do. I think so, too."

"I wonder. They told me to try doing my hair in Japanese style, but I didn't want to."

"And that ribbon?"

"This? I bought it myself at a shop in front of the Kannon Temple. Do you like it?" She turned her head away so that I could see the fluttering pink cloth as her clean, unoiled hair caught the wind.

"It's very becoming. Much better than doing it Japanese style."

With a toss of her button nose, she gave a little laugh, as though in agreement. This was a mannerism of hers. It was an impudent, nasal laugh, but I thought it made her look clever.

4

N A O M I was constantly begging me to take her to
Kamakura. We went at the beginning of August with the
intention of staying two or three days.

"Why does it have to be only two or three days?" she
asked. "It's no fun unless we go for a week or ten days."
Her face showed her displeasure as we left the house. But
I'd come back early from the country with the excuse that
I was busy at work, and out of deference to my mother, I
didn't want to risk my ruse being exposed. If I'd put it to
Naomi in this way, though, she'd have felt humiliated.
Instead I said, "Try to be content with two or three days
this year. Next year I'll take you for a longer stay some-
where else. All right?"

"But just two or three days . . ."

"I know, but if you want to swim when we get back,
you can go to the beach at Ōmori."

"I can't swim in a filthy place like that."

"You shouldn't say things like that when you don't really

know. Be a good girl. I'll buy you something to wear, instead. Didn't you say you wanted some Western clothes? I'll get some for you."

Caught with the bait of Western clothes, she finally agreed.

In Kamakura we stayed in the Golden Wave Pavilion at Hase, an unremarkable inn for bathers. It makes me laugh to think of it now. There was no need to economize, because I still had most of my semiannual bonus. Thrilled to be taking my first overnight trip with Naomi, I wanted to leave her with the most beautiful impressions possible: we'd stay in a high-class place and not worry about the cost. But when the day came and we boarded a second-class coach bound for Yokosuka, we were seized by a kind of timidity. The train was full of women and girls headed for Zushi and Kamakura, sitting in resplendent rows. In their midst, Naomi's outfit, to me at least, looked wretched.

As it was summer, of course the women couldn't have been particularly dressed up. But when I compared them to Naomi, I sensed an unmistakable difference in refinement between those who are born to the higher classes of society and those who aren't. Though Naomi seemed to have become a different person from the café girl she'd been, there's no concealing bad birth and breeding. And if this is what *I* was thinking, she must have felt it even more. How pitiful it looked now, that muslin kimono with the grape design, that had made her seem so stylish. Some of the women sitting around us were wearing simple summer robes, but their fingers glittered with gemstones and their luggage was luxurious; everything bespoke their wealth and station, while Naomi had nothing to show but her velvety skin. I can still remember how she hid her parasol self-consciously under her sleeve. And well she might—though the parasol was brand-new, anyone could see it was a cheap item, worth no more than seven or eight yen.

At first, then, we'd pictured ourselves staying at the Mitsu-hashi Inn, or even at the Kaihin Hotel. But when we approached the buildings, we were so intimidated by their magnificent gates that we walked up and down the Hase road two or three times until we finally found ourselves at the Golden Wave Pavilion, a second- or third-class establishment, by local standards.

There were too many noisy students staying at the inn to allow for any relaxation there, so we spent nearly all of our time on the beach. Tomboy that she was, Naomi cheered up as soon as she saw the ocean and forgot how dispirited she'd been on the train.

"I *must* learn how to swim this summer," she said, clinging to my arm and splashing about wildly in the shallows. I held her with both hands and showed her how to float on her belly, taught her how to kick, as she grasped a post in the water, and let her go suddenly, so that she tasted the brine. When she tired of that, we practiced riding the waves, played with the sand as we lay on the beach, and, in the evening, rowed out toward the bay in a rented boat. With a big towel wrapped around her bathing suit, she'd sit on the stern or lie back against the gunwale, gaze at the blue sky, and sing the Neapolitan boat song "Santa Lucia"—her favorite—in a shrill voice:

> *O dolce Napoli,*
> *O soul beato . . .*

As her soprano voice reverberated over the sea in the evening calm, I gently rowed the boat and listened, entranced. "Farther, farther," she cried, as though she wanted to travel across the waves forever. Before we knew it, the sun had set and the stars were sparkling; as the darkness gathered around us, Naomi's form, wrapped in a white towel, blurred into indistinctness. But her bright voice continued. She sang "Santa Lucia" over and over, then "Lorelei," "Zigeuner-leben," and a melody from *Mignon*. Song followed song as the boat moved gently forward.

I suppose that everyone experiences something like this in his youth, but for me it was the first time. Being an electrical engineer, I knew less than others did about literature and art and hardly ever read novels; but that evening, I thought of Natsume Sōseki's *Pillow of Grass*, which I'd read. The line "As Venice sank, as Venice sank" appears in that novel, and somehow I was reminded of it as Naomi and I, rocked by the boat, gazed from the offing and through the veil of evening haze toward the flickering lights on the shore. Moved to a tearful ecstasy, I wanted to drift away with Naomi to some uncharted, faraway world. For a rustic like me to experience this sensation was enough by itself to make our short stay in Kamakura worthwhile.

To tell the truth, our three days in Kamakura allowed me one other important discovery. Though I'd been living with Naomi, I'd never had a chance to observe her figure—the shape of her naked body, to put it bluntly—but on this trip I was able to. When she appeared on the beach at Yuigahama, wearing the dark green cap and bathing suit that we'd bought on the Ginza the evening before, I rejoiced at the beautiful proportions of her limbs. Yes, I rejoiced: from the way a kimono fit her, I'd already speculated on the curves of her body, and I'd been right. My heart cried out, "Naomi, Naomi, my Mary Pickford! What a fine, well-proportioned body you have. Your graceful arms! Your legs, straight and streamlined like a boy's!" And I couldn't help thinking of Mack Sennett's lively "bathing beauties," whom I'd seen in the movies.

I suppose that no one likes to advertise the details of his own wife's body. I don't enjoy boasting about the girl who later became my wife, and relating these details to so many people. But if I avoid the subject, it'll be hard to tell my story properly, and the point of making this record will be lost. I must note here, then, what kind of figure Naomi cut as she stood on the beach at Kamakura in August of her fifteenth year. At the time, she was about one inch shorter than I. (Please keep in mind that, though I had a robust physique, I was a small man, only about five feet, two inches tall.) But a striking characteristic of Naomi's frame was that her trunk was short and her legs long, so that from a distance she looked much taller than she was. Her short trunk tapered to a wonderfully slim waist, then swelled into richly feminine hips.

We'd seen a movie called *Neptune's Daughter*, about a mermaid, starring the famous swimmer Annette Kellerman. "Naomi," I said, "let me see you imitate Kellerman." She stood up with her arms straight over her head and showed me her "diving" pose. As she stood with her thighs together, her legs, so straight there was no space between them, formed a long triangle from her hips to her ankles.

She was pleased with her legs. "Jōji, are my legs crooked?" she asked. Taking a few steps, standing still, stretching out on the sand, she happily studied the shape of her legs.

Another distinctive feature of her body was the line from her neck to her shoulders. I had many opportunities to touch her shoulders: whenever she put on her bathing suit, she made me fasten the shoulder buttons. Normally a person like Naomi, with sloping shoulders and a thin neck, is rather thin; but she had surprisingly full shoulders and a thick chest that suggested strong lungs. When I tried to fasten the buttons for her, she'd take deep breaths and move her arms so that the muscles of her back rippled and swelled. The bathing suit, which already seemed at the bursting point, would stretch even more tightly across her bulging shoulders and threaten to split. In sum, her shoulders were powerful and brimming with youth and beauty. When I surreptitiously compared her with the other girls on the beach, it seemed to me that none of them had her combination of healthy shoulders and a graceful neck.

"Stand still, Naomi. If you move like that I can't fasten the buttons." I gripped the edge of her suit and pushed her shoulders into it, as though I were stuffing something large into a small sack.

With such a build, it's only natural that she was a tomboy and loved sports. She was good at everything athletic. After our three days at Kamakura, she went to the beach at Ōmori every day to practice swimming and by the end of the summer had mastered it. She also learned how to row and to sail. Having played all day, she'd come home clutching her wet bathing suit, cry "I'm starved!," and fling herself exhausted into a chair. Bored with cooking dinner every night, we sometimes stopped at a Western restaurant on the way home from the beach, and gorged ourselves as though we were in an eating contest. Beefsteak followed beefsteak, as she put away three or four helpings.

I could go on indefinitely about my happy memories of that summer, so I'll stop here. But there's just one more development that can't be omitted. Around that time, I got into the habit of bathing Naomi's arms, legs, back, and so on with a rubber sponge. The practice began when Naomi came home too sleepy to bother with the public bath. Instead, she'd rinse off the salt water by pouring water over herself in the kitchen, or by taking a sponge bath from a basin. "Naomi," I said, "if you go to bed that way your body'll be all sticky. Get in the washtub and I'll rinse you off." She did as I said and let me wash her. Gradually this became a habit. The washtub baths continued into the cool fall weather, until finally I installed a Western-style bathtub with a bathmat in a corner of the atelier and enclosed it with a standing screen. There I helped Naomi with her bath all through the winter.

5

S O M E of my more perceptive readers are probably
thinking that Naomi and I were already more than just
friends. We weren't though, in fact. It's true that a sort of
unspoken understanding developed between us as the months
went by. But not only was she still a girl of fifteen and I a
scrupulous "gentleman" who had had no experience with
women; I also felt responsible for her chastity, so I didn't
let the impulse of the moment push me beyond the bounds
of our understanding. Of course the notion had gradually
taken root in my mind that Naomi was the only woman I
could ever think of marrying, and that even if there were
someone else, I couldn't abandon Naomi now. This is another reason I didn't want to make the first move frivolously,
or in a way that might hurt her.

It was in the spring of the following year—April 26 of
Naomi's sixteenth year—that our relationship entered a new
phase. I remember the exact date because around that time—

no, it was when we began to use the washtub—I started a diary in which I recorded everything about Naomi that caught my attention. Her figure was growing strikingly more feminine every day. Like a new parent who keeps track of his baby's development with entries like "Laughed for the first time," or, "Spoke for the first time," I wrote down everything I noticed. I still leaf through it now and then. Here's what I wrote on September 21 in the fall of Naomi's fifteenth year:

At 8 p.m., I bathed her in the washtub. She still has her tan from the beach. She's very dark, except under the bathing suit. I'm dark, too, but Naomi has such a light complexion, the contrast is sharper. Even when she has nothing on, you'd think she was wearing a suit. "You look like a zebra," I said. She laughed.

About a month later, on October 17, I wrote:

Her tan is fading and her skin doesn't peel any more. It's even smoother and lovelier than before. When I washed her arms, she watched quietly as the soap bubbles dissolved and ran down against her skin. "Beautiful," I said. "Yes, isn't it?" she said. Then she added, "I mean the soap bubbles, you know."

On November 5:

We tried using the Western tub tonight for the first time. Not being used to it, Naomi slipped and slid around, shrieking with laughter. When I said, "Big baby," she called me "Papa."

After that, we sometimes called each other "Baby" and "Papa." She always called me "Papa" when she was trying to coax something out of me.

"Naomi Grows Up" was the title I gave my diary. Of course I only wrote about Naomi. Before long, I bought a camera and photographed her face, which was looking more and more like Mary Pickford's, in different lighting and from various angles. I pasted the photos here and there among the diary entries.

But the diary has taken me off the subject. According to the diary, she and I began a deeper relationship on April 26 of the year after we moved to Ōmori. Because of our unspoken understanding, it came about silently and spontaneously. Neither of us had taken the initiative, and we hardly exchanged a word. Finally she put her mouth to my ear.

"Jōji, don't ever leave me."

"Leave you? Absolutely not. You don't need to worry about that. I think you know how I feel."

"Yes, I do."

"How long have you known?"

"Let's see, how long has it been?"

"What did you think of me when I said I'd take care of you? Did you think that I intended to marry you eventually?"

"Yes, I thought that's what you had in mind."

"Then you agreed to come because you were willing to be my wife?"

Without waiting for her answer, I hugged her with all my might. "Thank you, Naomi, thank you. You understood. I'll be completely honest now. I never thought that you would come this close to my ideal woman. I'm so lucky. I'll always love you . . . only you. . . . I won't mistreat you the way so many husbands do. I live for your sake. Go on studying and grow up as a fine young woman, and I'll give you whatever you want."

"Oh, yes, I'll study hard. And I'll be the sort of woman you want, I promise." There were tears in her eyes, and I'd begun to weep, too. We talked all night about the future.

Shortly after that I spent a weekend at home and told my mother all about Naomi. There were several reasons for reporting to her quickly. I wanted to reassure Naomi, who seemed to be concerned about my family's reaction, and I wanted everything to be out in the open. I told my mother my ideas about marriage and, in a way that would make sense to an old woman, explained why I wanted to marry Naomi. My mother had always understood and trusted me. She said only, "If that's what you want, then you should marry her. But if she's from that kind of family, there might be trouble in the future. Be careful."

We decided to wait two or three years before announcing our marriage publicly, but I wanted to have her officially registered as my wife right away. I went to Senzoku to negotiate with her mother and brother. As before, they were nonchalant and everything went smoothly. They may have been a little negligent, but they weren't bad people, and they didn't say anything to suggest that they were motivated by greed.

Our relationship evolved rapidly after that. No one knew of the change yet, and outwardly we were just friends. But legally we were now married and had nothing to hide.

"Naomi," I said one day, "let's go right on living together like friends, shall we?"

"Then are you going to go on calling me 'Naomi'?"

"Of course. Or shall I call you 'wife'?"

"No, I wouldn't like that."

"And will I always be 'Jōji'?"

"Naturally. What else would I call you?"

Naomi lay down on the sofa with a rose in her hand. She pressed it to her lips and fingered it for a moment, then said suddenly, "Jōji?" Opening her arms, she dropped the blossom and embraced my head.

"My darling Naomi," I gasped from the darkness under her sleeves. "My darling Naomi, I don't just love you, I worship you. You're my treasure. You're a diamond that I found and polished. I'll buy anything that'll make you beautiful. I'll give you my whole salary."

"That's all right, you don't need to. My English and music lessons are more important."

"Oh, yes, yes. I'm going to buy you a piano soon. You'll be such a lady, you won't even be ashamed to mix with Westerners."

I often used phrases like "mix with Westerners" and "like a Westerner." Clearly this pleased her. "What do you think?" she'd say, trying out different expressions in the mirror. "Don't you think I look like a Westerner when I do this?" Apparently she studied the actresses' movements when we went to the movies, because she was very good at imitating them. In an instant she could capture the mood and idiosyncrasies of an actress. Pickford laughs like this, she'd say; Pina Menicheli moves her eyes like this; Geraldine Farrar does her hair up this way. Loosening her hair, she'd push it into this shape and that.

"Very good—better than any actor. Your face looks so Western."

"Does it? *Where* does it look Western?"

"Your nose and your teeth."

"My teeth?" She pulled her lips back and studied the row of teeth in the mirror. They were wonderfully straight and glossy.

"Anyway, you're different from other Japanese, and ordinary Japanese clothes don't do anything for you. How would it be if you wore Western clothes? Or Japanese clothes in some new style?"

"What kind of style?"

"Women are going to be more and more active in the future. Those heavy, tight things they wear now won't do."

"How about a narrow-sleeved kimono with an informal sash?"

"That'd be fine. Anything's all right as long as you try for original styles. I wonder if there isn't some outfit that's neither Japanese, Chinese, or Western . . ."

"If there is, will you buy it for me?"

"Of course I will. I'm going to get all sorts of clothes for you, and we'll switch them around every day. You don't need expensive stuff. Muslin and common silk will do. The important thing is to have original designs."

After this conversation, we often went to drapers and department stores together to look for fabric. We must have spent every Sunday at Mitsukoshi and Shirokiya. But it was hard to find patterns we liked, because neither of us was satisfied with the usual women's things. Run-of-the-mill drapers were of no use to us, so we went to cotton-print dealers, carpet shops, and stores that specialized in Western fabrics. We even went on full-day outings to Yokohama, where we dragged ourselves from shop to shop in China-town and to dry goods stores in the foreign settlement, foraging for the right fabrics. We studied the outfits of Westerners we passed on the street and scrutinized every shop window. If there was something unusual, one of us would cry, "Look, how about that?" We'd rush into the shop, have the fabric brought in from the window and see how it looked on Naomi, draping it from her chin and wrapping it around her torso. We had great fun walking around and window-shopping this way, even when we didn't buy anything.

Nowadays, it's fashionable for women to make summer kimonos out of organdy, Georgette, and cotton voile, but Naomi and I were probably the first to use these fabrics. For some reason the textures were very becoming to her. We weren't interested in conventional kimonos. Instead, she made the material into narrow-sleeved kimonos, pajama suits, and robes that looked like nightgowns. Sometimes she'd simply wrap a bolt of cloth around her body and fasten it with brooches. Dressed in one or another of these outfits, she'd parade around the house, stand in front of the mirror, and pose while I took pictures. Wrapped in gauzy, translucent clothing of white, rose, or pale lavender, she was like a beautiful large blossom in a vase. "Try it this way; now this way," I'd say. Picking her up, laying her down, telling her to be seated or to walk, I gazed at her by the hour.

Under the circumstances, her wardrobe grew enormously in the space of a year. She couldn't possibly store it all in her room; she hung things or rolled them up in piles everywhere. We could have bought a cabinet, but that would have cut into our clothes budget, and in any case there was no need to treat her clothes that carefully. She had lots of them, but they were all inexpensive and quick to wear out. It was more convenient to spread them around where we could see them and try various combinations whenever we were in the mood. They also served as decoration for the rooms. The atelier was just like a property room at the theater, with clothes strewn everywhere—on the chairs, on the sofa, in corners, even on the stairs and over the theater box rail. Most of them were soiled, because Naomi was in the habit of wearing them right against her skin, and we hardly ever laundered them.

Most of the designs were so outrageous that she could wear only about half of them outside the house. Her favorite, which she often wore when we went out, was a lined, cotton-padded satin kimono with a matching jacket. Both the jacket and the kimono were a solid, reddish brown, as were the thongs on her sandals and the cord on her jacket. Everything else—the neckpiece, the sash fastener, the lining of the underkimono, the sleeve ends, and the trim at the bottom—was pale blue. The narrow sash, too, was made of thinly padded satin; she wound it tightly, high on her chest.

For the neckpiece, she bought a ribbon, wanting something that looked like satin. She wore this outfit most often when we went to the theater in the evening. Everyone turned to look as she walked through the lobby of the Yūrakuza or the Imperial Theater in that glistening fabric.

"I wonder who *she* is?"

"An actress, maybe?"

"A Eurasian?"

Hearing the whispers, we'd move proudly toward them.

If *that* outfit amazed people, then Naomi could scarcely have gone out in her more fanciful creations, however much she liked to be unconventional. They were no more than containers—a variety of packages into which I'd put her when we were home, and gaze at her. I suppose it was like trying out a beautiful flower in one vase, then another. There's nothing so surprising about this. While she was my wife, she was also a rare, precious doll and an ornament. She never wore ordinary clothes at home. Her most expensive indoor outfit was a three-piece, black velvet suit that she said was inspired by a costume she'd seen a man wear in an American movie. When she put it on with her hair rolled up under a sports cap, she was as sensuous as a cat. Both summer and winter (when we heated the room with a stove), she often wore nothing but a loose gown or a bathing suit. She had countless pairs of slippers, including embroidered ones from China. She always wore them without socks.

6

E V E N while I was indulging her this way, I hadn't abandoned my original desire, which was to give her a good education and bring her up as a fine, respectable woman. I didn't have a clear idea of what "respectable" and "fine" meant, but I must have been thinking of something vague and simplistic like "a modern, sophisticated woman whom I wouldn't be ashamed to present in any company." Was "making Naomi a fine woman" compatible with "cherishing her like a doll"? It seems ridiculous now, but I was so befuddled by my love for her that I couldn't see such an obvious inconsistency.

"Naomi, play is play, study is study," I was always saying. "If you'll just work hard to make something of yourself, I'll buy you all kinds of other things."

She always responded in the same way: "Yes, I'll study, and I promise, I'll be a fine woman."

Every day after dinner I'd spend half an hour with her,

reviewing her English reading and conversation. No matter what I said, "play" and "study" had a way of merging. Wearing her velvet suit or a gown, she'd slouch in a chair and dangle a slipper from one toe, like a toy.

"Naomi, what are you doing! Mind your manners when you're studying!"

She'd sit up, bow her head, and assume the wheedling tone of an elementary-school student: "I'm sorry, teacher," or, "Excuse me, Mr. Kawai." Then she'd steal a glance at me and give me a peck on the cheek. I didn't have the courage to be firm with my adorable pupil; my scoldings always ended in childish horseplay.

I didn't know how Naomi was doing with her music, but she'd been studying English with Miss Harrison for about two years. It seemed to me that she should have made good progress by now. Having started with the first reader, she was now more than halfway through the second; her conversation text was *English Echo*, and for grammar she used Kanda Naibu's *Intermediate Grammar*. This would be equivalent to third-year level in middle school. Yet she still seemed to be below the level of a second-year student, at best. Puzzled, I called on Miss Harrison.

"No, nothing of the sort," said the kindly, stout spinster with a cheerful smile. Her Japanese was a little odd. "She is very bright. She is doing well."

"It's true that she's a bright child, but I don't believe her English is as good as it should be. She can read, but when it comes to translating into Japanese or analyzing the grammar . . ."

"No," she interrupted with a smile. "You have the wrong idea. Japanese people always think about grammar and translation. Very bad. When you study English, you must not think about grammar. Must not translate. Read it over and over as English—this is the best way. Miss Naomi has beautiful pronunciation. She is very good at reading. Her English will be very good soon."

She had a point. But I didn't mean that Naomi should systematically memorize the rules of grammar. Having studied for two years and completed the third reader, she should have known at least how to use the past participle, how to form the passive voice, and when to use the subjunctive. But when I had her translate from Japanese to English, it was clear that she hadn't learned any of these. She was no better than the most backward middle-school student. At this rate, she'd never speak English proficiently, however good she might be at reading. I wondered what on earth she'd been taught for two whole years. But the woman ignored my look of displeasure; she nodded with a confident, magnanimous air. "Miss Naomi is a very bright child," she said again.

My guess is that Western teachers have a certain bias with regard to their Japanese pupils. Or if "bias" is too strong, I might say that they have preconceived ideas. It seems to me that when they see a Westernized, sophisticated, sweet-faced boy or girl, they conclude without a second thought that the child is clever. This tendency is particularly strong among spinsters. That's why Miss Harrison was so lavish with her praise of Naomi—she'd made up her mind at the outset that Naomi was "a bright child." Naomi's pronunciation was extremely smooth, as Miss Harrison said. Her voice was beautiful to listen to, thanks to her singing lessons and her straight teeth. Her English sounded marvelous, and I was sure that I, at least, was no match for her in this respect. No doubt Miss Harrison was dazzled by Naomi's voice. I realized how much she loved Naomi when, to my astonishment, I saw photographs of Naomi tacked up all around Miss Harrison's dressing-table mirror.

While I was dissatisfied with Miss Harrison's opinions and

teaching methods, here was a Westerner who was partial to Naomi and who said that she was bright. This was just what I'd hoped for, and in spite of myself I was as pleased as if Miss Harrison had praised me directly. Not only that— like most Japanese, I tended to feel helpless when I came into contact with Westerners and lost the courage to state my opinions clearly. Undone by Miss Harrison's confident chatter, delivered in her odd Japanese, I didn't say what I ought to have said. It doesn't matter, I told myself. If that's how she feels, then I'll just fill in the gaps at home. To Miss Harrison I said, "Yes, that's very true. Just as you say. I understand now. I won't worry any more." And with an ambiguous, flattering smile, I excused myself and came home dispirited. I hadn't settled anything.

"Jōji, what did Miss Harrison say?" Naomi asked that evening. Her tone suggested that she was confident of the woman's backing and wasn't taking the matter seriously.

"She said you're doing very well. But Westerners don't understand Japanese students' psychology. She's wrong if she thinks that it's enough to have good pronunciation and be able to read smoothly. You're good at memorizing, but when I ask you to translate, you haven't understood the content at all. That's no better than a parrot can do. At this rate, your English will never be of any practical use."

That was the first time I gave Naomi a real scolding. I was irritated by her triumphant look and the way she sided with Miss Harrison, as if to say, "What did I tell you?" But more than that, I doubted now whether Naomi could become the "fine woman" we'd talked about. Her English aside, it wasn't hard to see what future there might be for a mind that couldn't even grasp the rules of grammar. Why do boys study geometry and algebra in middle school? The objective is not so much to provide them with a practical tool, as to cultivate their ability to use their minds with precision.

In the past, a woman could get along without an analytical mind; but not any more. A woman who wanted to be "the equal of Westerners" and a "fine woman" wasn't very promising if she had no aptitude for systematic thinking and analysis.

Formerly I'd spent only about thirty minutes a day reviewing her lessons. Now I was more obstinate and taught her Japanese-English translation and grammar for an hour to an hour-and-a-half and more every day. I no longer permitted the previous playful mood; I scolded her crossly. Since she was weakest in comprehension, I refrained from making detailed explanations and instead gave little hints so that she could figure out the rest for herself. If she were studying the passive voice, for instance, I'd immediately present her with an exercise. "All right, translate this into English," I'd say. "If you understand what you just read, you should be able to do this." Then I'd wait patiently for her to come up with the answer. If her answer was wrong, I wouldn't tell her where the mistake was. "You don't understand, do you? Read the grammar again," I'd say, and send her to the textbook over and over.

If she still couldn't do it, I said, "Naomi, how will you get anywhere if you can't do something this simple? How old are you now? You've been corrected again and again on the same point, and you still don't understand. Where's your head? Miss Harrison says you're bright, but I don't think so at all. If you couldn't do this, you'd be at the bottom of the class if you were in school." In the end I'd get too zealous and start shouting at her. Naomi would puff out her cheeks in a pout and start sobbing.

Normally, we were the happiest, most loving of couples— I laughed whenever she laughed, and we never quarreled. But when the time came for her English review, the mood darkened and became suffocating for both of us. Once a day, I'd lose my temper and she'd sulk. Cheerful until a moment before, suddenly we'd be sitting rigidly, staring each other down with hostile eyes. I'd forget my original desire to make her into a fine woman; frustrated by my own ineffectiveness, I'd begin to find her exasperating. If she'd been a boy, I might well have lost my temper and hit her. As it was, I was always shouting "idiot!" at her. Once I even rapped her on the forehead with my knuckles. Her reaction was to be perverse. She wouldn't respond even when she knew the answer. Fighting back the tears that streamed down her cheeks, she sat there as silent as a stone. Once she fell into this contrary mood, she was amazingly stubborn, and it wasn't in her nature to back down. In the end I'd give up and leave the matter unresolved.

Then, one day, the following happened. I'd told her repeatedly that the present participle ("doing," "going," and the like) has to be preceded by the verb "to be," but she couldn't grasp it. She was still making mistakes like "I going" and "He making." "Idiot!" I shouted again and again. I made myself hoarse explaining the various forms of "going," including the tenses—past, future, future perfect, and past perfect. To my astonishment, she didn't understand any of it. She'd write "He will going" and "I had going." In a rage, I cried, "Idiot! What an idiot! How many times do you have to be told that you can't say 'will going' and 'have going'? If you don't understand, then we'll keep at it until you do. I won't let you go until you can do it right, even if we have to stay up all night." Violently I thrust the pencil and notebook back at her. Naomi had gone pale. Her lips pressed tightly together, she glared up at me from her downturned face. Suddenly she grabbed the notebook, tore it in half and threw it on the floor. Then she fixed those frightening eyes on me again, as if to bore a hole in my face.

"What do you think you're doing!" Taken aback by the

brute ferocity of her stare, I needed a moment to collect myself. "You're feeling rebellious, are you? 'Who wants to study?' you're thinking. 'I'll study hard,' you said. 'I'll be a fine woman.' Have you changed your mind? Why did you tear up the notebook? Apologize. If you don't apologize, I'm through with you! Get out of this house today!"

Naomi remained stubbornly silent, her face white as a sheet. A faint smile played around her lips, as though she were going to cry.

"All right, don't apologize. Get out. Get out, right now!" Nothing short of this would make an impression on her, I thought, and so I stood up, gathered several pieces of her clothing and rolled them into a bundle. I brought my pocket-book from the second floor and took out two ten-yen notes. "Naomi," I said, thrusting it all at her. "I've put a few of your things in this bundle. Take it and go back to Asakusa tonight. And here's twenty yen. It's not much, but it'll do for the time being. I'll work out the details in a few days, and I'll send the rest of your things tomorrow. . . . Well? Naomi, why don't you say something?"

Despite her defiant look, she was still a child after all. Flinching at my determination, she hung her head ruefully and seemed to shrink in on herself.

"You're stubborn, but once I've said what I did, I'm not going to let it go. If you think you're in the wrong, then apologize. If you don't want to, then go home. Make up your mind. Are you going to apologize? Or are you going back to Asakusa?"

She shook her head.

"Then you don't want to go back?"

She shook her head again.

"Will you apologize?"

She nodded.

"In that case, I'll forgive you. Let's have a proper bow of apology."

She pressed her hands reluctantly to the table, but she still seemed to be mocking me as she made a careless little bow, her eyes averted.

Whether it had been there from the beginning or was a result of my spoiling her, her insolent, willful nature was clearly getting worse as the days went by. Or perhaps I'd let it pass as girlish charm when she was still fifteen or sixteen, and now that she was older it was proving more than I could handle. When she'd been fretful and demanding before, she'd always submitted tamely to a little scolding; but these days she'd start sulking as soon as anything displeased her. When she sobbed, she was still appealing; but at times, however fiercely I scolded her, she'd provoke me by playing the innocent, or take aim at me with her sharp upward glare. If there's such a thing as animal electricity, Naomi's eyes had it in abundance. It seemed beyond belief that they were a woman's eyes. Glittering, sharp, and frightful, they still brimmed with a certain mysterious allure. And sometimes when she shot her angry glance at me, I felt a shudder pass through my body.

7

MY HEART was a battleground for the conflicting emotions of disappointment and love. I'd made the wrong choice; Naomi was not as intelligent as I'd hoped. I couldn't deny it any longer, much as I wanted to. I could see now that my desire for her to become a fine woman was nothing but a dream. I was resigned to the situation: bad breeding is bad breeding; a girl from Senzoku ought to be a café hostess, and there's nothing to be gained from giving someone an inappropriate education. And so I abandoned my ambitions. But at the same time, her body attracted me ever more powerfully. I use the word "body" advisedly. It was her skin, teeth, lips, hair, eyes—the beauty of her entire form—that attracted me. There was nothing spiritual about it. She'd betrayed my expectations for her mind, but her body now surpassed my ideal. Stupid woman, I thought. Hopeless. Unhappily, the more I thought so, the more I found her beauty alluring. This was very unfortunate for me. Gradually I forgot my innocent notion of "training" her:

I was the one being dragged along, and by the time I realized what was happening, there was nothing I could do about it.

Things don't always turn out as you want, I told myself. I had wanted to make Naomi beautiful both spiritually and physically. I had failed with the spiritual side but succeeded splendidly on the physical. I never expected that she'd become so beautiful. My success here had more than compensated for my failure on the spiritual side. . . . Forcing myself to think along these lines, I tried to be satisfied with what I had.

"Jōji, you don't call me an idiot any more during our English lessons." Naomi quickly noted my change of heart. Though she had no talent for grammar, she was very sharp when it came to reading my face.

"I decided it doesn't do any good to yell at you, because you just get obstinate. I decided to change my tactics."

She snorted. "Of course. I won't do as you say if you yell at me like that. Actually, I could do most of those exercises, but I wanted to give you a hard time, so I pretended I didn't understand. Couldn't you tell?"

"What, really?" I knew that her boasting was just sour grapes, but I pretended to be startled.

"Naturally. Anybody could do those exercises. You're the dumb one if you really thought I couldn't do them. You're so funny when you get mad."

"Well, you certainly fooled me."

"What do you think now? Maybe I'm a little smarter than you thought?"

"You're the smart one, all right. I'm no match for you."

Pleased with herself, she laughed and laughed.

At this point I have an odd story to tell. I hope that my readers will listen patiently without laughing at me. When I was in middle school, we learned about Antony and Cleopatra in a history class. As you probably know, Antony engaged the forces of Augustus in a naval battle on the Nile. Cleopatra followed Antony into battle, but when she saw that things looked bad for her side, she immediately turned her ship and fled; whereupon Antony, realizing that the heartless queen was deserting him, withdrew from the battle at a critical moment and chased after her.

"Boys," the history teacher said to us, "this man Antony pursued a woman and lost his life. He is the greatest fool in history, truly the laughingstock of the ages. Alas! that a valiant hero should meet his end in this way . . ."

The teacher's manner was so odd that we burst out laughing in his face. Naturally, I laughed too.

But here is the point. I couldn't understand why Antony had fallen in love with such a heartless woman. And it wasn't only Antony; before him, the great Julius Caesar had disgraced himself by getting entangled with Cleopatra. There are many other instances. When you examine the great family quarrels of the Tokugawa period, or the rise and fall of states, you always find in the background the wiles of a terrifying enchantress. Now, are these wiles so ingeniously, so slyly contrived that anyone would be taken in by them? I think not. However shrewd Cleopatra may have been, it's unlikely that she was more resourceful than Caesar or Antony. If a man is alert, he doesn't have to be a hero to discern when a woman is sincere and telling the truth. A man who lets himself be deceived, even though he knows that he's destroying himself, is just too fainthearted. If this was really the case with Antony, then there's nothing so wonderful about heroes. . . . These were my secret thoughts at the time, and I accepted my teacher's judgment that Marc Antony was "the laughingstock of the ages," "the greatest fool in history."

Once in a while the teacher's words come back to me, and I can see myself laughing with the other students. Each time I recall the scene, I'm conscious that I'm no longer qualified to laugh at Antony, because now I understand why a Roman hero made a fool of himself—why Antony was taken in so effortlessly by an enchantress's wiles. I even find myself sympathizing with him.

It's often said that "women deceive men." But from my experience, I'd say that it doesn't start with the woman deceiving the man. Rather, the man, without any prompting, rejoices in *being deceived*; when he falls in love with a woman, everything she says, whether true or not, sounds adorable to his ears. When she puts her head on his shoulder and weeps false tears, he takes the generous view: "Ah, you're trying to put something over on me. But you're a funny, adorable creature. I know what you're up to, but I'll let you tempt me. Go ahead, make a fool out of me." He plays along, like someone trying to make a small child happy. He has no intention of being misled by her. On the contrary, he laughs to himself that he's deceiving her.

Naomi and I were a case in point. When she said, "I'm smarter than you are, Jōji," Naomi thought that she'd succeeded in deceiving me. I played the fool and pretended to be taken in. I was far happier letting her be pleased with herself and watching the joy in her face than I would have been if I'd exposed her silly lie. Doing so also satisfied the demands of my conscience. Even if Naomi wasn't a particularly clever woman, there was nothing wrong with giving her the confidence that she was clever. The greatest weakness of Japanese women is that they lack confidence. As a result, they look timorous compared to Western women. For the modern beauty, an intelligent, quick-witted expression and attitude are more important than lovely features. If she lacks true confidence, simple vanity is enough: to think "I'm smart," or "I'm beautiful," makes a woman beautiful. Believing this at the time, I was in no hurry to discourage

Naomi's pretensions to cleverness; indeed, I did everything I could to kindle them. Always cheerfully ready to be deceived, I maneuvered her toward ever greater confidence.

To give an example: if I'd tried, I could have won the children's chess matches and card games that we frequently played in those days, but I usually let her win. Finally she was vain enough to say, "I'm much better than you are at games." She'd challenge me contemptuously, "Come here, Jōji, it's time to give you another good beating."

"All right, I'll let you have a return match. You know, I wouldn't lose to the likes of you if I played seriously, but I get careless when I'm playing with a child."

"No excuses. I'll listen to your fine speeches after you've won."

"Done! I'll win this one, you'll see."

Deliberately playing badly, as usual, I let her win.

"Well, Jōji? How does it feel to lose to a child? There's no hope for you. No matter what you say, you're no match for me. Really, Jōji, a grown man of thirty-one losing to a child of eighteen! You just don't know how to play." Then, more and more puffed up with herself, she'd say, "I guess brains count more than age, don't they," or, "You might as well just accept it, you're the dumb one." And she'd give her impudent, scornful little snort of a laugh.

What's frightening is the upshot of all this. At first I was humoring Naomi, or at least I thought I was. But gradually, losing got to be a habit, and Naomi's confidence grew, until presently I couldn't beat her no matter how hard I tried.

Victory and defeat aren't determined solely by intellect. There's such a thing as spirit or, put another way, animal electricity. This is especially true in gambling. When we had a play-off game, Naomi would attack from the beginning with such marvelous concentration and vigor that I was pushed off balance and never had a chance to take the initiative.

"It's no fun unless we play for money," she said finally. "Here, I'll put something on it for you." Once she acquired a taste for it, she wouldn't play without betting. The more we bet, the more my losses piled up. Though she didn't have a penny to her name, she always set the ante herself— ten or twenty sen—and extracted as much spending money from me as she wanted.

"I could buy that kimono if I had thirty yen. Come on, I'll take it from you with the cards," she'd say by way of a challenge. Occasionally she lost, but when she did she knew other "moves" to get the money she wanted. When she was determined, she'd do whatever was necessary.

She generally wore a loose gown when we played, not quite fastened and a little bit revealing, so that she could employ her "moves" as soon as they were needed. When play was going badly for her, she'd slouch immodestly in her chair, unfasten the neck of her gown, stick out her legs and, if that failed, lie in my lap, stroke my cheek, tweak the corner of my mouth—in short, attempt every form of enticement. I had very little resistance to these moves. In particular, when she employed her move of last resort (which I can't very well describe in writing), my head would get all fuzzy and everything would go dark, and I'd lose track of the game completely.

"That's not fair, Naomi. You can't do that."

"Of course it's fair. There's this kind of move, too, you know."

As my attention drifted further and further from the game, everything became a blur in my eyes. I could dimly make out her coquettish face—nothing more—wreathed in an insinuating grin. . . .

"Not fair, not fair, that's no way to play cards. . . ."

"Isn't it? When men and women play, they use all kinds of tricks. I've seen them. When I was little, I used to watch my big sister play cards with men. She had all kinds of tricks."

I believe that when Antony was conquered by Cleopatra, it happened this way: little by little he was stripped of his resistance and became ensnared. It's fine to give confidence to the woman you love, but as a result you lose confidence in yourself. And when that happens, there's no way to overcome her sense of superiority. This leads to undreamed-of misfortunes.

8

I T   W A S   a hot early-September evening in the fall
of Naomi's eighteenth year. Things being slow at the office,
I left an hour early and went home. To my surprise, a boy
I'd never seen before stood in the garden, talking with Naomi.

He appeared to be about Naomi's age, or at most a year
older. He was wearing a whitish, unlined kimono and a
Yankee-style straw hat adorned with a bright ribbon. As
he spoke, he tapped the front of his wooden sandals with a
walking stick. His features were well formed and ruddy,
and he had thick eyebrows, but his face was covered with
pimples.

Naomi was crouching at his feet behind the flowerbed,
where I couldn't see her very well. I could just catch flickers
of her profile and her hair between the zinnia, phlox and
canna blossoms.

When the boy saw me, he took off his hat and bowed to
Naomi. "See you later," he said and walked briskly toward
the gate.

"Good-bye," said Naomi, standing up. He answered, "Good-bye," without looking back at her. When he passed in front of me, he touched the brim of his hat as if to hide his face.

"Who was that?" I asked, not so much from jealousy as from curiosity about the strange scene I'd just witnessed.

"Him? He's a friend of mine. His name is Hamada."

"How long have you known him?"

"Oh, a long time. He takes voice lessons at Isarago, too. His face is all pimply, but he's wonderful when he sings. A good baritone. We sang together in a quartet at the last recital."

I studied her eyes, my suspicions aroused by the unnecessary comment on his face, but she was quite relaxed and behaved exactly as she always did.

"Does he come here often?"

"No, this is the first time. He was in the neighborhood, so he dropped by. He says they're starting a social-dance club, and he came to ask me to join."

In fact I was somewhat troubled, but as I listened, I began to accept what she said. Maybe that was all the boy had come for. They'd been talking together in the garden at an hour I was likely to come home; that was enough to dispel my suspicions.

"Did you say you'd join?"

"I said I'd think about it. . . ." Then, suddenly shifting to a pleading, coaxing tone, she said, "Won't you let me? Oh, please do! Why don't you join, too, and we can go together."

"Could I join the club, too?"

"Anybody can join. The teacher is a Russian that Miss Sugizaki at Isarago knows. She escaped here from Siberia and she doesn't have any money, so Miss Sugizaki started the club to help her out. The more students the better. Oh, please let me!"

"All right. But I wonder if I can learn Western dancing."

"Of course you can. You'll learn right away."

"But I don't know anything about music."

"Oh, you'll get used to the music while you're learning. There's nothing to it. Jōji, you just *have* to join. I can't go dancing by myself. We'll go out together sometimes. It's no fun just staying in the house every day."

I'd sensed before that Naomi was beginning to be bored with the life we were leading. More than three years had passed since we set up our nest in Ōmori. Except for summer vacations, we'd spent all of our time alone together in our "fairy-tale house," avoiding contact with society at large; whatever games we might play together, it was natural that she'd get bored eventually. To make things worse, Naomi's attention strayed quickly. At first she'd be completely absorbed in a new activity, but her interest never lasted very long. On the other hand, she always had to be doing something, and so when she was tired of cards, chess, and movie actress imitations, she turned again to the flower bed that she'd neglected for so long. She fussed with the blossoms, busily turned over the soil, sowed seeds and watered them; but this too was just a passing whim.

"How boring," she'd say. "Isn't there something to do?" Lying on the sofa, she'd put aside the novel she'd just started and give a big yawn. Whenever I saw her like this, I wished for a way to bring a little variety into our monotonous lives. Since the dance proposal came at just such a time, I thought it might not be a bad idea to participate. Naomi wasn't the Naomi of three years before, when we'd gone to Kamakura together. Things were different. If I dressed her up and presented her in high society now, she could hold her own with most of the other ladies. I felt tremendously proud at the thought.

As I said before, I never had any particularly close friends, even in school, and I tried to avoid unnecessary relationships; but I certainly wasn't reluctant to mix in good society. Being from the country, clumsy at social pleasantries, and awkward in dealing with people, I'd become shy and withdrawn, but, for that very reason, glamorous society had a special allure. I'd married Naomi in the first place because I wanted to make her a beautiful woman, go out with her every day, and have people praise her. "Your wife is very chic," I wanted to hear them say in high society. Driven by this ambition, I didn't want to leave her in a "birdcage" forever.

According to Naomi, the Russian dance teacher was a countess named Aleksandra Shlemskaya. Her husband, the count, had disappeared during the Revolution. There'd been two children, but she didn't know where they were, either; she'd barely managed to escape to Japan by herself. Having no other means of support, she'd finally decided to teach social dancing. The club had been organized by Naomi's music teacher, Miss Sugizaki, to help the countess, and the club secretary was Naomi's friend Hamada, a student at Keio University.

Lessons would be held on the second floor of a shop called Yoshimura's that dealt in Western musical instruments. It was on Hijiri Slope in Mita. The countess would come twice a week, on Mondays and Fridays; club members could choose any convenient hour between four and seven in the evening. The fee was twenty yen per person each month, payable in advance. Naomi and I together would have to pay forty yen. It's silly to pay so much, I thought, even if she is a Westerner; but Naomi insisted that Western dance was like traditional Japanese dance—a luxury, and one had to pay accordingly. It wouldn't be necessary to take lessons for very long. One month would be enough for someone with talent, and even a bungler could learn in three months. It really wouldn't be expensive at all.

"To begin with, we have to help Madame Shlemskaya. The poor woman. She used to be a countess, and look how she's come down in the world. Hamada says she's a very good dancer. She can teach stage dancing, too, if anyone wants to learn. Professionals don't know how to dance. You have to learn from someone like her." Naomi talked as though she knew all about dancing and eagerly promoted the countess she'd never met.

So it was that Naomi and I joined the club. We agreed to meet every Monday and Friday at six o'clock at the music shop on Hijiri Slope. Naomi would go directly from her music lesson, and I from work. On the first day, Naomi met me at five o'clock at Tamachi Station and led me to the music shop. It was a narrow little store, halfway up the slope. Inside were rows of pianos, organs, gramophones and other instruments packed into a tiny space. A clamor of footsteps and gramophone music came from the second floor; dance lessons seemed to be under way already. Five or six boys—Keio students, from the look of them—were loitering at the foot of the stairs. The way they stared at Naomi and me made me uncomfortable. Then someone called out, "Naomi!" in a loud, friendly voice. It was one of the students. Holding an instrument that looked something like a Japanese moon-guitar—might it be called a flat mandolin?—he was plucking the wire strings as he tuned it.

"Hi, there," Naomi replied inelegantly. She sounded like a schoolboy. "How are you, Ma-chan? Aren't you going to dance?"

"Not me," the boy said with an insinuating grin. He put the mandolin on a shelf. "That sort of thing isn't for me. For starters, twenty yen a month's too much."

"But what else can you do if you're just a beginner?"

"Pretty soon you'll all know how to dance, and I'll get you to teach me. Why should I spend a lot of money? Pretty smart, eh?"

"You sneak, Ma-chan! You're just *too* smart. Say, is Hama upstairs?"

"Yeah, he's there. Go take a look."

The shop seemed to be a hangout for students in the neighborhood. Naomi must have come frequently; everyone seemed to know her.

"Naomi," I said, as she led me up the stairs, "who are those students?"

"That's the Keio Mandolin Club. They're rude, but they're not bad people."

"Are they all friends of yours?"

"Not really friends. I just got to know them because they're here when I come to buy things."

"Are they the sort of people who'll be in the dance club?"

"I wonder. Probably not. Don't you suppose they'll be older people, mostly? Anyway, we'll soon see."

The practice room was at the head of the corridor on the second floor. As soon as we reached the top of the stairs, we saw five or six people marking time with their feet as they repeated, "One, two, three," in English. The partitions between two Japanese-style rooms had been removed to form one large space, and a wood floor had been put down so that we could keep our shoes on. Hamada was scurrying around scattering powder on the floor—to make it more slippery, I suppose. It was the time of year when days are still long and hot, and the afternoon sun streamed through the open windows on the west side. Bathed in the pale red glow, a solitary figure stood in the middle of the room, wearing a white Georgette blouse and a dark blue serge skirt. It was, of course, Madame Shlemskaya. Since I'd heard that she had two children, I guessed she might be thirty-five or thirty-six, but she looked only about thirty. She had the grave dignity and firm features of a born aristocrat; and her dignity was enhanced by her pale, limpid complexion—so white it was a little frightening. Seeing her authoritative expression, her tasteful clothes, and the jewels glittering on her breast and fingers, I found it hard to believe that she was as poor as I'd been told.

Holding a short whip in one hand and scowling crossly, she glared at her students' feet and repeated, "One, two, tree" (in her accented English, "three" became "tree"), quietly but firmly. Following directions, her students formed a line and moved back and forth with uncertain steps. She looked like a woman officer drilling the troops; the scene reminded me of *The Woman's Army Is Off for the Front,* an opera I'd seen at the Golden Dragon Theater in Asakusa. One of her pupils was a young man in a suit—probably not a university student. Another was a modestly dressed young woman who looked to be the daughter of a good family and just out of Women's College; practicing earnestly with a man in Japanese dress, she appeared to be a very serious young lady and made a good impression. As soon as one of the students did a step wrong, the countess would utter a sharp "No!" and go over to the student to demonstrate. If someone had trouble learning and made too many mistakes, she'd cry "No good!" and snap her whip on the floor. Sometimes she'd lash mercilessly at a student's feet; it made no difference to her whether the offender was a man or a woman.

"My, she's a very enthusiastic teacher, isn't she? That's the best way."

"Yes, indeed, Madame Shlemskaya is *very* enthusiastic. Japanese teachers just aren't quite up to it, but Western people, even the ladies, are very exacting. It's so refreshing. She *will* go on with her lessons like that for hours on end without taking a break, even when it's hot like this. I offered to bring her some ice cream, but she refused. She said that she didn't want anything during the lessons."

"My, it's a wonder she doesn't get tired."

"Western people have strong bodies. They're not like us. But I do feel sorry for her. She used to be married to a count, you know, living in luxury, and now because of the Revolution she has to do this sort of thing."

Two women sitting on a sofa in the next room were watching the lesson in progress and discussing it admiringly. One was a lady of twenty-five or -six; her large, thin-lipped mouth, round face, and protruding eyes made her look like a Chinese goldfish. Her unparted hair was drawn up and back from her forehead to a high, billowing peak that looked like a porcupine's behind. At the nape of her neck she wore a huge hairpin of white tortoise shell. Her sash, woven with an Egyptian design, was held by a jade clip. This was the lady who had so much sympathy and praise for Madame Shlemskaya. The woman she was talking to looked about forty—tiny wrinkles and chapped skin showed through her thick white makeup, which was splotchy with perspiration. Whether by design or by nature, the reddish hair in her chignon was shaggy and frizzy. Tall and thin, she was gaily dressed but somehow had the look of an ex-nurse.

Some of the people surrounding these ladies were bashfully awaiting their turns; others, who seemed already to have had some lessons, were dancing in pairs around the edge of the room.

Hamada, the club secretary, rushed about, perhaps as the countess's representative, perhaps on his own initiative, changing records on the gramophone and offering himself as a partner to people dancing at the side. Wondering what sort of man would be inclined to take dancing lessons, I studied the men on the floor. To my surprise, Hamada was

the only one smartly dressed. Most of the others wore taste-
less blue three-piece suits and looked like poorly paid
workers with no sense of style. They all looked younger than
I. There was only one man who might have been in his
thirties. He wore a morning coat, thick glasses with gold rims,
and an old-fashioned long mustache. As he was the slowest
learner of all, the countess scolded, "No good," and cracked
her whip at him again and again. He'd give a pale, stupid
grin and start his "one, two, three" over again.

What brings a man of his age to take dancing lessons? I
wondered. But then it occurred to me that he and I were
probably not so different. In any case, I'd never been to such
a grand affair before. Although I was there merely as Naomi's
partner, when I imagined myself under the scrutiny of these
ladies and being scolded by that Westerner, I thought I'd
break out into a cold sweat. I dreaded the moment when our
turn would come.

"Hello. Welcome." It was Hamada. Having danced two
or three numbers, he came over to greet us, wiping his
pimply forehead with a handkerchief. "Nice to see you
again," he said to me, a little smugly. Then he turned to
Naomi. "Thanks for coming in this heat. Say, do you have
a fan I could borrow? It's not so easy being the assistant."

Naomi took a fan from her sash and handed it to him.
"But you're good, Hama-san, good enough to be her assistant.
When did you start taking lessons?"

"Me? About six months ago. But you're quick, you'll learn
fast. The man leads and all the girl has to do is follow."

"Who are the men here today?" I asked.

"Most of them are employees of Oriental Petroleum In-
corporated." He spoke to me more politely than he had to
Naomi. "One of Miss Sugizaki's relatives is on the board
of directors. I understand that he introduced them."

Oriental Petroleum and social dancing! An unlikely combination, I thought. "Then is the gentleman with the mustache an employee, too?"

"No, he is a doctor."

"A doctor?"

"Yes, he serves as a sanitation consultant with the company. He says that there is nothing like dancing for bodily exercise, and that's why he's taking lessons."

"Really?" Naomi cut in. "Hama-san, is it really good exercise?"

"Sure. You get all sweaty, even in winter, and your shirt gets sopping wet. It's good exercise, all right. Especially the way Madame Shlemskaya teaches."

"Does she understand Japanese?" I asked. It had been on my mind for some time.

"Hardly at all. She uses English, mostly."

"English? I'm afraid I'm not much good at spoken English, so maybe I'd better . . ."

"Nonsense. We're all in the same boat. Madame Shlemskaya herself speaks very broken English, even worse than ours. There's nothing to worry about. And for dance lessons, you don't need to talk anyway. It's just 'one, two, three,' and then you follow her movements."

"Oh, Miss Naomi. And when did you arrive?" It was the Chinese-goldfish lady with the white tortoise-shell hairpin.

"Hello, Miss Sugizaki." Catching my hand, Naomi led me toward the sofa where the music teacher was sitting. "Miss Sugizaki, this is Mr. Kawai Jōji. . . ."

"Oh, I see." Naomi was blushing, and so Miss Sugizaki, without waiting to hear more, stood up knowingly and bowed.

"And how do you do? I am glad to make your acquaintance. My name is Sugizaki. Thank you so much for coming today. Miss Naomi, bring that chair over here."

Turning to me again, she said, "Won't you please sit

down? Your turn will come shortly, and we wouldn't want you to get tired while you wait, would we?"

I don't remember how I responded. I probably just mumbled something. I don't know how to deal with women who use such stiff, formal language. In this case, I was all the more embarrassed because I'd neglected to ask Naomi how much the lady knew about our relationship.

"May I introduce you?" Paying no attention to my discomfort, Miss Sugizaki pointed to the lady with the frizzy hair. "This is Mrs. James Brown, from Yokohama. And this is Mr. Kawai Jōji, who is with an electric company in Ōimachi."

So the woman is the wife of a foreigner, I said to myself; come to think of it, she does look more like a foreigner's mistress than a nurse. I bowed, stiffer than ever.

"Excuse me for asking," she said, latching onto me immediately, "but is this your *foist time?*" I didn't like the affected way she pronounced the English "foist time," and besides, she spoke very fast.

"I beg your pardon?" I said, fidgeting.

"Yes, he is just beginning." Miss Sugizaki took charge.

"Oh, is that so? But, don't you know, it's *moa moa difficult* for a *gen'lman* to learn than a *lady*, but once you start, you'll catch on right away, don't you know."

What on earth is *moa moa*? I wondered. Finally I realized that it was "more, more." She was fond of inserting English words into her conversation. "Gentleman" became "gen'lman," "little" became "li'l," and so on. Her Japanese had a peculiar accent, too. She jabbered on and on, throwing out one "don't you know" after another.

She talked about Madame Shlemskaya again, then about dance, foreign languages, and music—Beethoven's sonatas were such and such, the Third Symphony was whatever, this company's records were better than that company's. Utterly dejected, I couldn't think of anything to say in reply, and so presently she directed her chatter toward the music teacher. I gathered that Mrs. Brown was taking piano lessons from Miss Sugizaki. Since I wasn't capable of seizing the proper moment to excuse myself gracefully, I had to remain sandwiched in between these two garrulous ladies, lamenting my misfortune.

When the mustachioed doctor and the rest of the petroleum company group finished their lesson, Miss Sugizaki led Naomi and me to Madame Shlemskaya and introduced us in fluent English—Naomi first, then me, presumably following the Western principle of ladies first. Miss Sugizaki called Naomi "Miss Kawai." I'd been waiting curiously to see how Naomi would react when she came face-to-face with a Westerner. Sure enough, conceited as she usually was, she panicked in front of the countess. Saying a word or two, Madame Shlemskaya allowed a smile to creep onto her dignified face and held out her hand. Naomi flushed bright red and shook hands furtively without saying a word. I was even worse when my turn came. To tell the truth, I couldn't look at the countess's pale, sculptured face. Her hand glittered with countless tiny diamonds as I touched it silently. I didn't raise my eyes.

9

THOUGH I had no sense for such things, my tastes ran to the chic and up-to-date, and I imitated the Western style in everything. My readers already know as much. If I'd had enough money to do whatever I pleased, I might have gone to live in the West and married a Western woman; but my circumstances wouldn't permit that, and I married Naomi, a Japanese woman with a Western flavor. Even if I'd been rich, I would have had no confidence in my looks. I'm only five feet two inches tall; I have a dark complexion, and my teeth are snaggly. I'd be forgetting my place if I hoped for a wife with the majestic physique of a Westerner. A Japanese should marry a Japanese, I concluded, and Naomi came closest to meeting my needs. I was satisfied.

Nevertheless, it was a pleasure—no, an honor—to come into such close contact with a Western lady. The truth is that I was so disgusted with my own awkwardness and ineptitude for languages that I'd given up all hope of ever actually meeting such a person. Instead, I'd gone to see Western opera companies and studied movie actresses' faces, cherishing their beauty as though I were seeing it in a dream. Then, unexpectedly, the dance lessons provided me with a chance to meet a Western woman, and a countess, at that. An old woman like Miss Harrison aside, this was the first time in my life that I had had the honor of shaking hands with a Western lady. When Madame Shlemskaya presented her white hand, my heart skipped a beat and I hesitated, uncertain whether it was all right to take it.

Naomi's hands were elegant, too—graceful and sleek, with long, slender fingers. But the countess's white hand was both sturdy and lovely: the palm was thick and fleshy, not fragile like Naomi's; and the fingers, while long and supple, didn't give the impression of being weak and thin. Her huge rings, glittering like so many eyes, would have looked tawdry on a Japanese; but they made the countess's fingers resplendently alluring and suggested refinement and luxury. What set her apart from Naomi most of all was the extraordinary whiteness of her skin. Her pale lavender veins, faintly visible beneath the white surface like speckles on marble, were weirdly beautiful. I'd often complimented Naomi on her hands as I toyed with them. "What exquisite hands you have. As white as a Westerner's." But now, to my regret, I could see that there was a difference. Naomi's hands weren't a vivid white—indeed, seen after the countess's hand, her skin looked murky. Something else that caught my attention was the countess's nails. All ten fingertips were perfectly matched, like a collection of sea shells. The nails were a glowing pink, handsomely aligned, and, perhaps in the current Western fashion, each tip was trimmed to a sharp triangle.

I've already reported that Naomi stood about an inch shorter than I. Though the countess appeared to be on the small side for a Westerner, she was still taller than I am.

It may have been because she wore high-heeled shoes, but when we danced together, my head came right up to her prominent chest. The first time she said, "Walk with me!," placed her arm around my back, and showed me the one-step, how desperately I tried to keep my dark face from grazing her skin! I'd have been satisfied just to gaze at her smooth, immaculate skin from a distance. It had seemed irreverent even to shake her hand. Now, drawn to her breast with only her soft, thin blouse between us, I felt as though I were doing something absolutely forbidden. Maybe my breath's bad, I fretted. She's offended by my greasy hands. And when a strand of her hair fell against me, I couldn't restrain the cold shiver that ran through my body.

What's more, her body had a certain sweet fragrance. "Her armpits stink," I heard the students in the mandolin club say later. I'm told that Westerners do have strong body odor, and no doubt it was true of the countess. She probably used perfume to hide it. But to me, the faint, sweet-sour combination of perfume and perspiration was not at all displeasing—to the contrary, I found it deeply alluring. It made me think of lands across the sea I'd never seen, of exquisite, exotic flower gardens.

"This is the fragrance exuded by the countess's white body!" I told myself, enraptured, as I inhaled the aroma greedily.

Why did I, a clumsy oaf totally unsuited to the gay atmosphere of social dancing, go on with the lessons for a month, then two months, without losing interest? It wasn't just for Naomi's sake. It was—I confess—because of Madame Shlemskaya. To dance in her embrace for that brief hour every Monday and Friday afternoon came to be my greatest pleasure. I utterly forgot Naomi when I stood before the countess. That hour intoxicated me as surely as a savory liquor.

"You're more enthusiastic than I expected, Jōji. I thought you'd get tired of it right away."

"Why?"

"Didn't you say, 'I don't think I can learn to dance'?"

I always had a bad conscience when the subject came up with Naomi. "I didn't think I'd be able to, but when I tried, it was fun. And, as the doctor said, it's good exercise."

"There, you see?" Naomi laughed. "You shouldn't think so much about things, just try them." She hadn't guessed my secret.

In the winter of that year, having practiced a lot, we went for the first time to the Café El Dorado in the Ginza. There were still very few dance halls in Tokyo at the time. Aside from the Imperial Hotel and the Kagetsuen, the Café must have been one of the first. We'd heard that the Imperial and the Kagetsuen, patronized mainly by foreigners, were fussy about dress and etiquette, so it seemed best to start out by going to the El Dorado. Naomi had heard about it from someone and came to me, urging that we go. But I didn't have the courage to dance in public yet.

"You're impossible, Jōji." Naomi glared at me. "Don't be so timid. You can't learn to dance just by taking lessons. You have to get out in society. Be daring, and you'll be a good dancer before you know it."

"I'm sure you're right, but I don't have it in me to be daring."

"All right, I'll go alone. I'll invite Hama-san or Ma-chan to go dancing."

"Ma-chan's the boy in the mandolin club, isn't he?"

"That's right. He hasn't had a single lesson, but he'll dance anywhere with anybody, and so now he's really good. Much better than you. You just have to be a little daring, or you lose out. . . . All right? Let's go, then. I'll dance with you. . . . Oh, please come with me. . . . There's a good boy, Jōji, there's a good boy."

Once it was decided that we'd go, a long discussion began on what Naomi should wear.

"Jōji, which one looks best?" A good four or five days before we were to go, the house was in chaos, as she brought all of her clothes out and went through them one by one.

"That one's fine," I said finally, not really meaning it. I didn't want to be bothered any more.

"I'm not so sure. Does it look all right?" She turned around and around in front of the mirror. "Something's wrong. No, I don't like it." Stripping it off, she kicked it aside in a heap and threw on the next one, then the next one. None of them pleased her. "Oh, Jōji, buy me a new outfit, won't you?" she said, finally. "I've got to wear something really flashy when we go dancing. These things don't show me off. Will you? Oh, get me a new one! We'll be going out all the time now, and I've got to have something to wear, haven't I?"

By then my monthly salary could no longer keep up with her extravagance. I'd always been scrupulous about finances; when I was still single, I'd budgeted my expenses and put the remainder, even if it was only a little, in the bank. By the time I began living with Naomi, I'd saved quite a bit. What's more, though I doted on Naomi, I never neglected my work; I continued to be the exemplary hard-working employee, and I earned the trust of the managers. My salary increased until I was earning about four hundred yen a month, including the usual semiannual bonuses. This amount would easily support two people living normally, but it wasn't enough for us. Perhaps I shouldn't go into detail, but our living expenses came to at least two hundred and fifty yen a month, sometimes as much as three hundred, by a conservative estimate. Rent accounted for thirty-five of this (in four years it had increased by fifteen yen); after subtracting expenses for gas, electricity, water, heating, fuel, and laundry, we were left with a balance of from two hundred to two hundred and forty yen, most of which went for food.

As a child, Naomi had been satisfied to eat beefsteak à la carte, but now she'd become something of a gourmet and at every meal demanded special delicacies out of keeping with her age. To make it worse, she didn't want to be bothered with shopping and cooking; she placed orders with nearby restaurants.

"I'd sure like something good to eat," she'd say whenever she was bored. Formerly she'd always preferred Western food, but now, for about one meal in three, she'd say impudently, "I think I'll see what the Japanese soup from A is like," or, "Let's get B to send around some sashimi."

Naomi ate lunch alone while I was at the office. This is when she tended to be the most extravagant. Arriving home from work in the evening, I often found wooden trays from Japanese caterers or plates and bowls from Western restaurants piled up in the kitchen.

"Naomi, you've had something brought in for lunch again! It costs a lot of money to cater all your meals, you know. Don't you think it's a bit much for a woman by herself?"

Naomi was undismayed. "But I ordered it *because* I was alone," she said. "It's too much trouble to cook." She sprawled on the sofa to sulk.

Under the circumstances, saving money was out of the question. There were times when she didn't even want to bother with boiling rice; she'd order it from the caterer along with the other dishes. When the bills came at the end of the month from the poulterer, butcher, Japanese restaurants, Western restaurants, sushi shops, eel shops, bakeries, and fruiterers, I was astonished at the total. How can she eat so much? I wondered.

Next to food, the highest bills were for laundry. This is

because Naomi, unwilling to wash so much as a sock herself, sent everything to the cleaners. As soon as I began to complain, she said, "I'm not your maid, you know. If I do the laundry, my fingers'll get fat and I won't be able to play the piano. What is it you called me? Your treasure? What'll you do if my hands get all fat?"

At first, Naomi had looked after the house and done the cooking, but this didn't go on for more than six months or a year. An even bigger problem than the laundry was the house: it got messier and dirtier every day. She left her clothes wherever they fell and her dishes wherever they happened to be when she stopped eating. The house was littered with plates, bowls, and tea cups, their contents half-consumed. There was soiled underwear everywhere. The floor, chairs, and tables were always covered with dust; the dingy India-print curtains had lost all of their original charm. The atmosphere of our bright "birdcage"—our fairy-tale house—had changed completely, and the stuffy rooms assaulted the nose with the smell of neglect. At one point I became so annoyed I said, "All right, I'll clean up. You go out into the garden." I set to work sweeping and dusting, but the more I cleaned, the dustier everything got. And I didn't know where to begin straightening up the things that were scattered all over the house.

Seeing no alternative, I hired a series of maids, but each in turn was appalled by the mess and left after a few days. I hadn't originally planned to have a maid, and there wasn't a suitable place for one to sleep. To make matters worse, with a maid around, Naomi and I couldn't flirt and play our games as freely as we had done before. And Naomi got even lazier: she'd drive the maid like a horse and never lift a finger herself. Her extravagance reached new extremes as ordering meals from the caterers got easier than ever. "Go to such and such a restaurant," she'd command, "and order so-and-so for me." In short, having a maid was not only extremely uneconomical, but it also interfered with our "playful" life. No doubt the women I hired were intimidated, and I was in no mood to insist on their staying.

This, then, is what we paid in living expenses. Of the hundred to hundred and fifty yen remaining each month, I wanted to save ten or twenty, but Naomi's reckless spending habits didn't permit it. For one thing, she had a new kimono made every month. Even if the material was muslin or common silk, she'd invariably buy additional material for the lining and then pay someone to do the sewing. The result was that each kimono cost fifty or sixty yen. If she didn't care for the finished product, she'd stuff it in a drawer and never wear it, or, if she liked it, she'd wear it until there were holes in the knees. Her closet was bursting with tattered old clothes. Another of her extravagances was footwear. She had to have straw sandals and wooden sandals of every variety—low ones, high ones, dry-weather ones, the kind that are carved from a single block of wood, formal ones, informal ones. They ranged from two to eight yen a pair, and, since she bought a new pair every ten days or so, they weren't cheap.

"You're spending a lot on sandals," I said. "Wouldn't shoes do just as well?" Formerly she'd enjoyed wearing the shoes and formal skirt of a student, but these days she went mincing off, even to her lessons, without changing.

"I'm a pure Tokyoite, you know," she declared, reminding me that I was from the country. "Whatever else I may wear, I'm very particular about what I put on my feet."

Every few days she'd spend three to five yen on concert tickets, streetcar fares, textbooks, magazines, and novels. Then there was the tuition for her English and music lessons, twenty-five yen that had to be paid every month. It wasn't easy to meet all these expenses on a monthly salary of four hundred yen; far from putting money aside, I was with-drawing from my savings account, and little by little the money I'd accumulated as a bachelor trickled away. Money goes fast once you begin to use it; in those three or four years I exhausted my savings, and presently there was nothing left at all.

To make matters worse, I wasn't any better at asking for credit than most other men of my sort. I went through agony at the end of every month, unable to rest until I'd paid all the bills. "If you keep on spending like this, I'll end up in debt," I'd say to Naomi reproachfully.

"If you can't pay, ask them to wait," she'd reply. "Who says you still have to pay at the end of every month, when you've been living in the same place for years? They'll wait if you promise to pay every six months. You're just too timid and strait-laced, Jōji." Whenever she went shopping, she paid in cash. The monthly bills were to be put off until I received my semiannual bonus, but she'd have no part of asking for credit herself. "I don't want to; that's a man's job," she'd say. When the end of the month came, she made herself scarce.

It'd be no exaggeration to say that I spent my entire in-come on Naomi. The desire I'd cherished all along was to make her more beautiful, to protect her from financial con-straints, and to let her grow and develop freely. I grumbled now and then, but I permitted her extravagances. This re-quired cutting and squeezing in other areas. Fortunately, I had hardly any social expenses of my own, and I avoided office parties whenever I could, even if it meant shirking my own social responsibilities. I kept my other expenses—cloth-ing, lunch, and so on—to a minimum. Naomi bought a second-class commuter pass for the line we rode every day; I settled for third class. Since Naomi didn't want to bother with boiling rice, and since it cost so much to call the caterer,

I sometimes boiled the rice myself and prepared side dishes. This arrangement didn't please Naomi either. "A man shouldn't work in the kitchen; it's not right," she said.

"Jōji, you ought to wear something a little smarter, instead of wearing the same old things year in and year out. I don't like it when I'm all dressed up and you look like that; I can't go anywhere with you."

I'd have had no fun at all if we couldn't go anywhere together, and so I was forced to buy some "smart" clothes for myself. When we went out together, I had to join her in second class. In short, I had to share in her extravagance.

Such being the case, I'd been having trouble making ends meet even before I began paying forty yen a month to Madame Shlemskaya. I'd really be in a pinch if I had to buy a dance wardrobe for Naomi besides. It was late in the month; I had cash in my pocket, and Naomi, not being one to listen to reason, wouldn't take no for an answer.

"But if I spend this money now, I'll be short on the thirtieth, when the bills are due. You understand that, don't you?"

"So what if you run short? It'll work out."

"What do you mean by that? There's no way for it to work out."

"Then why are we taking dance lessons? . . . All right, in that case, starting tomorrow I won't go anywhere at all." Tears welled up in her eyes as she glared at me reproachfully and lapsed into a silent pout.

"Naomi, are you angry? Naomi? Turn this way." In bed that night, I shook her shoulder as she lay with her back to me, pretending to be asleep. "Turn this way, Naomi." Gently, like turning over a fried fish, I rolled her toward me. Her unresisting, supple body faced me obediently, her eyes open just a crack.

"What's wrong? Are you still angry?"

She didn't respond.

"Here, don't be angry, I'll figure out something."

Still no response.

"Come on, open your eyes." As I spoke, I lifted the flesh of her trembling eyelids. Her plump eyes, peeking out like pearls from a shell, were wide awake and looking directly at my face.

"I'll buy something for you with that money, all right?"

"But won't you be left short, then?"

"That's all right, I'll find a way."

"But what will you do?"

"I'll ask them to send money from home."

"Will they send it?"

"Of course. I've never caused them any trouble, and I'm sure Mother will understand. There are all sorts of expenses when two people set up housekeeping."

"Really? But wouldn't it be wrong to ask her?" Naomi spoke as though she were concerned, but I sensed that for a long time she'd been thinking I should do just that. I was saying exactly what she wanted to hear.

"It wouldn't be wrong, but I didn't do it before because it's against my principles."

"Then why have you changed your principles?"

"I felt sorry for you when I saw you crying."

"Really?" She heaved her breast like a wave that rolls toward the beach. "Did I cry?" she asked with a sheepish smile.

" 'I won't go *anywhere*,' you said, and your eyes were full of tears. You'll always be a spoiled child, won't you—my big baby."

"My Papa! My dear Papa!" She threw her arms around my neck. Like a postal clerk urgently cancelling a flood of letters, she pressed her lips furiously to my forehead and nose, above my eyelids, behind my ears, and over every inch of my face.

This gave me the delicious sensation of countless camellia petals, heavy, dewy and soft, cascading onto my face, and inspired a daydream in which my head was submerged in the petals' fragrance.

"What is it, Naomi? You act as though you'd lost your senses."

"I have. . . . You're so loveable tonight, I've lost my senses. . . . Does it bother you?"

"Bother me? Oh, no, I'm happy, so happy that I'm losing my senses, too. I'll make any sacrifice for you. . . . What's wrong? Are you crying again?"

"Thank you, Papa. I'm grateful to my Papa, and that's why I'm crying. I can't help it. Do you understand? Do you want me to stop crying? If you want me to stop, then wipe my eyes for me."

She took some tissue from the folds of her kimono and put it in my hand. She was still gazing directly at me. Before I could wipe her eyes, they filled once again with tears. What clear, liquid eyes they were! I wished for some way to crystallize those beautiful teardrops and keep them forever. First I wiped her cheeks; next, taking care not to touch the round, swollen tears, I wiped around her eyes. As the skin stretched and then relaxed, the tears were pushed into various shapes, now forming convex lenses, now concave, until finally they burst and streamed down her freshly wiped cheeks, tracing threads of light on her skin as they went. I wiped her cheeks again and rubbed her damp eyes; then, as she was still sniffling, I held the tissue to her nose. "Blow," I said. She blew again and again, with a trumpeting noise.

The next day, Naomi went by herself to the Mitsukoshi with my two hundred yen. During my lunch hour, I wrote for the first time to ask my mother for money. I remember writing, ". . . The rise in prices over the past two or three years has been astonishing, and, though we are by no means extravagant, we are pressed by our monthly expenses. City life is not easy. . . ."

It frightened me that I'd grown reckless enough to lie so skillfully to my own mother. But Mother not only trusted me; she showed her affection for Naomi, too, in the reply that came two or three days later. "Buy a kimono for Naomi," she wrote, enclosing a draft that was for one hundred yen more than I'd requested.

10

THE DANCE at the El Dorado was on a Satur-
day evening and scheduled to start at seven-thirty. When I
got home from work around five, I found Naomi, fresh from
the bath, busily applying her makeup.

"Jōji, it's ready," she said the moment she saw my reflec-
tion in the mirror. Stretching one arm behind her, she pointed
to the sofa, where she'd spread out the kimono and one-piece
sash she'd rush-ordered from the Mitsukoshi. The kimono,
trimmed with cotton padding and lined, was of dark red silk
crepe with an overall pattern of yellow flowers and green
leaves. On the sash, old-fashioned pleasure barges floated on
delicate waves stitched in silver thread.

"Well? A good choice, don't you think?" Dissolving white
powder in her hands, she patted it vigorously on her steaming
shoulders and nape as she spoke.

To tell the truth, the soft, flowing material wasn't very
becoming on her full shoulders, large hips, and prominent
bust. Muslin or common silk cloth gave her the exotic beauty

of a Eurasian girl, but a more formal kimono, like this one, only made her look vulgar. And when she wore a bold pattern, she looked like a chophouse woman in one of those places in Yokohama that cater to foreign sailors. I didn't want to say anything when she was so pleased with herself, but I cringed at the thought of being seen on the train or in a dance hall with a woman dressed so gaudily.

When Naomi had finished dressing, she said, "Now, Jōji, you're going to wear your blue suit." For once, she got it out for me, brushed it off, and ironed it.

"I'd rather wear brown than blue."

"Jōji! Don't you know anything?" she scolded, shooting an angry look at me. "For an evening party, you have to wear a dark blue suit or a *tuxedo*. And you can't wear a *soft collar*; it has to be a *stiff* one." She used the English words. "That's *etiquette*, and you'd better remember from now on."

"Is that the way it is?"

"That's the way it is. How can you pretend to be chic if you don't even know that? Your suit is awfully soiled, but it doesn't matter with Western clothes as long as they hold their shape and there aren't any wrinkles. There, I've gotten it all ready for you, and that's what you'll wear tonight. You'll have to get a tuxedo soon, though. Otherwise I won't dance with you."

The necktie had to be dark blue or black, preferably tied in a bow; the shoes were to be of patent leather, or, lacking that, ordinary black shoes (red leather was improper); silk stockings were best, but any socks would do if they were solid black—wherever she may have picked up all the information in her lecture, she concerned herself with every detail of my preparations. It was a long time before we left the house.

It was past seven-thirty when we arrived, and the dance had already begun. We could hear a clamorous jazz band as we climbed the stairs to the dance hall, which had been created by clearing away the chairs from a dining room. At the entrance was a sign in English: "Special Dance—Admission: Ladies Free, Gentlemen ¥3.00." A waiter collected the admission fee. Since it was actually a café, the "hall" wasn't very grand. I saw about ten couples dancing, enough to make the place seem fairly crowded. Tables and chairs were arranged in two rows on one side of the room. The idea seemed to be that after buying an admission ticket you claimed a seat and could rest in it now and then while you watched the other dancers. Several groups of unfamiliar men and women were seated, talking. When Naomi entered the room, they whispered furtively to each other and scrutinized her showy outfit with that strange, suspicious look, half-hostile and half-contemptuous, that can only be seen in this kind of setting. I had a feeling that they were saying, "Hey, look at the dame that just walked in," and "What do you think of the joker she's got with her?"

I could distinctly feel their gaze falling not only on Naomi, but also on me, as I made myself small behind her. The music echoed noisily in my ears, and I saw that the dancers— every one of them more skillful than I—had formed a large ring and were circling round and round. Meanwhile I was reminding myself that I'm only five feet two inches tall, dark as a savage, snaggle-toothed, and wearing a two-year-old blue suit that was far beyond its prime. I flushed hot and trembled. I'll never come to a place like this again, I said to myself.

"There's no point in just standing here. . . . Let's go over . . . over toward the tables." Maybe Naomi was embarrassed, too; she spoke in a small voice with her mouth pressed to my ear.

"Yes, but do you think we should just cut through all these people?"

"I don't think it matters. . . ."

"But what if we bump into somebody?"

"We'll just have to be careful not to. . . . Look, that man just cut across. It's all right. Let's go."

I followed her through the crowd. My legs shook, and the floor was slippery; it was no easy task to reach the other side of the room safely. I remember that Naomi scowled at me once when I almost fell over with a crash.

"There's an empty place. Let's take that table." More daring than I, Naomi passed nonchalantly through the staring crowd to a table on the far side. As much as she'd been looking forward to the evening, though, she didn't want to start dancing right away. She seemed a little agitated as she took a mirror from her handbag and touched up her face, then whispered, "Your necktie's twisted to the left," as she peered toward the dance floor.

"Naomi, Hamada's here, isn't he?"

"Don't say 'Naomi.' Say 'Miss Naomi.' " She scowled at me again. "Hama-san's here, and so is Ma-chan."

"Where?"

"Over there . . ." Suddenly she lowered her voice. "It's rude to point," she scolded. "Over there, dancing with the young lady in the pink dress. That's Ma-chan."

"Hello," said Ma-chan, moving toward us and grinning over his partner's shoulder. The woman in the pink dress was tall and plump, and her long, voluptuous arms were fully exposed. Her thick, raven black hair—not simply abundant, but heavy and oppressive—was chopped shoulder length, frizzled in a negligent sort of way, and adorned with a ribbon wrapped around her head and over her forehead. Her cheeks were red, her eyes large, and her lips thick, but the oval outline of her face, with its long, thin nose, was in the pure Japanese style of the *ukiyoe* prints. I pay close attention to women's faces, and I'd never seen such an ill-sorted face as this. It occurred to me that the woman was probably distressed by her Japanese face and had worked overtime to look like a Westerner. She'd whitened every bit of exposed skin until she looked as though she'd been dusted with rice flour, and applied shiny, blue-green pigment around her eyes. The bright red on her cheeks was obviously rouge. Unfortunately, with that ribbon twisted around her head, she looked like a monster.

"Naomi . . ." I said, without thinking. Correcting myself to "Miss Naomi," I continued. "*She's* a 'young lady'?"

"Yes, she is. She looks like a whore, though."

"Do you know her?"

"No, but I've heard about her from Ma-chan. You see that ribbon? Her eyebrows are way up on her forehead, so she wears the ribbon to cover them and paints new eyebrows below it. Look carefully—those eyebrows are fake."

"But her face isn't bad. She doesn't need to slop on all that red and green stuff."

"She's stupid, that's all," Naomi declared in her usual conceited tone. She seemed to be regaining her confidence. "And she's not so good-looking. Is that your idea of a beauty?"

"She's not beautiful, but her nose is nice and high, and her figure's not bad. If she wore normal makeup, she'd be attractive enough."

"Ugh! Attractive? Don't be ridiculous! You see faces like that everywhere. And look at the way she's dressed. I don't mind if somebody tries to look like a Westerner, but *she* doesn't look like one at all. Pathetic. She's a monkey."

"Now, that woman dancing with Hamada looks familiar, doesn't she?"

"She ought to. That's Haruno Kirako of the Imperial Theater."

"Really? Does Hamada know her, then?"

"Sure. He's a good dancer, so he meets lots of actresses."

Dressed in a brown suit and chocolate-colored, box calf shoes with spats, Hamada was clearly the most skillful dancer on the floor. The outrageous thing was the way he pressed his face right against his partner's. No doubt this was one of the styles of dancing. Kirako was delicately built and had slender, ivorylike fingers; she looked as though she'd bend and snap in Hamada's firm embrace. Far more beautiful here than on stage, she wore a gorgeous, alluring kimono and a one-piece damask sash with a dragon figured in gold and dark green thread on a black ground. Being taller than she, Hamada held his head down at a sharp angle, with his ear against Kirako's sidelock. He looked as though he were sniffing her hair. Kirako, for her part, was pressing her forehead hard enough against his cheek to make deep creases at the corners of her eyes. The two heads and four blinking eyes danced on and on, never separating for an instant, even when their bodies weren't touching.

"Jōji, do you know that style of dancing?"

"No, but it's not very dignified, is it?"

"No. In fact, it's vulgar." She spat out the words. "It's called 'cheek dancing.' You just don't do it in nice places. In America they ask you to leave if you try it—that's what I heard. Hama-san's all right, but he's a show-off."

"But the woman's doing it, too."

"Well, what do you expect from an actress? They shouldn't let actresses in here. If they carry on like that, real *ladies*'ll stop coming."

"Hardly any of the men are wearing blue suits, and you made such a fuss about it. Look at what Hamada's wearing." I'd noticed this at the outset. In her know-it-all way, Naomi had forced me to wear a dark blue suit on the basis of something she'd heard about *etiquette*. But here at the dance, only two or three of us were dressed in blue, and there wasn't a single tuxedo. The other men were wearing stylish suits in unorthodox colors.

"Yes, but Hama-san's in the wrong. You're supposed to wear blue."

"That's what you say, but . . . well, look at that Westerner. He's wearing homespun, isn't he? I guess it doesn't matter what you wear."

"That's not true. You should always wear the proper thing, even if you're the only one who does. That Westerner came dressed that way because Japanese people don't know how to dress. And anyway, Hama-san's special, because he's had a lot of experience and he's a good dancer. But you'd look awful if you weren't dressed just right."

On the dance floor, the flow of movement slowed to a halt, and there was enthusiastic applause. The orchestra had stopped playing, but the dancers wanted to go on; the most eager of them whistled, stamped their feet, and called "encore!" The music started up and the undulating flow began again. After a while it stopped, and there were more cries of "encore." This was repeated two or three times, until, finally, no amount of applause had any effect on the musicians. Then the men followed their partners like bodyguards back to their tables. Hamada and Ma-chan escorted Kirako and the Pink Dress, each to her own table, seated them, bowed politely, and then came over to where we were sitting.

"Good evening," said Hamada. "You came rather late, didn't you."

"What's the matter, aren't you gonna dance?" Ma-chan spoke in his usual crude way. He stood directly behind Naomi and stared down at her dazzling attire. "If you haven't made any promises, why don't you dance the next one with me?"

"No, thanks. You're too clumsy."

"Nonsense. I didn't pay for lessons, but I know how to dance anyway. Funny, huh?" Flaring his nostrils, he gave a vulgar, insinuating giggle. "It just comes natural, you know."

"Humph! Don't talk so big. You didn't make such a pretty picture dancing with Pinky out there." It was astonishing the way Naomi's speech suddenly coarsened when she spoke with the boy.

"That bad, huh?" Ma-chan scratched his head in embarrassment and glanced toward the Pink One, seated at her table some distance from us. "I thought I was as nervy as anyone, but I'm no match for her, barging in here dressed like that."

"She's a monkey, that's what."

"A monkey? That's good. She's a monkey, all right."

"You're a fine one to talk. Didn't you bring her? Really, Ma-chan, she looks just awful and you ought to tell her so. She'll never look Western with that face. It has 'Japan,' 'pure Japan.' written all over it."

"In other words, a pitiful effort."

"That's right, a monkey's pitiful effort. Some people look Western even when they wear Japanese clothes, you know."

"Like you, right?"

Naomi gave her impudent nasal laugh. "That's right, I look more like a Eurasian than she does."

"Kumagai." Apparently in deference to me, Hamada addressed Ma-chan by his family name. He seemed a little uneasy, hesitant. "Kumagai, you've never met Mr. Kawai before, have you?"

"No, I haven't. I know his face, though. . . ." From where he stood behind Naomi's chair, Ma-chan—now "Kumagai"—darted an ironical glance at me. "Let me introduce myself. I'm Kumagai Seitarō."

"Real name, Kumagai Seitarō; alias, Ma-chan." Naomi looked up at Kumagai. "Well, Ma-chan, introduce yourself a little better."

"Nah, I'd give myself away. . . . Kindly ask Miss Naomi for the details, if you will."

"Of all things! What do I know about the details?"

I was uncomfortable surrounded by this bunch, but Naomi had gotten into a playful mood, and I saw no alternative but to smile and say, "Mr. Hamada, Mr. Kumagai, would you care to join us?"

"Jōji, I'm thirsty. Order something to drink, would you? Hama-san, what do you want? A lemon squash?"

"Anything's fine with me. . . ."

"Ma-chan, how about you?"

"If you're paying, I'll have a whisky and soda."

"Disgusting. I hate drinkers. Their breath stinks."

"What if it does? That's part of a man's appeal, they say."

"Who says? That monkey?"

"Oh, you've got me. I give up."

Oblivious to the people around us, Naomi rocked back and forth with laughter. "Jōji, call the waiter. One whisky and soda, three lemon squashes. . . . No, wait, wait! Cancel the lemon squash. I'd rather have a *fruit cocktail*."

"*Fruit cocktail*?" I wondered how Naomi knew about a drink I'd never heard of. "If it's a *cocktail*, it has liquor in it, right?"

"No, Jōji. You wouldn't know. Hama-chan, Ma-chan, listen to this. This guy is such a bumpkin." Naomi patted me on the shoulder with her index finger as she said "this guy." "That's why I feel funny coming to a dance with him. He's in such a daze, he almost fell down a minute ago."

"The floor's very slippery," said Hamada in my defense. "And everyone feels out of place at first. Once you get used to it, you'll feel right at home."

"Then what about me? Don't I feel at home?"

"You're different, Naomi, you've got spunk. . . . You're a genius in the social arts."

"You're something of a genius yourself, Hama-san."

"Who, me?"

"Sure, making friends with Haruno Kirako, before we knew what was happening!"

"That's right." Kumagai thrust out his lower lip and nodded. "Hamada, have you made a play for Kirako yet?"

"Quit kidding. I don't do that sort of thing."

"But it's cute the way you blush when you defend yourself," said Naomi. "You've got an honest streak somewhere. . . . Say, Hama-san, why don't you call Kirako over here? Come on, call her over! Introduce me to her."

"So you can make fun of her? That tongue of yours is too sharp for me."

"Don't worry, I won't make fun of her. Call her over. The more the merrier."

"Should I call the Monkey, then?"

"Oh, yes, yes." Naomi turned to Kumagai. "Call the Monkey, Ma-chan. Let's all sit together."

"All right. But the music's started again. I'll call her after I've danced one with you."

"I didn't want to dance with you, Ma-chan, but I guess there's no getting out of it."

"Who're you to talk like that? You're just a beginner."

"Now, Jōji, I'm going to dance, so watch me. I'll dance with you later."

I'm sure I had a strange, sad expression on my face, but Naomi jumped up, took Kumagai's arm and joined the stream of dancers who had once again begun their lively movements.

"Ah, this is the seventh dance, a fox trot," said Hamada, taking a program from his pocket. Left alone with me, he seemed to be at a loss for something to talk about. Hesitantly, he rose. "Excuse me, but I promised this dance to Kirako."

"Not at all. Please don't bother about me."

After the three of them had departed, the waiter arrived with a whisky and soda and the "fruit cocktails." There was nothing for me to do but sit alone, with the four drinks in front of me, and gaze absently at the scene on the dance floor. Of course I hadn't come to dance; I was mainly interested in seeing whether Naomi was shown to advantage in a place like this and how well she danced, and so I was more comfortable where I was than I would have been on the floor. Feeling liberated, I eagerly watched Naomi's figure bob in and out among the waves of people.

She's dancing well! I said to myself. Nothing to be ashamed of there. . . . She *is* good when I let her do this sort of thing.

Her colorful, long sleeves waved and danced as she spun around on tiptoe in her little dance sandals and formal white socks. With each step she took, the front flap of her kimono rose, fluttering like a butterfly. In every detail she stood out in the crowd like a blossom: her white fingers, grasping Kumagai's shoulder the way a geisha holds a plectrum; the ornate sash, wound thick and heavy about her torso; the nape of her neck; her profile; her full face; her hair. Looking at her now, I realized that Japanese clothing has its own appeal. And, perhaps because of the Pink Dress and the other women in their wild creations, Naomi's gaudy taste, which had secretly worried me, didn't seem so cheap after all.

"Oh, I'm so hot! How was it, Jōji? Did you watch me dance?" The number having ended, she came back to the table and reached for her fruit cocktail.

"Yes, I was watching. I can hardly believe it's your first time."

"Really? Then I'll dance the next one with you. It's a one-step. All right? The one-step's easy."

"Where're the others, Hamada and Kumagai?"

"They're coming. They're going to bring Kirako and the Monkey. You'd better order two more fruit cocktails."

"That reminds me. The Pink One was dancing with that Westerner just now."

"Yes, wasn't it funny?" Naomi gulped down her drink, moistening her dry mouth. "They're not friends or anything; he just walked over and asked the Monkey to dance with him. He's making a fool of her, don't you see? Doing something like that without being introduced first! He must have taken her for a whore or something."

"Couldn't she just have refused?"

"But that's what's so funny—she couldn't refuse because he's a Westerner! What an idiot! She's a disgrace!"

"But you shouldn't be so harsh. It makes me uncomfortable to hear you talk like that."

"It's all right, I know what I'm doing. A woman like that ought to be told. Otherwise, she'll make trouble for all of us. Ma-chan said so too—she's going too far, and he's going to warn her."

"Well, I suppose it's all right for a man to tell her, but . . ."

"Shhh! Here comes Hama-chan with Kirako. You have to stand up when a *lady* comes."

"Let me introduce you." Hamada stood in front of us like a soldier at attention. "This is Miss Haruno Kirako."

At times like this, I used Naomi's beauty as a standard— is this woman superior to Naomi, or inferior? Gracefully, coquettishly, Kirako stepped from behind Hamada with a self-composed smile. She must have been a year or two older than Naomi, but in her vitality and girlishness she was no different. If anything, her gorgeous clothing surpassed Naomi's.

"How do you do?" she said modestly, lowering her intelligent, round, bright eyes and inhaling slightly as she bowed. Her movements, as one would expect of an actress, had none of Naomi's roughness.

Naomi exceeded the bounds of mere liveliness; she was too rough in everything she did. Her speech, supercilious and lacking in feminine gentleness, was often vulgar. In short, she was a wild animal, whereas Kirako was refined in every way—in the way she spoke, used her eyes, inclined her head, and lifted her hands. She gave the impression of a precious object that's been scrupulously polished with the highest art. For instance, when she sat down at the table and picked up her cocktail glass, her hand, from the palm to the wrist, looked wonderfully slender, so light it could barely support the weight of her softly draping sleeve. Neither the smoothness of her skin nor the warmth of her complexion were inferior to Naomi's, and I don't know how many times my eyes moved back and forth between the two pairs of hands resting on the table. But their faces were very different—if Naomi was Mary Pickford, a *Yankee girl*, then the other was a subtle beauty from Italy or France, graceful and vaguely flirtatious. If they'd been flowers, Naomi would have bloomed in a field, Kirako indoors. How thin, almost transparent was that little nose on her firm, round face! Not even a baby—only a doll made by the greatest master—could have such a delicate nose! Last of all, I noticed her teeth: Naomi had always been proud of hers but Kirako's were rows of pearls, like seeds in the bright red melon that was her lovely mouth.

I felt small and insignificant, and Naomi surely did, too. Suddenly, when Kirako joined our group, Naomi ceased to be arrogant. Far from making fun of Kirako, she fell silent. Conversation at the table dried up completely. But Naomi was a bad loser, and she *had* told Hamada to bring Kirako over. Finally, regaining her usual sauciness, she said, "Hama-san, don't just sit there, say something. . . . Miss Kirako, when did you meet Hama-san?" She'd taken the first steps toward getting a conversation going.

"Oh," said Kirako, her clear eyes suddenly brightening. "It was only very recently."

"I was watching you dance just now." Under Kirako's influence, Naomi's tone had become more polite. "You dance so beautifully; you must practice a great deal."

"Not at all. Well, I have been at it rather a long time, but I don't seem to get any better. I'm so clumsy."

"Nothing of the sort. Hama-san, what do you think?"

"Of course she's good. She learned the real thing at the actresses' training school."

"Oh, my, you say such things." Kirako shyly lowered her eyes.

"But you really are good," Naomi persisted. "When I looked around, Hama-san was the best dancer of the men, and you were the best of the women."

"Oh, my."

"What's this, some kind of dance competition? I'm the best of the men, aren't I?" Kumagai squeezed into our group with the Pink Dress in tow.

According to Kumagai's introduction, the Pink One was the daughter of an Aoyama businessman. Her name was Inoue Kikuko and she was twenty-five or -six, almost beyond marriageable age. (I heard later that she'd been married two or three years before, but the marriage had recently ended because of her obsession with dancing.) No doubt she'd intended to capitalize on her voluptuous beauty by wearing an evening gown that exposed her shoulders and arms, but at close range the effect was more that of a fat matron than of a sensuous woman. Of course a plump figure is better suited to Western clothes than a scrawny one; the real problem was her face. Like a Western doll with the head of a Kyoto doll, her clothes and her features just didn't go together. It wouldn't have been so bad if she'd accepted the situation, but she'd been at pains to harmonize them with all sorts of devices, only to spoil her good looks. I could see now that her real eyebrows were indeed concealed behind her headband; those drawn in above her eyes were clearly artificial. The green makeup around her eyes, the rouge, the beauty spots, the line of her lips, the line of her nose—almost every part of her face was contrived.

"Ma-chan, do you like monkeys?" Naomi asked abruptly.

"Monkeys?" Kumagai fought back a guffaw. "That's a strange question, ain't it?"

"I have two monkeys at home, and I thought I'd give one of them to you, if you like. Well? You do like monkeys, don't you?"

"Think of that. Do you really have monkeys?" Kikuko asked gravely.

Encouraged by her success, Naomi forged ahead, her eyes shining. "Yes, I do. Are you fond of monkeys, Miss Kikuko?"

"Oh, I like all kinds of animals—dogs, cats, and . . ."

"And monkeys?"

"Yes, monkeys, too."

The conversation was so comical that Kumagai turned away holding his sides, while Hamada giggled into a handkerchief and Kirako grinned knowingly. But Kikuko, a surprisingly good-natured woman, didn't seem to realize she was being ridiculed.

As soon as the eighth dance, a one-step, had begun and Kumagai and Kikuko had headed for the dance floor, Naomi announced coarsely, "Humph. What a fool. She must have cotton between her ears. Don't you think so, Miss Kirako?"

"Oh, my, well . . ."

"Doesn't she look like a monkey? I talked about monkeys on purpose."

"Oh, my."

"She didn't catch on, even with everyone laughing like that. It proves she's an idiot."

With a half-startled, half-contemptuous look, Kirako stole a glance at Naomi's face, but "Oh, my" was all she would say.

II

"ALL RIGHT, Jōji, it's the one-step. I'll dance
with you now. Come on." Finally I was to have the honor
of dancing with Naomi.

Though I felt awkward, I was happy—this was a chance to
apply what I'd learned, and my partner was my dear Naomi.
Even if I were so clumsy that people laughed at me, my
clumsiness would make Naomi look even better and I'd be
satisfied. A certain vanity was also involved. I wanted people
to see me and say, "He must be that woman's husband." To
put it another way, I wanted to boast to everyone, "This
woman is mine. Take a look at my treasure." The thought
made me self-conscious and at the same time gave me the
most intense satisfaction. I felt as though I had been justly
compensated for all the sacrifices and hardships I had under-
gone for her sake.

She'd given the impression that she didn't want to dance
with me that night—not until I got a little better. If she
didn't want to, then I'd wait quietly until she did. I'd pretty

much resigned myself, then, when suddenly she'd said, "I'll dance with you." How happy those words made me.

I remember taking Naomi's hand and beginning the one-step, feverish with excitement; but after that, I lost all sense of what was going on. I couldn't hear the music any longer; my steps were chaotic; my eyes were dazed; my heart pounded. It was all so different from dancing to records above Yoshimura's music shop. Once I'd paddled out into this vast sea of people, there was no turning back and no going forward. I didn't know what to do.

"Jōji, why are you shaking? Get hold of yourself!" Naomi scolded in my ear. "Watch out! You slipped again! It's because you turn so fast! Take it easy! Take it easy, I said!" I grew more and more excited as she spoke. To make matters worse, the floor had been specially polished for tonight's dance; if I forgot for a moment and danced as though I were in the practice room, I began to slide all over.

"Here! I told you not to raise your shoulder, didn't I? Lower this shoulder! Lower it!" Shaking her hand loose from my frantic grip, she gave my shoulder a cruel push. "And why do you have to fasten yourself to me like that! . . . Hey, hey, your shoulder again!" Nothing good could come of this; it was as if we were dancing only so that she could shout at me. I was in such a state that I scarcely heard her nagging.

"Jōji, I've had enough," she said angrily. The other dancers were still crying "encore" as she abandoned me and went back to her seat.

"Well! I never! I can't possibly dance with you yet, Jōji. You'll have to practice at home." Hamada and Kirako came back, as did Kumagai and Kikuko, and so the table was lively again; but I was too lost in grief and disillusionment to say anything as Naomi made me the target of her derision.

"Listening to you, a timid fellow wouldn't be able to

dance at all. Stop talking like that. Go ahead and dance with him. Do the guy a favor." I was stung by Kumagai's words. "Do the guy a favor"! Is that any way to talk? Who does this brat think he is?

"He's not as bad as you say, Naomi." It was Hamada. "There're a lot of people who can't dance as well as he can, aren't there? Miss Kirako, how would you like to dance this next fox trot with Mr. Kawai?"

"Yes, that would be fine." Kirako nodded, with all the charm one expects of an actress.

"Oh, no, I couldn't, I couldn't." I was so rattled it was comical.

"Of course you could. You mustn't be so reserved. Don't you think so, Miss Kirako?"

"Oh, yes. . . . Really, it would be fine."

"No, no, it wouldn't do. Please, after I've improved."

"She says she'll dance with you; you ought to take her up on it." Naomi spoke emphatically. It was as though she thought I was passing up an honor that was far more than I deserved. "You mustn't refuse to dance with everybody but me. Go ahead, the fox trot's starting. It'll be good for you to see how other people dance."

"*Will you dance with me?*" A man walked straight up to Naomi and spoke in English. He was a slim young foreigner with white makeup on his prissy face—the man who'd been dancing with Kikuko. Bending over in front of Naomi and smiling, he spoke very quickly. He was probably flattering her. All that I could catch was a shameless "*please, please.*" Naomi looked perplexed and turned bright red, but she couldn't get angry; she just simpered. She wanted to refuse but, caught off guard, she couldn't think of how to refuse delicately in English. The foreigner, apparently encouraged by her smile, waited with an impatient look, as if to say, "Well?"

"Yes . . ." As Naomi reluctantly rose, her cheeks flamed an even brighter red than before.

"She was full of herself a minute ago, but she crumbled in front of that Westerner, didn't she?" Kumagai was in stitches.

"Westerners are so pushy," said Kikuko. "I was at my wits' end."

"Well, shall we, then?" Kirako was waiting; there was nothing else I could say.

Strictly speaking—and not only on the day in question— I had no eyes for any woman other than Naomi. Of course, when I saw a beautiful woman, I sensed her beauty; but I only wanted to look at her quietly, from a distance, without touching her. Madame Shlemskaya was an exception, but even in that case the rapture I experienced was not ordinary sexual desire. It was too sublime, too elusive, too dreamlike to be called that. And then, she was different from us, being a foreigner and a dance instructor; compared with Kirako—a Japanese actress at the Imperial Theater, who wore dazzling clothes—the Countess was easy to be with.

But when I danced with Kirako, I was surprised to find how light she was. Her whole body was soft, like cotton, and her hands were as smooth as new leaves. She quickly got the knack of dancing with me, awkward as I was, and adapted herself to me the way an intelligent horse does to its rider. Lightness carried to this degree is indescribably pleasant. I cheered up immediately; my feet began to move briskly; I glided around as smoothly and effortlessly as if I were riding a merry-go-round.

This is fun! It's wonderful, what a joy! I said to myself.

"Oh, my, you're very good. You're so easy to dance with." Kirako's voice grazed my ear as we spun around and around like a mill wheel. It was a gentle, faint, sweet voice, as became Kirako.

"It's not that; it's because you're so skillful."

"Oh, no, really, . . ."

A moment later, she spoke again. "The band tonight is very good, isn't it?"

"Yes."

"Somehow, dancing doesn't seem worth the effort if the music isn't good."

I noticed that Kirako's lips were just below my temple. This seemed to be a habit with her: just as with Hamada a few minutes before, her sidelock touched my cheek. The caress of her soft hair . . . the faint whispers that escaped from her lips from time to time . . . For me, having been trampled so long by that unruly colt Naomi, this was a height of feminine refinement that I'd never before imagined. I felt as though a sympathetic hand were tending the wounds where thorns had stabbed me. . . .

"I was about to turn him down, but Westerners don't have any friends. You've got to sympathize with them." This was Naomi's defense when she finally came back to the table, looking depressed.

It was about eleven-thirty when number sixteen, a waltz, came to an end. There were still a number of encores to come. Naomi suggested going home by automobile if it got too late; but at length I calmed her down, and we set off toward Shimbashi in time to catch the last train. Kumagai, Hamada, and the women walked with us along Ginza Street. The jazz band still echoed in everyone's ears; when one person started to sing a melody, all the rest joined in. Not knowing the songs, I envied their skill, their good memories, and their young, cheerful voices.

"La, la, la-la-la." Naomi kept time shrilly as she walked. "Hama-san, which do you like best? 'Caravan' is my favorite."

"Oh, 'Caravan'!" shrieked Kikuko. "It's divine!"

"But I rather like 'Whispering,' " said Kirako. "It's so very easy to dance to."

"How about 'Madame Butterfly'? That's my favorite." Hamada began to whistle "Madame Butterfly."

Parting from them at the ticket gate, Naomi and I went to stand on the windy platform in the late winter night. We spoke very little as we waited for the train. My heart was full of the loneliness that follows merriment.

Naomi didn't feel anything of the sort. "That was fun, wasn't it?" she asked. "Let's go again soon." To her attempts to start a conversation, I could only mumble, "yeah," with a glum face.

Is this what they call a *dance*? Did I deceive my mother, fight with my wife, and wear myself out crying and laughing just for this stupid dance party? for that vain, bootlicking, conceited, pretentious crowd?

But, then, why did I go? To parade Naomi in front of them?—if so, then I was as vain as they were. And what about this treasure I'd been so proud of! How about it, fellow? I couldn't help asking myself derisively. When you went out with her, did the world exclaim in wonder, as you had hoped? The proverbial blind man who isn't afraid of snakes —that's you. What if she is the greatest treasure in the world, as far as you're concerned? How did your treasure look when you took her out in public? A vain, conceited bunch! You put it well; but wasn't she the vainest, most conceited one of all? Looking at it objectively, who do you think was the most offensive person there?—so proud of herself, and recklessly calling people names! Kikuko wasn't the only one to be mistaken for a prostitute by that Westerner. And then she couldn't say the simplest thing in English—all flustered, she danced with him. And her language! She may put on the airs of a *lady*, but she talks like a roughneck. Both Kikuko and Kirako are far more refined than she is. . . . These unhappy thoughts—I don't know whether to call them regret or despair—clutched my heart all the way home that night.

On the train, I deliberately sat opposite her so I could take another good look at this woman named Naomi. What was it about her that made me love her so much? Her nose? Her eyes? It's strange, but when I inspected each of her features in turn that night, the face that had always been so appealing to me seemed utterly common and worthless. Then, from the depths of memory, the image of Naomi as I'd first met her in the Diamond Café came back to me dimly. She'd been much more appealing in those days than she was now. Ingenuous and naïve, shy and melancholy, she bore no resemblance to this rough, insolent woman. I'd fallen in love with her then, and the momentum had carried me to this day; but now I saw what an obnoxious person she'd become in the meantime. Sitting there primly, she seemed to be saying, "*I* am the clever one." Her haughty expression said, "No woman could be as chic, as Western-looking as I. Who is the fairest of them all? I am." No one else knew that she couldn't speak a syllable of English, that she couldn't even tell the difference between the *active* and the *passive* voice; but I knew.

As I was secretly heaping abuse on her, she threw her head back, and I could see into the darkness of that button nose of which she was so proud—her most Western feature. The flesh was thick on either side of her nostrils. It occurred to me that I was intimately familiar with these nostrils. Every night when I embraced her, I'd peer into them from this angle. Just the other day I'd helped her blow her nose; I'd caressed it; at times I'd pressed my nose against hers, like a wedge. In other words, this nose, this small lump of flesh attached to her face, was like a part of me. I couldn't think of it as belonging to someone else. But when I looked at it now, with all this in mind, her nose turned into something hateful and filthy. Often a hungry person will wolf down unpalatable food; but as his stomach swells, he'll suddenly notice how bad the food is and feel nauseated. I was experiencing something like this, and when I pictured myself lying face to face with this nose again tonight, I felt bloated, fed up. Enough of this feast.

It's my mother's punishment, I thought. No good comes of cheating your mother to have some fun.

But, readers, you mustn't conclude that I'd lost interest in Naomi. It's true that I thought so myself for a while, because I'd never felt this way before; but when we returned to the house at Ōmori and were alone together, the feeling of satiety that I'd had on the train evaporated, and every part of Naomi—her eyes, nose, hands, feet—was full of enchantment once again. Each part was a supreme delicacy, and I was insatiable.

After that I often went to dances with Naomi. Each time, I'd be confronted with her shortcomings and feel unhappy on the way home. But it never lasted for long, and in the space of a night my love for her would change again and again, like the eyes of a cat.

12

THE HOUSE at Ōmori had always been quiet,
but as time went by, Hamada, Kumagai, and their friends—
most of them young men we'd met at dance parties—came
visiting with increasing frequency.

They usually came in the evening about the time I got
home from work, and they'd play the gramophone and dance.
It wasn't just that Naomi was fond of company; there were
no servants or old people to inhibit them, and the atelier was
perfect for dancing. They enjoyed themselves so much they
were hardly conscious of the passage of time. At first, they
were polite enough to leave at dinnertime; but then Naomi
started forcing them to stay: "Hey! Where're you going!
Have a bite to eat before you go." In the end, it got so that
we'd always order Western food for them from Ōmori House.

It was a humid, mid-June night at the beginning of the
rainy season. Hamada and Kumagai had come and were still
chatting after eleven o'clock, when a driving rain began to

beat against the windows. Both of them spoke of going home, but they hesitated for a bit.

"The weather's terrible. You can't go home in this. Stay here tonight," Naomi said abruptly. "Why not? Ma-chan, you can, can't you?"

"Sure. Either way's okay with me. But if Hamada goes home, I'll go too."

"Hama-san can stay, can't you?" Naomi glanced at me. "It's all right, Hama-san, no need to be bashful. If it were winter, there wouldn't be enough bedding, but we can handle four people now. And tomorrow's Sunday, so Jōji'll be home, and we can sleep as late as we want."

"Yes, why don't you stay? The rain's awful." I had no choice but to join in the invitation.

"How about it, then? And we can have some more fun tomorrow. I've got it! In the evening we can go to the Kagetsuen."

When it was finally decided that they'd stay, I said, "What shall we do about the mosquito net?"

"There's only one, so we'll all sleep under it together. That'll be more fun, won't it?" Naomi squealed happily, like a child on a school trip. Perhaps sleeping in a group was something terribly novel for her.

I wasn't prepared for this. I'd thought that we'd offer the net to the other two while Naomi and I burned mosquito incense and slept on the sofa in the atelier. I hadn't counted on the four of us sharing one small room. But that's what Naomi wanted to do, and I didn't want to appear to be a spoilsport in front of the other two. As usual, Naomi decided everything while I shilly-shallied.

"I'm going to lay out the bedding now, and I want all three of you to help," she commanded as she led us up to the larger of the attic rooms.

I wondered how she'd arrange the quilts. The net wasn't large enough for all of us to sleep under it side by side. The solution was that three of us would sleep in a row, with the fourth at a right angle.

"We'll do it this way—you three men sleep there together, and I'll sleep here by myself."

"This isn't gonna work too well," said Kumagai, peering into the net we'd just finished constructing, "all jumbled together like pigs in a sty."

"So what if we're jumbled together? You shouldn't expect luxury all the time, you know."

"Even when I'm enjoying the hospitality of friends?"

"Of course. You won't be able to sleep tonight, anyway."

"Oh, I'm gonna sleep. I'll sleep and snore." Still in his kimono, Kumagai leaped into bed, shaking the house as he landed.

"Maybe you think you're going to sleep, but I won't let you. Hama-san, don't let Ma-chan sleep. If he gets drowsy, tickle him."

"Who can sleep when it's so muggy?" To the right of Kumagai, who was sprawled on the middle set of bedding with his knees raised, Hamada lay face up in his trousers and undershirt. His belly formed a sharp depression in his thin body. With one hand resting on his forehead and the other flapping a fan, he looked as though he were listening quietly to the rain outside. The sound of the fan seemed to emphasize his discomfort. "And then, I have a feeling I won't be able to sleep very well with a girl in the room."

"But I'm a boy, not a girl. You said so yourself, Hama-san— that I didn't seem like a girl to you." In the shadows beyond the mosquito net, Naomi's back shone white for an instant as she changed into her nightgown.

"Well, that's what I said, but . . ."

". . . if I lie down next to you, I'll seem like a girl?"

"I guess so."

"And how about you, Ma-chan?"

"Doesn't bother me. I don't think of you as a girl."

"What, then?"

"Let's see—you're a seal."

"That's funny. Which is better, a seal or a monkey?"

"Don't like either one," said Kumagai, trying to sound sleepy. I lay to Kumagai's left, silently listening to their chatter. I was wondering which way Naomi would lie down when she came under the net—with her head toward Hamada, or toward me. Her pillow lay in an ambiguous position, neither here nor there. I suspected that she'd put it there deliberately when she spread out the bedding, so that she could go either way. Finally, having changed into her pink crepe gown, she came under the net and stood erect.

"Shall I turn off the light?" she said.

"Yeah, wish you would." It was Kumagai's voice.

"All right, then."

"Oh! Ow!" said Kumagai. Naomi had jumped onto his chest and used him as a footstool while she turned off the switch.

The room darkened, but the street light in front of the house reflected against the window, illuminating the interior just enough for us to make out each other's faces and clothing. Stepping over Kumagai's head, Naomi jumped to her own bedding. The skirt of her nightgown flew open for a moment, brushing a tantalizing gust of air across my nose.

"Ma-chan, how about a smoke?" Instead of lying down right away, Naomi sat on her pillow with her knees apart like a man and looked down at Kumagai. "Hey! Turn this way!"

"Damn, you're just not gonna let me sleep, are you?"

Naomi snickered. "Here! Turn this way! If you don't, I'll be mean to you."

"Ow! Stop, stop! Stop, I said! I'm alive, you know; treat me with a little respect. I may be strong, but it's too much when you stand on me and kick me."

More snickering.

I was looking up at the top of the net, and so I can't be certain; but apparently Naomi was pressing down on his head with her toes.

"I give up," Kumagai said, finally turning over.

"Ma-chan, are you up?" It was Hamada.

"Yeah, she's been tormenting me."

"Hama-san, you turn this way, too. Otherwise, I'll torment *you*."

Hamada turned over and lay on his stomach.

At the same time, I heard a box of matches rattle as Kumagai took them out of his kimono. He struck one, and a light flared above my eyes.

"Jōji, why don't you turn this way, too? What're you doing all by yourself?"

"Uh, what? . . ."

"What's the matter? Are you sleepy?"

"Uh, umm, I guess I was dozing off."

She sniggered. "Nice try, but you're just pretending. Well? Am I right? Aren't you just a little nervous?"

She'd hit the bull's eye. My eyes were closed, but I could feel my face turning red.

"I'll be all right. We're just having some fun, so you can relax and go to sleep. . . . Or, if you really *are* nervous, why don't you turn this way? You don't have to play the martyr."

"I think he wants to be tormented." It was Kumagai. He lit a cigarette and took a puff.

"Oh, no! There's no point in tormenting *him*; I do it to him all the time."

"He's a lucky man," Hamada said, but he didn't mean it; I could only take it as flattery directed at me.

"Jōji? You know, if you want me to torment you, I will."

"No, I've had enough."

"In that case, turn toward me. It's queer for just one person to be different like that."

I turned over and rested my chin on the pillow. Naomi was sitting with her knees up and her legs spread in a V. One foot was planted in front of Hamada's nose, one in front of mine. Kumagai's head was thrust between her legs; he was puffing serenely on his Shikishima.

"Well, Jōji, what do you think of the view?"

"Ummm . . ."

"What do you mean, 'umm'?"

"I don't like it much. You really are a seal, aren't you?"

"That's right, I'm a seal, and I'm resting on the ice. And these three stretched out in front of me—they're male seals."

The pale green net hung overhead like a dense cloud; . . . Naomi's long hair, black even against the darkness of night, fell loosely around her white face; . . . her breasts, arms, and calves were exposed here and there by gaps in her careless gown; . . . this was one of the poses that Naomi always struck to seduce me. When confronted with it, I turned into baited prey. I could feel her staring down at me in the pale darkness with her usual alluring expression, smiling with malevolent eyes.

"And you're lying when you say you don't like it. You always say you can't control yourself when I wear a gown, but tonight you're going to tough it out, because of the others. Am I right, Jōji?"

"Don't be ridiculous."

She snickered. "If you're going to talk so big, I'll make you give in. Shall I?"

"Hey, hey, you're going too far," said Kumagai. "I wish you'd save that for tomorrow night."

"Me, too," Hamada chimed in. "You've got to treat everybody equally tonight."

"I *am* treating you equally. Just to be fair, I have this foot in front of you, Hama-san, and this one in front of Jōji."

"And what about me?"

"You've got the best deal of all, Ma-chan. You're the closest to me, and you've got your head stuck in here, don't you?"

"I'm greatly honored."

"That's right, you're getting the best treatment."

"But you're not going to stay up like that all night, are you? What's going to happen when you lie down?"

"Well, let's see, Hama-san. Where shall I put my head? Toward you, or toward Jōji?"

"It's no big deal where you put your head."

"Yes, it is," said Hamada. "You're in the middle, Ma-chan, and it doesn't matter to you, but it's a problem for me."

"Really, Hama-san? Then shall I lie with my head toward you?"

"That's the problem. If your head's this way, I'll worry; but I'll also be nervous if you lie with it toward Mr. Kawai."

"She tosses around in her sleep," Kumagai interjected. "Whoever gets the feet might get kicked in the middle of the night."

"Mr. Kawai, does she really toss in her sleep?"

"Yes, far more than most."

"Hey, Hamada."

"Yeah?"

"I hear you licked the sole of somebody's foot in your sleep." Kumagai guffawed.

"And what's wrong with licking feet? Jōji does it all the time. He even says my feet are more loveable than my face."

"That's a kind of fetishism, isn't it?"

"But it's true. Right, Jōji? You really do prefer my feet, don't you?"

After that, Naomi would put her feet toward me, then toward Hamada, saying, "Got to be fair." Every five minutes she'd reverse herself and stretch out in the opposite direction. "Now it's Hamada's turn for the feet!" Without getting up, she'd twirl her body around like a draftsman's compass, raise her feet as she turned, and kick at the top of the net as she'd throw her pillow from one end to the other. The seal's activity was so violent that the bottom of the net, from which half of her mattress extended anyway, flapped up and down, letting in any number of mosquitoes.

"Confound it! There's a million of them in here!" Kumagai sat up abruptly and began to battle the mosquitoes. Somebody stepped on the net, breaking its holders and pulling it down on top of us. Inside the fallen net, Naomi flopped about even more wildly than before. Fixing the holders and rehanging the net took a long time. When the commotion finally died down a little, the eastern sky was already aglow.

The sound of the rain, the howl of the wind, the snoring of Kumagai as he lay beside me, . . . Listening to these, I dozed off at last, only to wake up again right away. The room was cramped when just the two of us were in it, and it was permeated with the sweet fragrance and the smell of sweat that clung to Naomi's skin and clothing. With two extra men in the room that night, the musty body odor was worse than ever; and the air within the wind-tight walls had that suffocating mugginess it has just before an earthquake. Now and then, when Kumagai turned over in his sleep, a clammy arm or leg would rub against me. Naomi's pillow was at my end, but she had one foot resting on it. The other knee was raised, and the foot thrust under my mattress. Her head angled toward Hamada; her arms were thrown out to the sides. Exhausted, the tomboy was sleeping happily.

"Naomi," I murmured, checking the others' quiet breathing. I stroked the foot that rested under my mattress. Ah, this foot: this peacefully sleeping, white, beautiful foot; this was mine—I'd washed it with soap in the bath every night since she was a girl. And its soft skin! Her body had shot up since she was fifteen, but this foot was as loveable as ever. It hardly seemed to have developed at all. Yes, the big toe was just as it had been. The shape of the little toe, the roundness of the heel, the swelling flesh of the instep— all were just as they had been. . . . Before I realized it, I was pressing my lips softly to the top of her foot.

I dozed off again after sunrise, only to be awakened by a burst of laughter. Naomi was dangling a string of twisted paper in my nostril.

"Jōji? Are you awake?"

"What time is it?"

"Ten-thirty. But there's no reason to get up yet. Let's stay in bed until the midday gun."

The rain had stopped and the Sunday sky was blue; but the musty, human smell lingered in the room.

13

I T H O U G H T it unlikely that anyone at work
knew of my dissipation. My life was sharply divided between home and office. It's true that Naomi's image hovered
in my mind while I was working, but not enough to inter-
fere with my performance, let alone attract attention. I was
sure that my colleagues still saw me as a gentleman.

But then one gloomy evening late in the rainy season, a
farewell party was held at the Seiyōken in Tsukiji for a
fellow engineer named Namikawa, whom the company was
sending overseas. As usual, I went only for courtesy's sake.
After finishing dinner, we filed from the dining room into
the smoking room and began our after-dinner small talk
over liqueurs. Thinking it would be all right to leave now,
I stood up.

"Hey, Kawai, come sit down." A man named S stopped
me with a grin. Slightly drunk, he occupied a sofa with T,
K, and H and was trying to get me to sit with them, right

in the middle. "Come on, don't run off like that. Do you have someplace to go in this rain?" S grinned again, looking up at me as I stood there noncommittally.

"No, it's not that, but, . . ."

"Then you're going right home?" It was H.

"Yes, please excuse me. I live in Ōmori, and the roads are bad in this kind of weather. If I don't leave early, I won't be able to find a ricksha."

"That's pretty good." It was T this time and he was laughing. "Listen, Kawai, the cat's out of the bag."

"What?" Not knowing the significance of the "cat," I didn't understand what T meant. I felt a little panicky.

"We really didn't expect it—always thought you were such a gentleman, . . ." Now it was K, cocking his head to one side as if he were terribly impressed. "The times are moving ahead, all right, if Kawai's taken up dancing."

"Listen, Kawai." S spoke close to my ear so as not to be overheard. "Who's that fantastic beauty you've been going out with? We'd like to get to know her, too."

"She's not that kind of woman."

"But I hear she's an actress at the Imperial. Isn't that right? There's a rumor going around that she's a movie actress, too. A Eurasian, according to one theory. Where does she hang out? We won't let you go until you tell us." Paying no attention to my sour expression and my confused spluttering, S sat forward and questioned me with great earnestness. "What is it, then? Can you only call her when you go dancing?"

A little more, and I might have shouted, "Idiot!" I'd thought that no one at work would find out. But to my surprise, they hadn't just gotten wind of Naomi—judging from the way this notorious playboy S talked, they didn't even believe that Naomi and I were married. They thought she was the kind of woman they could summon whenever they pleased. "Fool!" I was on the point of shouting, pale with rage, in response to this intolerable affront. "How dare you talk that way about a man's wife!" Indeed, for a moment my face did go white.

"Come on, Kawai, tell us!" H pressed me relentlessly, counting on my soft-heartedness. He turned to K. "Where did you say you heard about her?"

"From a Keio student."

"And what did he say?"

"He's a relative of mine, crazy about dancing. He spends all his time in dance halls, and that's where he got to know her."

"What's her name?" T asked, leaning over toward K.

"Her name . . . let's see . . . it was something odd . . . Naomi . . . I think it was Naomi."

"Naomi? . . . Then maybe she *is* a Eurasian." S threw me a teasing glance. "If she's a Eurasian, then she must not be an actress."

"Anyway, I hear she's a real fast one. They say she's been playing fast and free with some Keio students."

I was twitching, displaying a strained smile, my mouth trembling; but when K's account reached this point, the smile froze on my face, and my eyes seemed to roll back into their sockets.

"Oh! Oh! Sounds good," cried the delighted S. "Does this student you're related to have something going with her?"

"Not that I know of, but he said that two or three of his friends did."

"Stop, stop. Kawai'll worry. Look at his face!" As T said this, they all looked up at me and laughed.

"Why not let him worry a little? He's a poor sport to monopolize a beauty like that and keep her hidden from us."

"How about it, Kawai? A gentleman ought to have something spicy to worry about once in a while, eh?"

They all laughed.

I was no longer angry. I couldn't hear what anyone was saying. I was conscious only of the laughter echoing in my ears. My confusion at the moment was about how best to get out of the situation. Should I cry? Should I laugh? If I said the wrong thing, wouldn't I be ridiculed all the more?

I ran from the smoking room in a daze. My feet didn't touch the ground until I reached the muddy street and was struck by the cold rain. I fled toward the Ginza, afraid that something was following me.

At the first intersection beyond Owarichō, I turned and walked toward Shimbashi. More precisely, my legs moved unconsciously in that direction; my head had nothing to do with it. The street lights reflected brightly off the wet pavement into my eyes. Despite the weather, there seemed to be a number of people on the street. A geisha under an umbrella; a young woman wearing flannels; streetcars and automobiles . . .

Naomi's a fast one? She plays fast and free with students? . . . Was it possible? Yes, definitely possible. Given Naomi's behavior recently, it would have been odd not to think so; even I had been secretly concerned. But I was reassured by the presence of so many male friends around her. Naomi was a child; she was very active. As she herself said, "I'm a boy." It's just that she liked to bring a lot of boys together and roughhouse with them innocently and cheerfully. If she'd had an ulterior motive, she wouldn't have been able to hide it from so many eyes. Surely she . . . But I shouldn't have been thinking "surely."

But *surely*, . . . *surely* it wasn't true. Naomi was too forward, but she had a noble character. I knew that very well. Outwardly she looked down on me, but she was grateful to me for rearing her since she was fifteen. In bed late at night, she'd told me again and again, with tears in her voice, that she'd never betray me. I couldn't doubt her words. That story of K's—maybe some scoundrels in the office had made it up to play a joke on me. What a relief that would be. . . . Who was the student related to K? She'd had relationships with two or three of his friends? Two or three? . . . Hamada? Kumagai? . . . Those two looked the most suspicious. But in that case, why didn't they quarrel? Why would they come to the house together, not separately, and play happily with Naomi? Could it have been a device to trick me? Or was Naomi manipulating them so well that neither one knew about the other? No, more important—was it possible that Naomi had fallen so far? If she'd been involved with both of them, could she have pulled off that shameless, brazen-faced performance the night of the slumber party? If so, then she was a better actress than any prostitute. . . .

Before I realized it, I'd crossed the Shimbashi Bridge and walked along the Shibaguchi Road as far as Kanasugi Bridge, splashing through the mud as I went. Rain walled in the world and enclosed me on all sides; the water spilling off my umbrella splashed the shoulders of my raincoat. It had rained like this the night we all slept together. And the night I first opened my heart to Naomi at the Diamond Café, too—the season had been spring, but it had rained like this. Could it be that someone was at the house in Ōmori tonight, again, even as I walked along, drenched? Another slumber party? Suddenly I had misgivings. Hamada and Kumagai would be slouching on the sofa with Naomi between them, telling their stupid jokes. The lewd scene in the atelier came vividly before my eyes.

Naomi, Naomi! Why had I deserted her tonight? She wasn't with me—that was the problem; that was the worst thing. . . . I thought that if I could just see Naomi, my nerves would calm down somewhat. I prayed that when I heard her generous voice and saw her guiltless eyes, my doubts would vanish.

But then, what should I say if she wanted to have another slumber party? What attitude should I take toward her from now on, and toward the riffraff who approached her— Hamada, Kumagai, and the others? Should I defy her anger and dare to supervise her more strictly? It'd be fine if she submitted, but what if she resisted? No, that wouldn't happen. I'd say, "Some men from the office said the most insulting things to me tonight. I want you to conduct yourself a little more carefully, so that people won't misunderstand you." This was different from other situations. She'd probably obey for the sake of her own good name. But if she were indifferent about her good name and about the misunderstandings, then she really was suspect. K's story would be true. If . . . oh, if that were the case . . .

Calming myself as much as I could and struggling to be dispassionate, I envisioned this last scenario. *If it turns out that she has deceived me, will I be able to forgive her?* The truth is that I was already incapable of going on without her for even a day. If she repented and apologized for her past misconduct, I wouldn't want to criticize her further, nor would I have the right to, because I shared the blame for her going astray. But she was stubborn, and she tended to get particularly obstinate with me: would she give in readily, even if I confronted her with evidence? This is what worried me. And even if she did give in, how could I be sure that she wouldn't go on unreformed, thinking of me as a pushover, and repeat her mistakes again and again? What if our mutual pigheadedness forced us to separate? This is what frightened me most of all. To be blunt, it caused me far more anxiety than her chastity did. If I were going to grill her, or govern her, I'd have to prepare myself for that eventuality. If she said, "In that case, I'm leaving," I hoped that I'd be ready to say, "Then leave, if you like."

I knew that on this score Naomi was in as weak a position as I. She could live extravagantly as long as she was with me, but if she were thrown out she'd have no place to go but that squalid house in Senzoku. Then there'd be no one to make a fuss over her, unless she really did become a prostitute. It may have been different before; but now, spoiled and proud, she wouldn't be able to bear that kind of life. Hamada or Kumagai might offer to take her in, but she would know that a student couldn't provide her with the luxury that I had. From that point of view, it was a good thing that I'd given her a taste for luxury.

Come to think of it, she'd backed down that time she tore up her notebook during our English lesson and I told her angrily to get out. It would've been hard on me if she'd walked out, but it would've been even harder on her. What would have become of her without me? If she had left me she'd have ended up in the lower depths of society, at the bottom of the heap again. That prospect must terrify her as much today as it did then. She's already in her nineteenth year. Now that she's older and knows the world a little better, she'll understand the danger all the more keenly. If I'm right, she might threaten to leave me, but she won't be able to go through with it. She knows well enough I wouldn't be deceived by such a transparent bluff.

I'd regained some of my courage by the time I reached Ōmori Station. No matter what happened, Naomi and I weren't destined to separate. Of that much I could be sure.

When I arrived in front of the house, I saw that my ominous imaginings had been completely off the mark. The atelier was dark and perfectly quiet—there didn't seem to be a single visitor; there was only a light in the attic.

She's here by herself. I was relieved. What a blessing, I couldn't help thinking.

I unlocked the front door, stepped inside, and immediately turned on the light in the atelier. Though the room was as cluttered as usual, there were no signs that there'd been company.

"Naomi, I'm home. . . ." She didn't answer. I climbed the stairs and found her sleeping peacefully in the larger of the attic rooms. There was nothing unusual in this—she often crawled under the covers when she was bored, day or night, and fell asleep over a novel. I was reassured by the sight of her guiltless face.

"Is she deceiving me? Is it possible? . . . This girl, breathing peacefully here before my eyes? . . ."

Taking care not to awaken her, I sat by her pillow, held my breath, and stealthily gazed at her sleeping form. In the old days, a fox might deceive a young man by taking the form of a princess, only to reveal its true form when it slept and give itself away. I recalled hearing such stories in my childhood. Rough sleeper that she was, Naomi had shed her coverlet and was gripping it between her thighs. One elbow was raised, and the hand rested like a bent twig on her exposed breast. The other arm was extended gracefully toward my knees. Her head inclined toward the extended arm, threatening to slip off of the pillow at any moment. A book lay open at her nose. It was the novel *Descendants of Cain* by Arishima Takeo, "the greatest writer today," in Naomi's judgment. My eyes moved back and forth between the pure white Western paper in the book and the whiteness of her breast.

Naomi's skin looked yellow one day and white another; but it was extraordinarily limpid when she was fast asleep, or had just awakened, as though all the fat in her body had melted away. *Night* is usually associated with *darkness*; but to me, night always brought thoughts of the whiteness of Naomi's skin. Unlike the bright, shadowless whiteness of noon, it was a whiteness wrapped in tatters, amid soiled, unsightly, dusty quilts; and that drew me to it all the more. As I sat gazing, her breast, in the shadow thrown by the lampshade, loomed vividly, like an object lying in the depths of pellucid water. Her face, too, radiant and kaleidoscopic by day, now wore a mysterious cast, a melancholy frown, like that of one who's just swallowed bitter medicine, or of one who's been strangled. I loved her sleeping face. "You look like a different person when you're asleep," I often told her, "as though you're having a terrible dream." "Her death-face would be beautiful, too," I often told myself. If she were a fox and her true form were this bewitching, then I'd eagerly let myself be enchanted.

I sat there quietly for about thirty minutes. Naomi's hand, extending palm up from the shadow of the lampshade into the light, was loosely clenched, like a blossom about to open. I could clearly see the pulse beating calmly at her wrist.

"When did you get back? . . ." Her peaceful, regular breathing stirred slightly, and she opened her eyes. A trace of melancholy remained.

"Just now, . . . a little while ago."

"Why didn't you wake me up?"

"I called, but you didn't wake up, so I kept still."

"And what were you doing, sitting there? Watching me as I slept?"

"Yes."

"What a funny man you are!" She laughed artlessly, like a child, and put her outstretched hand on my lap.

"I was bored here all by myself. I thought somebody might come, but no one did. . . . Papa, are you coming to bed?"

"I guess I might."

"Oh, do! Falling asleep like that, I've been bitten all over by mosquitoes. Look at this! Scratch me here!"

Doing as I was told, I scratched her arms and back for a while.

"Thanks. Oh, it itches. . . . Would you get my night-gown from over there, please? And then would you put it on me?"

I fetched the gown, embraced her as she lay with her arms outstretched, and scooped her up. While I loosened her sash and changed her kimono for the nightgown, she relaxed and let her arms and legs dangle limp as a corpse.

"Put up the mosquito net, Papa, and then come to bed quickly. . . ."

14

THERE'S no need to go into detail about our pillow talk that night. When Naomi heard what had happened at the Seiyōken, she didn't make much of it. "How rude!" she said severely. "They don't know anything!" The problem was that people didn't understand social dancing yet. If a man and a woman danced with their arms around each other, people assumed that they were having an improper relationship and started to spread the word. Reactionary newspapers wrote groundless articles that gave social dancing a bad name, and so most people had made up their minds that it was unwholesome. We'd just have to resign ourselves to hearing that sort of talk.

"And, Jōji, I've never once been alone with another man. Isn't that right?"

We went dancing together, we played at home together, and she never entertained a lone guest when I was out. If someone did come alone, she'd say, "Sorry, I'm by myself today," and the visitor would respectfully leave. None of her friends was ill-mannered enough to stay. Then she added, "I may be selfish, but I know what's right and what's wrong. I could deceive you if I wanted to, but I'd never do anything like that. Everything's open and aboveboard, Jōji. I've never kept anything from you."

"I know. It's just that it was unpleasant to have people say that sort of thing to me."

"Then what do you want to do about it? Are you saying that we give up dancing?"

"We don't need to give it up, but you ought to be careful so that people won't misunderstand."

"But I just told you how careful I've been with my friends."

"That's right. But *I'm* not the one who's misunderstanding."

"If you understand, then I'm not afraid of what other people say. They all dislike me anyway, because I'm coarse and I have a dirty mouth."

Then she repeated, in a sentimental, sugary voice, that she only wanted me to trust her and love her, that it was natural for her to make male friends, because she wasn't like a woman. She preferred men because they were more open and uncomplicated, and that was why all of her friends were men. But she didn't have improper feelings for them at all—not sensual, not romantic. And finally, weeping copiously, she delivered her usual lines: "I've never forgotten the debt I owe you for raising me," and, "I think of you as both father and husband." Then, she had me wipe her tears and rained kisses on me.

But strangely, whether by design or by coincidence, she never spoke of Hamada or Kumagai in the course of that long conversation. I'd actually planned to mention their names and watch her face for a reaction, but I missed my chance. Naturally I didn't believe everything she said, but once you start doubting, it's hard to know what to believe. There was no need to scrutinize the past so closely; all I had to do now was be attentive and supervise her more closely. . . . No, at first I'd intended to be firm, but gradually she brought me around to this vague position. Drowned in tears and kisses, I still thought twice when I heard her whispers between the sobs; I suspected that she was lying; but in the end her words began to sound true.

After that, I kept a casual eye on Naomi's behavior. Little by little, slowly enough so that it didn't seem calculated, she appeared to be reforming. We still went dancing, but not as often as before; and when we went, we'd dance less and leave earlier. Visitors were no longer a nuisance. When I returned home from the office, she'd be there alone, reading a novel, knitting, listening quietly to the gramophone, or planting flowers in the garden.

"Did you stay home alone again today?"

"Yes, all by myself. Nobody came to visit."

"Weren't you lonely, then?"

"If I know from the start that I'm going to be alone, I'm not lonely. It doesn't bother me."

Then she added, "I like to have a good time, but I don't mind being alone, either. I didn't have any friends when I was little. I always played by myself."

"It did look that way, now that you mention it. You hardly ever talked with the others at the Diamond Café. You even looked a bit gloomy."

"That's right. I act like a tomboy, but my real personality is gloomy. . . . You don't like me to be gloomy?"

"It's fine if you're quiet, but I'd rather you weren't gloomy."

"But isn't it better than being rowdy, the way I used to be?"

"I can't tell you how much better."

"I'm good now, aren't I?"

Suddenly she ran to me, threw her arms around my neck, and kissed me so violently that my head swam.

"What do you think," I'd say, "we haven't gone dancing in a while. Shall we go tonight?"

"Well, whatever—if you want to, Jōji," she'd reply vaguely, with a glum face; or, often, "Why don't we go to the movies instead? I don't feel like dancing tonight."

The innocent, happy life we'd shared four or five years before now returned. All by ourselves, Naomi and I went to Asakusa almost every night. We'd go to a movie theater and have dinner at a restaurant on the way home. As we ate, we'd recall our past together nostalgically. "You were so small that you sat on the rail at the Imperial movie theater and watched the picture with your hand on my shoulder," I'd say. And Naomi would say, "The first time you came to the café, you just sat there looking moody and staring at my face. It made me nervous."

"By the way, Papa, you don't bathe me any more. You were always washing my body in those days."

"Yes, that's right, come to think of it."

"What do you mean, 'come to think of it'? Aren't you going to wash me any more? I suppose you're not interested in bathing me now that I've gotten so big?"

"It's not that at all. I'd bathe you right now, but the truth is, I was holding myself back."

"Really? Then wash me. I'll be the baby again."

Luckily, this conversation took place right at the start of the hot season. I moved the Western bathtub back to the atelier from the corner of the storeroom where I'd left it and started bathing Naomi again. "My big baby," I'd said in those days; but now, when I stretched her out full-length in the tub, I saw that she had matured into a splendid adult. Loosened, her voluptuous hair spread out richly, like evening rain clouds; her rounded flesh formed dimples here and there at her joints. Her shoulders were fuller; her chest and hips rose higher and more resilient; and her legs seemed even longer than ever.

"Have I grown some, Jōji?"

"Oh, yes, you have. You're almost as tall as I am, now."

"Pretty soon I'll be taller than you. When I weighed myself the other day, I was one hundred and seventeen pounds."

"Amazing. I only weigh about one hundred and thirty."

"Are you really heavier than I am? You're such a little shrimp."

"Of course I'm heavier. Maybe I'm a shrimp, but men have heavier frames."

"Then do you still have the courage to be a horse and give me a ride? We used to do that a lot when I first came, ride around the room, . . ."

"You were light then, around one hundred, I guess."

"You'd collapse, now."

"Don't be silly. If that's what you think, then just get on and see."

The result of our joking was that we played horse, just as we had before.

"The horse is ready," I said, getting down on all fours. Naomi plumped her hundred and seventeen pounds on my back and put the towel reins in my mouth.

"What a wobbly little horse you are! Look sharp! Giddap! Giddap!" she cried happily, wrapping her legs around my belly and jerking on the reins. I was determined not to collapse under her. Heaving and struggling, I sweated my way around the room. She kept up her mischief until I was worn out.

"Jōji, this summer couldn't we go to Kamakura again? It's been a long time." This was at the beginning of August. "I want to go; we've never been back."

"You're right. We haven't gone since, have we?"

"No, so let's make it Kamakura this year. It's our special place."

How happy her words made me! As she said, our honeymoon—yes, it was a honeymoon—had been at Kamakura. No other place was special for us the way Kamakura was. Every year since then we'd gone somewhere else to escape from the heat, but I'd completely forgotten about Kamakura. Naomi had hit on a wonderful idea.

"Yes, let's go, let's definitely go!" I agreed without a second thought.

As soon as we'd decided, I took ten days off from the company. Closing up the house at Ōmori, the two of us set out for Kamakura early in the month. We rented a cottage attached to a plant nursery called Shokusō, on the street that runs from the Hase road toward the Emperor's villa.

At first, I'd thought we might stay at a good inn this time—certainly not at a place like the Golden Wave Pavilion again. We ended up with a rental because Naomi came to me with word of the nurseryman's cottage. "I heard about something just right for us, from Miss Sugizaki," she began. Inns were expensive and lacked privacy. It was always best to rent a place if possible. As luck would have it, Miss Sugizaki's relative, the one who was a director at Oriental Petroleum, would let us have a place that he'd rented but wasn't using. It would be an ideal arrangement. The director had reserved the place for June, July, and August for a total of five hundred yen; he'd used it through July but was tired of Kamakura now and would gladly rent it to anyone who wanted it. If it were to a friend of Miss Sugizaki's, then he didn't care about the money. This was Naomi's story.

"Oh, let's take it," she said. "We'll never find another place as good. And it won't cost anything, so we can stay all month."

"But I can't be away from work that long."

"So, from Kamakura you can commute by train. Why don't you? All right?"

"Shouldn't you take a look at it and see whether you like it?"

"Right, I'll go tomorrow. Can we take it if I like it?"

"Yes, but I wouldn't feel right if we didn't pay for it. We'll have to resolve that somehow."

"I know. You're busy, so if we decide to take it I'll go to Miss Sugizaki and ask her to accept some money. We'll have to pay a hundred or a hundred and fifty, anyway."

And so Naomi speeded things along by herself. One hundred yen was agreed on, and she took care of making the payment.

I had misgivings, but the house, once I saw it, was better than I'd expected. It was a one-story building, separate from the main house, with two matted rooms, twelve-by-twelve and nine-by-nine, respectively, an entryway, a bath, and a kitchen. It had its own entrance leading directly to the garden and the street, and there was no need to come in contact with the nurseryman's family. It was as though the two of us were setting up a new household. For the first time in a long time, I sat down on new mats in pure Japanese style. Crossing my legs in front of the brazier, I felt refreshed.

"This is wonderful. I feel right at home."

"Isn't it a nice house? Which do you like better, this one or the one at Ōmori?"

"This one's far more comfortable. I feel as though I could stay here indefinitely."

"There, you see? That's why I said we should take it." Naomi was pleased with herself.

One day, perhaps three days after we'd arrived, we went to the beach in the afternoon, swam for about an hour, and were lying on the sand when someone called out, "Miss Naomi!" right above our heads.

It was Kumagai. Apparently he'd just come out of the water: his wet bathing suit clung to his chest, and the salt water was dribbling down his hairy calves.

"Ma-chan. When did you come?"

"Today. I thought it was you." Then he turned toward the water and raised his arm. "Hey," he called.

"Hey," replied someone from the water.

"Who's that, swimming out there?"

"Hamada. Hamada, Seki, and Nakamura—the four of us came together."

"How exciting. Where's your inn?"

"We're not that fancy. It's hot, so we came for the day. That's all."

Hamada came up as they were talking.

"Hello! It's been a long time; sorry I've been out of touch. Mr. Kawai, you never go dancing any more, do you?"

"Well, that's not quite it. Naomi says she's tired of dancing."

"I see. That's a shame. And how long have you been here?"

"Only two or three days. We're renting a cottage at a nursery near Hase."

"It's a wonderful place," Naomi said. "Thanks to Miss Sugizaki, we have it for the whole month."

"Very snazzy," said Kumagai.

"Then you'll be here for a while?" said Hamada. "They have dances in Kamakura, too, you know. Actually, there's one tonight at the Kaihin Hotel. I'd go if I had a partner."

"I don't want to go," Naomi said bluntly. "I don't even want to think about dancing when it's so hot. Maybe when the weather cools down."

"I guess you're right. Summer's not the time to go dancing."

Then, hesitantly, Hamada said, "What shall we do now, Ma-chan? Do you want to go back into the water?"

"Not me, I'm too tired. Let's go. Even if we go over now and rest a little, it'll be dark by the time we get back to Tokyo."

"If you go *where* now?" Naomi asked Hamada. "Is there something interesting going on?"

"Hardly. It's a villa that Seki's uncle has in Ōgigayatsu. We all got dragged there today, and they say they're going to treat us to dinner, but it's so stiff and formal, we're planning to run away without eating."

"Really? Is it that formal?"

"Unbearable. The maid gets down and does that ceremonial, three-fingered bow. It's depressing. Even if they treated us, we wouldn't be able to swallow. . . . Hamada, let's get going. We can get something to eat in Tokyo."

But Kumagai made no move to stand up. Still seated on the beach, he was scooping up handfuls of sand and pouring it on his legs.

"Well, then, how would it be if you ate with us this evening? Since you've come all this way . . ."

Naomi, Hamada, and Kumagai had lapsed into silence; I thought I had to say something to relieve the awkwardness.

15

W E H A D a lively meal that night, for the first time in many days. The six of us, including Hamada, Kumagai, Seki, and Nakamura, sat around the low table in the larger room and chatted until about ten o'clock. At first I hadn't felt good about this bunch invading our new lodgings, but seeing them like this after a long interval, I enjoyed their youthful dispositions, so lively, open and easygoing. Naomi was tactful and charming; the way she entertained our guests without being flippant was just right.

"I had a good time tonight," I said. "It's nice to see them once in a while." After sending them off on the last train, Naomi and I talked as we strolled hand in hand under the summer-night sky. The stars were bright, and a cool breeze blew in from the sea.

"Did you really have a good time?" Naomi sounded pleased that I was in such a good mood. After thinking for a moment, she said, "Once you've spent some time with them, you see they're not bad people."

"No, they really aren't."

"But aren't you afraid they'll come barging in again one of these days? Seki's uncle has that villa, you know. Didn't Seki say he'd be coming back with all of them now and then?"

"Yes, but I don't think they'll come barging into our place, will they?"

"I wouldn't mind once in a while, but it'll be irritating if they come too often. We shouldn't be so hospitable if they come again. They don't have to stay for dinner."

"But surely we can't just send them away."

"Of course we can. I'll tell them they've overstayed their welcome and send them away in a hurry—it's all right to say that, isn't it?"

"We'd be in for another good ribbing from Kumagai."

"What difference does that make? It's their fault if they come around intruding when we've come all this way to Kamakura."

We arrived at a dark place under the pines. Naomi stopped walking and stood still. "Jōji?"

When I grasped the significance of her sweet, faint, pleading voice, I wrapped her silently in my arms. It was like taking a gulp of sea water as I tasted those strong, passionate lips.

My ten-day vacation passed in a twinkling, and we were still happy. As we'd planned, I began to commute daily from Kamakura to the office. Seki and his friends, who'd said that they'd be "dropping by now and then," had come only once, about a week later.

Toward the end of the month, something urgent came up at the office that forced me to work late. Usually I was able to get home by seven o'clock and have dinner with Naomi, but for the next five or six days I'd be staying at work until nine and arriving home after eleven. It was now the fourth day of this new schedule.

I'd expected to work until nine that evening, but I finished early and left the office around eight. As always, I took the National electric line to Yokohama, where I changed to a steam line. It must have been before ten when I got off at Kamakura. I was more impatient than usual to rush home, see Naomi's face, and relax over dinner, because I'd been getting home late night after night—though actually it had only been three or four days; and so I got a ricksha at the station and took the road past the Emperor's villa.

To someone coming home after putting in a hot day's work and being flung about on the train, the night air at the shore was indescribably soft and refreshing against the skin. To-night, as so often, there'd been a brief shower at sunset; and there was a secretive, quiet fragrance in the mist that rose softly from the damp foliage and pine branches dripping with dew. Here and there puddles glistened brightly, even in the darkness; but the sandy road was just damp enough to keep down the dust, and the puller's footfalls on the ground were as light and soft as if he were treading on velvet. I could hear the sound of a gramophone coming from beyond the hedge of a house that seemed to be some-one's villa; figures clad in white summer kimonos were strolling about, one here, two there. It felt just as a summer resort should.

I got out at the gate and sent the ricksha back, then walked through the garden toward the veranda. I expected Naomi to slide open the shōji and greet me there as soon as she heard my shoes in the garden; but while the light burned brightly inside, there was no sign that she was there. It was perfectly quiet.

"Naomi, . . ." I called two or three times. There being no answer, I stepped up on the veranda and opened the shōji. The room was deserted. As usual, it was a jumble of bathing suits, towels, and robes hanging everywhere—on the walls, on the sliding doors, and in the alcove—and of tea cups, ashtrays, and cushions strewn about; but the room was somehow mute and lifeless. With that special sense a lover possesses, I could tell that it had been quiet for some time.

"She went out, . . . probably two or three hours ago," I said to myself.

All the same, I peered into the privy, checked the bath, and, just to be sure, stepped down into the kitchen and turned on the light by the sink. The remains of some Western food and a large bottle of Masamune sake, the aftermath of heavy eating and drinking, greeted my eyes. Come to think of it, the ashtrays had been full of cigarette butts. Those fellows must have come barging in again.

I ran to the main house. "Naomi doesn't seem to be here. Did she go out?" I asked the nurseryman's wife.

"The young lady?" She always referred to Naomi as "the young lady." (Naomi was unhappy if she was called anything else. Though we were married, she wanted people to think that we were just living together, or perhaps engaged.) "The young lady came back in the evening, and then went out with everyone after dinner."

"Everyone?"

"Well, . . ." She hesitated a moment. "Young Mr. Kumagai and all the others . . ."

I thought it odd that the landlady knew Kumagai's name and, what's more, called him "young Mr. Kumagai"; but I didn't want to take the time to ask about that now.

"You said that she came back in the evening. Was she with them during the day, too?"

"She went bathing by herself in the afternoon, then she came back with young Mr. Kumagai, and . . ."

"Alone with Kumagai?"

"That's right . . ."

I hadn't started to panic yet, but the landlady's awkward answers and the uneasiness in her face troubled me. I didn't want to give myself away, but my tone inevitably betrayed my anxiety.

"Then they weren't all together!"

"No, it was just the two of them. They said there was an afternoon dance today at the hotel, and they went off together."

"And then?"

"And then in the evening she came back with all of them."

"Did they all eat dinner together at the cottage?"

"Yes. It was ever so lively . . ." Reading the look in my eyes, she forced a smile.

"About what time was it that they went out after dinner?"

"Let's see, around eight o'clock, I think it was."

"Two hours ago," I said without thinking. "Then do you suppose they're at the hotel? Did you overhear anything?"

"I'm not sure, but they might be at the villa."

I remembered that Seki's uncle had a villa at Ōgigayatsu. "So they went to the villa. In that case, I'll go meet her there. Do you know where it is?"

"Oh, it's not far—it's on the beach at Hase."

"At Hase? I thought I heard that it was at Ōgigayatsu. . . . Listen, the villa I'm talking about belongs to the uncle of a friend of Naomi's named Seki. I don't know whether he came here tonight, too, but . . ."

A look of surprise flashed across the landlady's face.

"Is it a different villa then?"

"Yes . . . well . . ."

"Whose villa is on the beach at Hase?"

"Well, . . . Mr. Kumagai's relative . . ."

"Kumagai's?" I suddenly went pale.

The landlady told me to take the Hase road away from the

station, bear left, and go straight down the road past the Kaihin Hotel. The road came to an end at the beach. The Ōkubo villa, on the last corner, belonged to Kumagai's relative. This was the first I'd heard of the place. Neither Naomi nor Kumagai had ever breathed a word about it.

"Does Naomi go there often?"

"Well, let's see . . ." Despite her words, I could see she was uncomfortable.

"Of course tonight wasn't the first time, was it?" I was short of breath and my voice shook, but there was nothing I could do about it. Maybe the landlady was frightened by the look on my face, because she paled, too. "Don't worry, I won't do anything to trouble you. Please, speak freely. How about last night? Did she go last night, too?"

"Yes . . . I believe she did . . ."

"How about the night before last?"

"Yes."

"She went then, too?"

"Yes."

"And the night before that?"

"Yes, the night before that, too."

"Then she's gone every night since I started coming home late?"

"Well, I don't remember exactly, but . . ."

"And about what time has she usually been coming back?"

"Usually . . . well, just before eleven . . ."

Then the two of them had been taking me for a ride from the very start! That's why Naomi had wanted to come to Kamakura!—My head began to spin like a tornado. With extraordinary swiftness, everything that Naomi had said and done in recent days flashed through my mind. In an instant, the web of trickery that encircled me became astonishingly obvious. It was so complex that a simple person like me could barely grasp it—multiple lies, a meticulously planned conspiracy, and who knows how many accomplices. From level, secure ground I'd been flung into a deep pit, and from the bottom of the pit I looked up enviously at Naomi, Kumagai, Hamada, Seki, and countless others laughing far above me as they went by.

"I'm going now. If I miss her on the way and she comes back, please don't tell her that I've been here. I have an idea." With these words, I ran toward the street.

I went to the front of the Kaihin Hotel and, staying in the shadows as much as possible, followed the road the landlady had told me about. Large villas lined the way on both sides. The road was hushed and still, almost deserted, and, fortunately, rather dark. I took out my watch under a gatelight. Whether Naomi was alone with Kumagai at the Ōkubo villa or partying with the regular crew, I wanted to catch her red-handed. I'd try to gather my evidence stealthily, without their noticing, and see what kind of cock-and-bull story they'd come up with later. Then I'd nail them and teach them a good lesson. My steps quickened at the thought.

I found the house easily. For a few minutes I walked up and down the street in front, studying the layout. There was a fine stone gate, beyond which the grounds were densely wooded. A gravel path weaved through the trees and shrubs to a secluded entrance. The faded writing on the nameplate, "Ōkubo Villa," and the mossy stone wall surrounding a spacious garden gave the place the look of a venerable estate, rather than of a summer residence. The more I saw, the more astonished I was that the owner of this imposing mansion, occupying such a splendid site, was related to Kumagai.

I stole through the gate, making as little noise as possible on the gravel path. Because of the heavy growth of trees, I hadn't been able to see the main house very well from the street; but as I approached, I was surprised to find that everything—the formal entrance, the family entrance, both floors, and all the rooms that I could see from where I stood—was silent, closed, and dark.

Well, then, I thought, Kumagai's room must be around in back. I crept to the rear of the house. Sure enough, lights were on in a second-floor room and at the service entrance beneath it.

I could tell at a glance that the room was Kumagai's. Not only was his flat mandolin leaning against the rail of the veranda; inside, a Tuscan hat that I remembered having seen before was hanging on a post. The shōji were open, but there were no voices. It was clear that no one was in the room.

The shōji at the service entrance had been left open, too, as if someone had just gone out. My eyes followed the faint band of light that the open door threw onto the ground, until I discovered a back gate, consisting of two old wooden posts, only fifteen or twenty feet away. Between the posts, I could see waves tracing a vivid white line in the darkness as they broke on Yui Beach. The smell of the sea assaulted me.

They must have gone out through here, I said to myself.

Just as I was going through the back gate toward the beach, I heard Naomi's unmistakable voice nearby. The wind must have prevented me from hearing it before.

"Hey, wait! There's sand in my shoe. I can't walk like this. Would somebody clean out this sand for me? . . . Ma-chan, take off my shoe!"

"Not me, I'm not your slave."

"If you talk like that, I won't be nice to you any more. . . . Oh, Hama-san, you're so kind. . . . Thank you, thank you. Hama-san's the only one for me. I like Hama-san the best."

"Come on! Don't make fun of me just because I'm being nice."

Naomi's voice broke into giggles. "Stop it, Hama-san, stop tickling my foot!"

"I'm not tickling it. Look at all this sand. I'm just brushing it off for you."

"If you start licking it, you'll turn into Papa," said Seki. Four or five men burst out laughing.

From where I stood, the sand dunes began a gentle downward slope. A tea cottage stood on the slope, sheltered by reed blinds; the voices were coming from inside. Less than thirty feet separated me from the cottage. Still dressed in the brown alpaca suit that I wore to work, I turned up the lapels of my coat, fastened all the buttons so that my shirt and collar wouldn't attract attention, and hid my straw hat under my arm. Bending into a low crouch, I scurried toward the darkness by the cottage's well. Just then, Naomi spoke. "It's all right, now. Let's go over there." They all came out with Naomi in the lead.

They went from the cottage down to the shore; they hadn't seen me. Hamada, Kumagai, Seki, and Nakamura—the four men—were all casually dressed in summer kimonos, while Naomi, right in the middle, wore a black mantle and high-heeled shoes. That's all I could make out. She hadn't brought a mantle or shoes with her to Kamakura; she must have borrowed them from someone. The mantle flapped in the wind. She seemed to be holding it around her body from the inside so that it wouldn't blow off. With every step, her plump bottom moved under the mantle. She walked like a drunk, purposely bumping her shoulders into the men, right and left, as she teetered along.

Until then, I'd been crouching motionless and holding my breath. Only when they were about sixty feet away and I could barely make out their white kimonos in the distance did I stand up and begin to follow them. At first I thought they'd walk straight down the coast toward Zaimokuya, but they bore left and headed over a sand hill toward town. As soon as they were completely out of sight beyond the hill, I ran up the slope with all my strength, because I knew they'd come to a dark residential street with a lot of pine groves and shady places that would be perfect to hide in. I could get closer to them without much fear of being discovered.

When I reached the bottom of the hill, their cheerful singing voices reverberated in my ears. They were walking in unison only four or five paces away as they sang,

> Just before the battle, Mother,
> I am thinking most of you . . .

It was one of Naomi's favorite songs, always on her lips. Kumagai walked in front, waving his arms like a conductor. Naomi was still staggering, first this way, then that, and bumping shoulders. As they were bumped, the men reeled from side to side as if they were sculling a boat.

"Yo-heave-ho! Yo-heave-ho!"

"Hey! What're you doing? If you push like that we'll crash into the wall."

There was a rapping sound as one of them struck the wall with his walking stick. Naomi shrieked with laughter.

"Next we'll do 'honika ua wiki wiki'!"

"Right! The Hawaiian hip dance. You wiggle your ass as you sing!"

"Honika ua wiki wiki! Sweet brown maiden said to me, . . ." They all wiggled their hips together.

"Seki's the best when it comes to shaking his ass," Naomi said with a laugh.

"Of course. I've been practicing, you know."

"Where?"

"At the Ueno Peace Exposition. There were natives dancing at the International Pavilion, remember? I went ten days in a row."

"How dumb can you get!" said Kumagai.

"You should've gone instead of me. They'd have taken you for one of the natives, with that mug."

"Hey, Ma-chan. What time is it?" It was Hamada. Not much of a drinker, he seemed to be the most sober.

"I dunno. Anybody got a watch?"

"Yeah, I do," said Nakamura. He struck a match. "Hey, it's already twenty past ten."

"Don't worry. Papa won't be back before eleven-thirty. Let's take the Hase road all the way around. I want to walk along a busy street in this outfit."

"Let's do it!" shouted Seki.

"But what'll I look like, walking around in this?"

"No question about it—a female gang leader."

"If I'm a female gangster, then all of you are my henchmen."

"The four thieves of the Kabuki stage."

"And I'm their leader, Benten Kozō."

"And the female gang leader, Kawai Naomi, . . ." Kumagai began, imitating a movie narrator, ". . . under the cloak of night, robed in a black mantle . . ."

Naomi snickered. "Quit using that crude voice!"

". . . Four scoundrels in tow, she leads the way from the shore at Yui Beach . . ."

"Stop it, Ma-chan! Stop it, I said!" She slapped him on the cheek.

"Ow! . . . My voice's naturally crude. It's one of the tragedies of our time that I didn't become an Osaka balladeer."

"But you know, Mary Pickford can't be a gangster."

"Who, then? Priscilla Dean?"

"Yeah, that's good. Priscilla Dean."

Singing again, Hamada began to dance. That's when it happened. Expecting that his dance steps would turn him toward me, I darted behind a tree, but at that moment he said, "Hey—who's that? It's Mr. Kawai, isn't it?"

A hush fell over them as they stopped in their tracks and looked back toward me through the darkness. "Darn," I thought, but it was too late.

"Papa? Is it you, Papa? What're you doing in there? Come join the rest of us."

Naomi came clattering over to me, threw her mantle open and put her arms on my shoulders. She had nothing on under the mantle.

"What're you doing! You humiliate me! Slut! Tramp! Whore!"

Naomi giggled. Her breath reeked of sake. I'd never known her to drink before.

16

IT TOOK me that night and all the next day
to overcome Naomi's obstinacy and wring from her a general
idea of the scheme she'd hatched to deceive me.

As I suspected, she'd wanted to come to Kamakura so she
could have a good time with Kumagai. It'd been a bold-faced
lie that Seki had a relative in Ōgigayatsu; the truth was that
the Ōkubo villa in Hase was the home of Kumagai's uncle.
Not only that, but we could thank Kumagai for the cottage
I was renting. The Ōkubo mansion was one of the nurseryman's regular customers. Kumagai had used pressure and
somehow arranged for the previous tenant to vacate so that
we could move in. Needless to say, it had all been planned
by Naomi and Kumagai. The talk about Miss Sugizaki's
good offices and the Oriental Petroleum director was nothing
more than a lie. That's why she took care of all the arrangements herself. According to the nurseryman's wife, Naomi
had been with "young Mr. Kumagai" when she first came
to inspect the cottage and had acted as though she were a

member of the family. In fact, she'd always pretended as much. The landlady had no choice but to turn out the previous occupant and surrender the rooms to us.

"I'm awfully sorry to involve you in this mess," I said to the landlady. "But please tell me everything you know. I'll never use your name, under any circumstances. I have no desire to lodge a protest with Kumagai. I just want to know the truth."

I stayed home from work the next day, something I'd never done before, and kept a close watch on Naomi. "Don't take a step from this room," I said firmly. Packing up all of her clothes, footwear, and her wallet, I carried them to the main house. There I questioned the landlady.

"Then the two of them have been seeing each other all along, when I was out?"

"Oh, yes, all the time. The young gentleman would come here, or the young lady would go there . . ."

"Then, who lives at the Ōkubo villa?"

"They all moved back to their main residence this year. They come once in a while, but young Mr. Kumagai is usually there by himself."

"And how about Kumagai's friends? Did they come, too?"

"Yes, they often came."

"Did Kumagai bring them, or did they come separately, on their own?"

"Well . . ." I didn't realize it until later, but the landlady seemed troubled at this point. ". . . Sometimes they came by themselves, sometimes with the young gentleman, I think . . ."

"Did anyone other than Kumagai ever come alone?"

"The one called Mr. Hamada came alone, I think, and some of the others . . ."

"Would they take her out someplace, then?"

"No, they usually talked in the house."

This was the most baffling part. If there was something going on between Naomi and Kumagai, then why drag along the others to get in the way? And what did it mean for one of them to come calling by himself and talk with Naomi? Why didn't they quarrel if they were all after Naomi? The four of them had been cheerfully horsing around together last night, hadn't they? The picture seemed to be getting fuzzy again. I even began to think that Naomi and Kumagai might not be involved with each other after all.

Naomi wasn't about to answer my questions on this point. She kept insisting that there was no deep plot; she just liked to have a lot of friends around her. Then why had she tricked me so cunningly?

"But Papa, you've never trusted them. You'd have been worried."

"In that case, why did you make up that story about Seki and his uncle's villa? What difference does it make whether it's Seki or Kumagai?"

Naomi seemed to be at a loss for an answer. She lowered her head abruptly, chewed her lips, and glared up at me as if to bore a hole in my face.

"You distrusted Ma-chan the most. I thought it'd be better to make it Seki."

"Quit saying 'Ma-chan'! His name is Kumagai!"

I'd been restraining myself so far, but I finally exploded. It made my skin crawl to hear her call him "Ma-chan."

"Listen! You had relations with Kumagai, didn't you? Tell the truth!"

"Of course not. If you're so suspicious of me, do you have any proof?"

"I don't need proof. I know."

"How do you know?" Naomi was frighteningly calm. An annoying smile played on her lips.

"What about that spectacle last night? Do you mean to

say that you're chaste and innocent, even when you go out looking like that?"

"They got me drunk and made me dress that way. I was just walking around, wasn't I?"

"So you still insist you're innocent?"

"Yes, chaste and innocent."

"You'll swear to it?"

"Yes, I swear."

"All right! Don't forget what you just said. I don't believe anything you say anymore." I didn't speak with her after that.

Fearing that she might write to Kumagai, I collected all the stationery, envelopes, ink, pencils, fountain pens, and stamps and entrusted them, along with Naomi's other things, to the landlady. Then, to make sure that Naomi couldn't go out while I was away, I gave her just the red crepe gown to wear. On the third day, I was ready to go to work and set out from Kamakura; but on the train I did some hard thinking about how to find proof, and finally decided that I'd start by going to the house at Ōmori, now vacant for a month. If Naomi was involved with Kumagai, the relationship hadn't started this summer. I might find some letters if I went through her things.

Having left Kamakura one train later than usual, I reached the Ōmori house around ten o'clock. I stepped onto the porch, unlocked the door, crossed the atelier, and went upstairs to search her room. Opening the door, I took one step inside and let out a gasp. I stood speechless. Hamada was sprawled out on the mats.

When I entered the room, Hamada turned bright red, said "Oh," and got up. Following the "Oh," the two of us stared at each other for a moment, each trying to read the other's thoughts.

"Hamada . . . what are you doing here?"

He mumbled as though about to say something, then fell silent again and hung his head as if to plead for mercy.

"Well? How long have you been here, Hamada?"

"Just now, . . . I just got here." He spoke more clearly this time, apparently recognizing that there was no escape.

"But the house was locked, wasn't it? How'd you get in?"

"Through the back door."

"But the back door must have been locked, too . . ."

"It was. I have a key." Hamada's voice was so faint I could barely make out what he said.

"A key? Where did you get a key?"

"From Miss Naomi. . . . Now that I've said that much, I'm sure you've figured out why I'm here."

Hamada quietly lifted his head and, squinting with embarrassment, looked directly at my face as I stood there dumbfounded. In a crisis, the simple honesty and refinement of a naïve, pampered young man showed in his face. Today he wasn't the punk that I was used to.

"And Mr. Kawai, I can guess why you came here today, all of a sudden. I've been deceiving you. And for that I'm ready to accept any punishment. It's too late for me to be saying this now, but for a long time, even if you hadn't caught me like this, I've been wanting to tell you the truth."

As he spoke, tears filled his eyes and trickled down his cheeks. It was all totally unexpected. I gazed at him silently, blinking my eyes. Even if I believed his confession, there were still a lot of things that didn't sit right.

"Mr. Kawai, please say that you forgive me."

"But I don't understand, Hamada. Why did Naomi give you a key? And what did you come here for?"

"Today . . . today . . . I was to meet Miss Naomi here."

"What? Meet Naomi here?"

"That's right. And not only today. We've done it many times before."

Little by little, his story came out. He and Naomi had met here secretly three times since we moved to Kamakura. After I'd left for work, Naomi would come to Ōmori one or two trains later. She always arrived around ten and left at eleven-thirty. That brought her back to Kamakura by one o'clock at the latest, so that it never occurred to anyone at the nursery that she'd been to Ōmori and back in the meantime. The two of them had arranged to meet at ten o'clock this morning, too, and so when Hamada had heard me coming up the stairs, he'd thought it was Naomi.

At first, all I felt in response to this astonishing confession was a dazed numbness filling my heart. My mouth hung open; I couldn't think of anything to say. Please keep in mind that I was thirty-two years old and Naomi, nineteen. To think that a girl of nineteen would deceive me so audaciously, so craftily! Until that moment, I'd never suspected that Naomi was such a terror. In fact, I still could hardly believe it.

"When did you and Naomi start having this kind of relationship?" Putting off the question of whether or not to forgive Hamada, I was consumed by a desire to learn every detail of the truth.

"It started a long time ago, probably before you knew me."

"Let's see, when did I meet you the first time? Wasn't it last fall, when I came home from work and found you standing by the flower bed, talking with Naomi?"

"That's right, almost a year ago."

"Was that when it started?"

"No, it was before that. Beginning in March last year, I went to take piano lessons at Miss Sugizaki's place. I met Miss Naomi there. Shortly after that—probably about three months later . . ."

"Where did you meet in those days?"

"Here at your house. Miss Naomi said she didn't have

any lessons in the morning and was lonely here all by herself. She asked me to visit, and so at first I just came to
keep her company."

"Naomi asked you to come?"

"That's right. I didn't know about you at all. Miss Naomi
said that her home was in the country and she was staying
with a relative in Ōmori. She said you were her cousin. I
realized it wasn't true when you came to the dance at the
El Dorado the first time. But by then . . . by then there
was nothing I could do."

"Was going to Kamakura this summer something that you
and Naomi planned?"

"No, Kumagai's the one who suggested Kamakura to Miss
Naomi." Hamada raised his voice as he continued. "Mr.
Kawai, you're not the only one who's been deceived! I have
been, too!"

"Then, Naomi and Kumagai . . ."

"Yes. Right now, Kumagai's the one who has a free hand
with Miss Naomi. I sensed a long time ago that Miss Naomi
liked Kumagai. But I never dreamed that she'd get involved
with Kumagai when she already had a relationship with me.
She said that she just liked to play innocently with her
friends. That's all there was to it, she said, and I thought,
well, maybe that's all . . ."

"Yes," I said with a sigh, "that's Naomi's line. She said
the same thing to me, and I believed her. . . . When did
you find out she was having an affair with Kumagai?"

"Do you remember that rainy night when we all slept here
together? I realized it then. I truly sympathized with you
that night. I could tell from their brazenness that something
was going on between them. The more jealous I became,
the better I understood your feelings."

"When you say you realized it that night, you mean that
you just guessed from their attitude?"

"No, something happened to confirm my suspicions. It was at dawn. You were asleep and didn't notice, but I couldn't sleep. I was drowsy, but I saw them kissing."

"Does Naomi know you saw them?"

"Yes, she does. I told her later. I asked her to break up with Kumagai. I told her that I didn't want to be toyed with. If I didn't marry her after this . . ."

"*Marry* her?"

"That's right. I intended to tell you honestly of our love for each other and marry Miss Naomi. She said that you're an understanding person, that if we told you how we were suffering, you'd surely consent. I don't know if it's true, but according to Miss Naomi, you only wanted to educate her. You were living together, but it wasn't as though you were pledged to marry each other. And then, even if you did get married, you might not be happy because of the difference in your ages."

"Naomi said that?"

"Yes. She promised me again and again that if I'd wait a little longer, she'd talk to you and we could get married. She also said that she'd break with Kumagai. But it was all a lie. She never intended to marry me at all."

"Do you think Naomi has made promises like that to Kumagai, too?"

"I don't know, but I think she probably has. Miss Naomi is fickle, and Kumagai's not very dependable, either. He's much trickier than I am."

Strangely, I hadn't felt any bitterness toward Hamada; and after hearing his story, I felt as though we were sharing the same pain. On the other hand, I detested Kumagai more than ever. I felt very strongly, now, that Kumagai was our mutual enemy.

"In any case, Hamada, we can't go on talking here. Let's get some lunch somewhere and have a good talk. I still have a lot of questions." We would have felt awkward in a Western restaurant; I took him to the Matsuasa on the Ōmori shore.

"Did you take the day off today, Mr. Kawai?" Hamada asked on the way. No longer excited, his tone was relaxed and familiar, as though he'd put down a heavy burden.

"Yes. I took yesterday off, too. Unfortunately, things are busy at the office these days, and I shouldn't be taking time off; but I've been so edgy since the day before yesterday that work is out of the question."

"Does Miss Naomi know that you came to Ōmori today?"

"I stayed home all day yesterday, but today I said I was going to work. Knowing her, I think she may have been suspicious, but I doubt that she really thought I'd come here. I decided to come on the spur of the moment. I thought if I searched her room, I might find love letters or something."

"Oh, I see. I thought that you came to catch me. But in that case, don't you think Miss Naomi might come?"

"Don't worry. I took away her wallet and all of her clothes. She can't even go to the door, dressed as she is."

"How is she dressed?"

"You know that pink crepe gown?"

"Oh, that one."

"That's all. She doesn't even have a sash. There's nothing to worry about. She's like a ferocious dog in a pen."

"But what would've happened if she'd walked in on us back there? What a commotion there would've been."

"Say, when was it that Naomi arranged to meet you today?"

"It was the day before yesterday. The night you caught us. I was sulking that night, and to cheer me up Miss Naomi said to come to Ōmori the day after tomorrow. Of course it was my fault, too. I should have broken up with Miss Naomi or else confronted Kumagai, but I couldn't do either. I called myself a coward; I was too weak to do anything but drift along with them. I said that I was taken in by Miss Naomi, but the truth is, it was my own foolishness."

I felt as though he were talking about me. When we'd been shown to a room at the Matsuasa and I sat down facing him, I even found him rather appealing.

17

"Y O U ' V E been honest with me, Hamada. I feel much better. Let's have a drink." I held out a sake cup to him.

"Do you forgive me, then, Mr. Kawai?"

"There's nothing to forgive. You were taken in by Naomi, and you didn't know about my relationship with her. You've done nothing wrong. I won't give it another thought."

"Oh, thank you. It takes a load off my mind to hear you say that."

But Hamada still seemed uncomfortable. Without making any move to drink the sake I poured for him, he spoke in snatches, hesitantly, with his eyes downcast.

"Then, well, it's rude of me to ask, but does this mean that you and Miss Naomi aren't related?"

"No, we're not related at all. I was born in Utsunomiya, but she's a pure Tokyoite and her family lives in Tokyo even now. She wanted to go to school, but her family's circumstances wouldn't permit it; I felt sorry for her and took charge of her when she was fifteen."

"And are you married now?"

"Yes. We got the consent of our parents and went through the formalities. But she was only sixteen then. I thought she was too young for me to treat her as a 'housewife,' and I guessed that she wouldn't like it either, and so we decided that we'd live together like friends for the time being."

"I see. And that was the beginning of the misunderstandings, wasn't it? To look at her, one wouldn't think she was a married woman, and she never said that she was. That's why we were all taken in."

"Naomi shares the blame, but it's partly my fault. The usual notion of 'husband and wife' had no appeal for me, and I wanted to avoid the ordinary 'husband-and-wife' way of life as much as possible. That was a terrible mistake, and I'll correct it now. I've learned my lesson."

"That would be best. And Mr. Kawai, I don't mean to overlook my own faults, but Kumagai's a bad one. Please be careful. It's not that I bear a grudge against him. They're all bad—Kumagai, Seki, Nakamura. Miss Naomi's not a bad person. They've been a bad influence on her." Hamada's voice was choked with emotion, and tears glistened in his eyes again. This youth truly loves Naomi, I said to myself. I felt grateful, even apologetic, toward him. Unaware of our marriage, he'd been ready to ask me to give her to him. Even now, if I said that I'd given up on her, he'd take her in without any hesitation. The ardor on this youth's brow, so intense that it moved me, left no doubt of his resolve.

"Hamada, I'll take your advice and settle this somehow in the next two or three days. If Naomi makes a clean break with Kumagai, that's fine. If not, I don't want to be with her another day, and . . ."

"But . . . but please don't leave her," Hamada interrupted. "If you leave her, she'll go to ruin. She's so innocent."

"Thank you! I can't tell you how happy your support makes me. I've been looking after her since she was fifteen and I don't want to leave her now, even if people do laugh at me. She's stubborn, though. I just have to find a way to get her to break off with her bad friends."

"She really is stubborn. She'll start a quarrel over the littlest thing, and then it's hopeless. Please handle it with all the skill you can. It's out of place for me to say this sort of thing, but . . ."

I thanked Hamada over and over. If it hadn't been for the difference in our ages and positions, and if we'd known each other better before, I probably would have taken his hand, and we might have wept in each other's arms. In any case, that's how strongly I felt.

"Please continue to visit us, Hamada. You, at least, will always be welcome," I said as we parted.

"Thank you. But I may not be able to for a while." He looked down uneasily, as though he didn't want me to see his face.

"But why?"

"For a while . . . until I'm able to put Miss Naomi out of my mind." Hiding his tears, he put on his hat, said good-bye, and started toward Shinagawa. He could have boarded a streetcar in front of the Matsuasa, but he walked.

I went to the office after that, but of course I couldn't get any work done. I wondered what Naomi was doing now. I'd left her with just that one robe; she couldn't possibly go anywhere. As soon as my thoughts reached this point, I started to worry. After all, there'd been one surprise after another. The realization that I'd been deceived again and again wore on my nerves—now morbidly sensitive—and I was beginning to imagine all sorts of situations. It started to look as though Naomi were endowed with magical powers far beyond my ability to comprehend. There was no telling what she might be doing; I couldn't take anything for granted. I mustn't hang around here; anything might have come out of the blue while I was away from home. Making short shrift of my work, I rushed back to Kamakura.

"Hello, I'm back early," I said as soon as I saw the land-lady standing at the gate. "Is she home?"

"Yes, I believe she is."

I was relieved. "Did anyone come to visit?"

"No one at all."

"How is she?" I pointed toward the cottage with my chin. I noticed that the room Naomi was most likely to be in was all closed up; the interior was dark beyond the glass and there was no sound. It was as though no one were home.

"Well, . . . she's been inside all day."

So she'd spent the whole day in the house. But why this disturbing silence? What would be the look on her face? With these forebodings, I stepped softly up onto the veranda and opened the shōji. It was a little past six o'clock in the evening. Naomi was sprawled immodestly in a dark corner of the room, sound asleep. No doubt the mosquitoes had been after her, and she'd rolled this way and that; she'd taken out my cravenette and wrapped it around her waist, but only her belly was successfully covered. Now, of all times, the sight of her white arms and legs protruding from the red gown, like stems in a pot of boiled cabbage, clawed seduc-tively at my heart. Without saying a word, I turned on the light, changed quickly into Japanese clothes, and shut the closet door noisily; but Naomi's steady breathing continued, undisturbed. I couldn't tell whether she knew I was back or not.

"Hey, aren't you going to get up? It's evening already." After needlessly leaning over my desk for thirty minutes, pretending to write a letter, I finally ran out of patience and spoke to her.

"Hmmm . . ." came a sleepy, half-hearted answer after I'd shouted at her two or three times.

"Hey! Aren't you going to get up?"

"Hmm . . ." She gave no sign of getting up.

"What're you doing! Hey!" I stood up and jostled her waist roughly with my foot.

She stretched her supple arms straight out and thrust her small, red, tightly clenched fists forward. Suppressing a yawn, she got up slowly, stole a glance at my face, and looked away. She began to scratch fiercely at the mosquito bites that covered the tops of her feet, her legs, and her spine. Whether as a result of sleeping too much, or, perhaps, of weeping, her eyes were bloodshot, and her disheveled hair hung ghostlike on her shoulders.

"Here, don't stay like that; put on a kimono." I brought her clothes back from the main house and set them down in front of her. She changed frostily. Dinner was brought in. Neither of us said anything as we ate.

All I could think about during this long, gloomy, glaring confrontation was how to get her to come clean, how to find a way to elicit a meek apology from this stubborn woman. Of course I kept Hamada's advice in mind—Naomi was stubborn, and when she got into a quarrel it was hopeless. No doubt his advice was based on personal experience; I could think of many instances myself. The worst thing would be to get her angry. I'd have to broach the subject carefully, so that she wouldn't be perverse and start to argue, but I mustn't appear to be too lenient. The most dangerous course would be for me to cross-examine her like a judge. She wasn't the sort of woman to answer respectfully, "Yes, sir," if I pressed her with direct questions: "You're involved with Kumagai, aren't you?" or, "You're involved with Hamada, too, aren't you?" She'd resist; she'd say she didn't know what I was talking about. I'd get impatient and lose my temper, and that would be the end of it. No, that kind of questioning wouldn't do. It'd be better to drop the idea of getting her to confess, and instead tell her outright what I'd learned today. No matter how stubborn she was, she couldn't deny it then. I made up my mind.

For openers I said, "I stopped at Ōmori around ten o'clock this morning and ran into Hamada."

Taken by surprise, Naomi grunted and avoided my gaze.

"Pretty soon it was time to eat. I took him to the Matsuasa for lunch."

Naomi made no reply after that. Watching her face closely, I patiently said what I had to say, trying not to be too sarcastic. Naomi sat motionlessly and listened with her head bowed until I finished. She maintained her composure, though her cheeks paled slightly.

"Now that Hamada's told me, there's no need to hear it from you. I know all about it. There's no point in your being perverse. If you were wrong, then all you need to do is say so. . . . How about it? Were you wrong? Do you acknowledge that you were wrong?"

She didn't answer. Was it going to turn into the sort of interrogation I'd feared? "How about it, Naomi?" I said as gently as I could. "If you'll just acknowledge that you were wrong, I won't condemn you for what happened in the past. I'm not going to force you to get down on your knees and apologize. I just want you to swear that there won't be any more mistakes like this. Do you understand? You'll admit that you were wrong, won't you?"

Naomi nodded.

"You understand, then, do you? You won't play with Kumagai and the others any more?"

"No."

"For sure? Do you promise?"

"Yes."

With this yes, we reached an accommodation that allowed each of us to save face.

18

N A O M I and I talked in bed that night as though nothing had happened; but to tell the truth, I hadn't been able to put it out of my mind completely. She was no longer chaste: not only did this thought cast a dark shadow over my heart; it also lowered the value of Naomi, who'd been my treasure, by more than half. This is because most of her value to me lay in the fact that I'd brought her up myself, that I myself had made her into the woman she was, and that only I knew every part of her body. For me Naomi was the same as a fruit that I'd cultivated myself. I'd labored hard and spared no pains to bring that piece of fruit to its present, magnificent ripeness, and it was only proper that I, the cultivator, should be the one to taste it. No one else had that right. But then, when I wasn't looking, a total stranger had ripped off the skin and taken a bite. Once defiled, she couldn't apologize enough to undo what had happened. The precious, sacred ground of her skin had been imprinted forever with the muddy tracks of two thieves. The more I thought about it, the more complete were my regret and chagrin. I didn't hate Naomi; I hated what had happened.

"Jōji, forgive me, . . ." Naomi said when she saw me weeping quietly. Her attitude had changed completely. I could only nod as I wept. I might say, "I forgive you," but I couldn't erase the anguished realization that what had happened couldn't be undone.

Thus our summer at Kamakura came to a cruel end, and we returned to the house at Ōmori. We didn't get along well; I wasn't always able to hide my feelings. Though on the surface we'd settled our differences, I still didn't trust her. When I was at work, I worried about Kumagai. I was so concerned about Naomi's conduct during my absence that I'd pretend to leave for work in the morning, then sneak around to the back door; I followed her when she went to her English and music lessons, and I read her mail on the sly. I began to feel like a secret agent. Naomi seemed to be laughing scornfully to herself at my persistence. She didn't quarrel with me, but she started to get cantankerous.

"Hey! Naomi!" I said one night, shaking her. (I wasn't speaking to her as though she were a child any more.) She was feigning sleep and had a particularly cold expression on her face. "What're you doing, pretending to be asleep? Do you hate me that much?"

"I'm not pretending to be asleep. I just wanted to go to sleep, so I closed my eyes."

"Then open them. You have no business keeping your eyes closed when I talk to you."

Reluctantly, she opened her eyes slightly. The narrow line of her eyes, peering at me through her lashes, made her face look all the more cold and cruel.

"Well? Do you hate me? If you do, say so."

"Why do you ask such a thing?"

"I can tell by the way you act. We don't quarrel any more,

but we're lashing out at each other in our hearts. Can we still call ourselves man and wife?"

"You're the one who's lashing out. I'm not."

"I think it's mutual. Your attitude keeps me on edge. I start getting suspicious, and . . ."

Naomi interrupted with her sarcastic, nasal laugh. "Let me ask you, then. Is there something suspicious about my attitude? If there is, let's see some evidence."

"I don't have any evidence, but . . ."

"Isn't it unreasonable to suspect me without any evidence? You can't expect us to live like man and wife when you won't trust me or let me have any freedom and my rights as your wife. Do you think I don't know anything? I know you've been reading my mail and following me around like a detective."

"That was wrong of me, but I'm all raw nerves because of what happened before. You've got to understand that."

"What do you want me to do? Didn't we promise not to talk about the past?"

"I want you to open your heart to me. I want you to love me so that my nerves will settle."

"I can't, if you don't trust me."

"I'll trust you. From now on I'll trust you."

Here I have to acknowledge how base males are. Whatever transpired in the daytime, I always gave in to her at night. Or, rather than "gave in," I should say that the animal in me was subdued by her. The truth is that I still didn't trust her at all, but the animal in me forced me to submit blindly to her; it led me to abandon everything and surrender. Naomi wasn't a priceless treasure or a cherished idol any more; she'd become a harlot. Neither lovers' innocence nor conjugal affection survived between us. Such feelings had faded away like an old dream. Why did I still feel anything for this faithless, defiled woman? Because I was being dragged along by her physical attractions. This degraded me at the same time it degraded Naomi, because it meant that I'd abandoned my integrity, fastidiousness, and sincerity as a man, flung away my pride, and bent down before a whore, and I no longer felt any shame for doing so. Indeed, there were times when I worshipped the figure of this despicable slut as though I were revering a goddess.

Naomi knew my weakness all too well. When she began to realize that her body was irresistibly alluring to men, and that, once night came, she could bring a man to his knees, she became incredibly uncivil in the daytime. She made it clear that she was selling the "woman" in herself to this man and that she had no other interest in him, no ties to him. She was sullen, curt, and indifferent, as if I were a stranger she'd passed on the street. She never gave a satisfactory answer when I spoke to her. If absolutely necessary, she'd answer yes or no. I could only take her behavior as a sign of indirect defiance and extreme contempt for me. "Jōji, you have no right to be angry, however cold I may be. You're taking everything you can from me. Aren't you satisfied with that?" This is what her glaring eyes seemed to say whenever I was in her presence. And the expression in her eyes often said, "What a disgusting man—as low and mean as a dog. I only put up with him because I have to."

This situation couldn't go on for very long. Even as we probed each other's hearts and continued our gloomy, smoldering feud, we knew that sometime it would explode into the open. One evening, I called to her in a more gentle, affectionate tone than usual. "Say, Naomi. Why don't we both drop this silly stubbornness? I don't know about you, but I can't take it any more—this cold life we've been living."

"What do you want to do about it?"

"Let's be a real couple again. We can't go on living in

despair like this. We should be trying to bring back our former happiness."

"Even if we try, feelings can't change that easily."

"Maybe so, but I think there's a way for us to be happy again. If you'll only go along with it. . . ."

"What way are you talking about?"

"Won't you have a baby? Become a mother? If we have a child—just one—we can be man and wife in the real sense. We can be happy. I beg you. Please say you will."

"No. I don't want to." Her answer was instant and emphatic. "Didn't you tell me not to have children? To stay young forever, like a girl? That nothing was more frightening than a man and wife having a child?"

"I did feel that way once, but . . ."

"Then you don't love me the way you did before, do you? You don't care how old and ugly I get, do you? No, I'm right. You're the one who doesn't love me."

"You're misunderstanding me. Before, I loved you as a friend. Now I'll love you as a real wife."

"And do you think that'll bring back our 'former happiness'?"

"Maybe it won't be the same, but real happiness . . ."

"No, no, I've heard enough." She shook her head violently before I could finish. "I want the kind of happiness we had before. I don't want anything else. That was the agreement when I came to live with you."

19

I F N A O M I wouldn't agree to have a child, I had
another resource. We'd move out of the "fairy-tale house"
at Ōmori and set up a more sedate, sensible household. I'd
lived in our strange, impractical artist's atelier because I was
drawn to it by the alluring idea of the *simple life*; but there
was no doubt that the house had contributed to making
our lives disorderly. It was inevitable that a young couple
living without a maid in such a house would get selfish,
abandon the simple life, and fall into careless ways. To keep
an eye on Naomi while I was out, I'd hire a maid and a
cook. No more "Culture Homes"—we'd move to a pure,
Japanese-style house, suitable for a middle-class gentleman
and just large enough for a husband, wife, and two servants.
I'd sell the Western furniture we'd been using and buy
Japanese-style furniture instead. I'd buy a piano for Naomi.
We could ask Miss Sugizaki to come to the house for
Naomi's music lessons. We'd have Miss Harrison come for
the English lessons, too. Naomi wouldn't have to leave the

house any more. But I'd need a good deal of capital to carry out my plan. I decided that I'd ask my family for the money and say nothing to Naomi until all the preparations were complete. With this in mind, I was spending a lot of time by myself looking for a house to rent and appraising furniture.

My family immediately sent a money order for fifteen hundred yen. In response to my request for a maid, my mother wrote in the letter that accompanied the order, "We have just the right person for you. You'll remember Sentarō, who used to work for us. His daughter, Ohana, turned fifteen this year. Since you already know her, you'll be comfortable with her. I'm still looking for a cook. I'll send one by the time you've found a new place."

Naomi must have sensed that I was secretly planning something, but at first she was frighteningly calm, as if to say, "I'll just watch and see what happens." Then, one night, two or three days after the letter had come from my mother, "Jōji, I'd like some Western clothes," she purred. "Won't you buy some for me?" Her tone was both coquettish and strangely scornful.

"Western clothes?" Astonished, I stared hard at her face. "Aha, she knows that a money order came, and she's probing," I said to myself.

"Won't you? Japanese clothes would be all right, too. Get me something nice for winter."

"I won't be buying you anything like that for a while."

"Why not?"

"You're already rolling in clothes, aren't you?"

"But I'm tired of them. I want some new ones."

"I'm not going to allow you that kind of luxury any more."

"Really? Then what are you going to use that money for?"

She finally came out with it! I said to myself. Feigning ignorance, I said, "Money? What money?"

"Jōji, I read the registered letter that was under the book-case. You read my mail, so I thought it'd be all right if I did the same."

I hadn't expected this. I thought she'd just seen the registered envelope and guessed that it contained a money order. I'd never anticipated that she'd read the letter I'd hidden under the bookcase. No doubt she'd hunted around for it in hopes of sniffing out my secret. If she'd read it, then she'd seen the amount of the money order. She knew about my moving plans, the maid, and everything else.

"With all that money, you can afford to buy me one kimono. What was it you used to say? 'I'll live in a tiny house and put up with any inconvenience for your sake. With the money I save, I'll let you live in luxury.' Have you forgotten what you said? You've changed completely since then."

"My heart hasn't changed. I still love you; it's just that I show it differently."

"Then why did you keep it a secret that we're moving? Were you just going to issue a decree?"

"I was going to talk with you about it when I'd found a good house, of course." Assuming a softer tone, I tried to soothe her with an explanation. "Naomi, I'll tell you how I really feel. I still want you to live in luxury. Not only luxurious clothes—I want you to live in a suitable house. I want to make everything in your life appropriate for a fine lady. There's nothing for you to complain about."

"Really? Thank you."

"Maybe you'd like to come with me tomorrow to look at houses. Any place will be all right if it has more rooms than this, and if you like it."

"In that case, I'll take a Western house. I won't stand for a Japanese house."

While I was fumbling for an answer, her face said, "I told you so," and she snapped, "As for the maid, I'll ask them to find me one in Asakusa. You can turn down that country bumpkin. It'll be my maid, you know."

The storm clouds gradually thickened over us as quarrels like this one multiplied. Often there were days when we didn't speak to each other at all. The explosion finally came early in November, two months after we'd returned from Kamakura, when I found positive proof that Naomi hadn't broken off with Kumagai.

There's no need to describe in detail the events leading up to my discovery. Even though I was preoccupied with my preparations for moving, I'd been intuitively suspicious of Naomi all along and kept up my investigative activities, with the result that one day I caught her on the way home from an audacious secret rendezvous with Kumagai at the Daybreak Pavilion, near our house in Ōmori.

That morning, my suspicions aroused by her unusually showy makeup, I doubled back after leaving the house and hid behind a sack of charcoal in the shed at the back door. (I was taking a lot of time off from work those days.) Sure enough, at nine o'clock she emerged, all dolled up, even though it wasn't one of her lesson days. Instead of going toward the station, she walked quickly in the opposite direction. I let her get ten or twelve yards ahead, then rushed into the house, dragged out the mantle and cap I'd worn as a student, put them on over my suit, slipped my bare feet into wooden sandals, ran outside, and followed Naomi at a distance. I watched her go into the Daybreak Pavilion; Kumagai came along about ten minutes later. I settled down to wait for them to come out.

They left separately, just as they'd arrived. It was around eleven o'clock when Naomi appeared on the street, leaving Kumagai inside. I'd been loitering near the Daybreak Pavilion for almost an hour and a half. Just as she had when she'd come, she walked the two-thirds of a mile to our house briskly, without glancing right or left. I gradually quickened my pace as I followed her. When she opened the back door and went inside, I was less than five minutes behind her.

The moment I stepped inside, I saw Naomi's eyes, fixed and grim, as she stood there stock-still, glaring at me. My hat, overcoat, shoes, and socks lay at her feet, scattered just as I'd left them when I'd taken them off. They must have told her everything. Her face, catching the glorious, autumn-morning light in the atelier, was calm and pale and showed the deep tranquility of total resignation.

"Get out!" I shouted so loud that my ears rang. I said nothing more, and Naomi didn't reply. Like two men with drawn swords pointed at one another's eyes, each of us watched the other for an opening. I truly felt the beauty of Naomi's face at that moment. I realized that a woman's face grows more beautiful the more it incurs a man's hatred. Don José killed Carmen because she became all the more beautiful as his hatred for her grew. I felt as he did. The muscles of her face perfectly motionless, her eyes fixed, her bloodless lips pressed tightly together, Naomi looked like evil incarnate as she stood there. Her face was the perfect expression of a whore's defiant look.

"Get out!" I shouted again. Driven by hatred, fear, and beauty, I grabbed her wildly by the shoulders and thrust her toward the door. "Get out! Go on! Get out, I said!"

"Forgive me, Jōji! From now on . . ." Her expression suddenly changed; her voice shook prayerfully; her eyes filled with tears; and she fell to her knees, looking up at my face imploringly.

"Jōji, I was wrong, forgive me! Forgive me . . . forgive me . . ."

I hadn't expected her to be so quick to beg for forgiveness. Taken by surprise, I grew even more enraged. I began to pummel her with my fists.

"Dog! Fiend! I'm finished with you! Why don't you get out when I tell you!"

Naomi suddenly changed her attitude again, as if she were saying to herself, "I botched that one, didn't I?" She rose quickly to her feet and said, "I'm going, then," in a perfectly normal tone of voice.

"Good! Right now!"

"Yes, I'll leave right away. Can I go upstairs and get a change of clothes?"

"No! Send someone later! I'll give all your things to him!"

"But there are some things I'll need right away."

"Then do as you like, but make it fast!" I spoke sharply because I interpreted Naomi's "right away" as a threat and wasn't about to give in. She went upstairs, noisily ransacked the rooms, and put together more baskets and bundles than she could carry. She briskly hailed a ricksha by herself and loaded it.

"Good-bye, then. Thanks for everything." Her parting words were simple in the extreme.

20

A S S O O N as her ricksha left, something made me
take out my watch and look at the time. It was 12:36 in
the afternoon. She'd left the Daybreak Pavilion at eleven;
there'd been a fight, and everything had changed in a flash;
she'd stood here until a moment before, but now she was
gone. All of that had taken one hour, thirty-six minutes.
People often look at the time unconsciously when the person
they've been nursing draws his last breath or when they feel
an earthquake. Taking out my watch on this occasion was
the same kind of instinct. At 12:36 on a certain November
day in a certain year, I'd parted with Naomi. This hour
might very well mark the end of our relationship. . . .
  "What a relief!" I said to myself. Exhausted from our continuing feud, I sank into a chair in a sort of daze. My immediate reaction was to feel relaxed and refreshed. I felt
liberated. I was tired not only spiritually, but physiologically;
my body demanded a rest most insistently. It was as though
Naomi were a strong wine. I knew it'd be bad for me to

drink too much, but I was shown the brimming, richly fragrant cups every day and I couldn't help myself. As I drank, the poisonous liquor spread to every joint in my body, until I was weary and listless, and the back of my head was as heavy as lead; and I thought that if I stood up I'd get dizzy and topple over backwards. It was like a permanent hangover: my stomach was bad, my memory was weak, I was indifferent to everything and as sluggish as an invalid. Strange visions of Naomi floated constantly in my head, sometimes making me queasy, like a latent belch; and the smell of her perspiration and her hair oil clung to my nose. "What the eye sees not, the heart rues not," they say. Now she was gone, and it was as though a rainy sky had suddenly cleared.

But this was just my immediate reaction. The feeling of relief lasted only about an hour. However robust I may have been, my body couldn't have recovered from its fatigue in one short hour; yet what came to mind after I'd caught my breath was Naomi's terrifying expression during our quarrel, at the moment I'd thought that a woman's face grows more beautiful the more it incurs a man's hatred. Seared indelibly on my mind was the face of a whore so loathsome that killing her wouldn't be enough. As time passed, the image grew clearer and clearer. I felt her glaring eyes still fixed on me. Little by little, the loathsomeness changed into an unfathomable beauty. It occurs to me that, even to this day, I've never seen her face so voluptuous as it was then. It was evil incarnate, without any question, and at the same time it was all the beauty of her body and spirit elevated to its highest level. Why hadn't I fallen to my knees when I was struck by her beauty in the midst of our quarrel, when my heart cried out, "How beautiful!" No matter how enraged I was, how could I have turned on that awesome goddess, heaped abuse on her, and raised my hand to her? I'm usually so weak and indecisive—where had that reckless courage come from? It was a mystery to me now. I even began to resent my own recklessness and courage.

I began to hear voices, saying, "What an idiot you are. Look what you've done. Do you really doubt that a little inconvenience is a fair price to pay for that face? You'll never see beauty like that again." That's right, I thought; I've done a stupid thing. I've always been careful not to anger her; an evil spirit must have been at work for things to have turned out as they have—coming from nowhere, this notion gained strength in my mind.

Until an hour before, I'd thought of Naomi as a burden. I'd cursed her existence. Why was I cursing myself now and regretting my hastiness? Why was I longing for someone who'd been so loathsome? This abrupt change of heart is something I can't explain; probably it's a riddle that only the god of love understands. Unconsciously, I'd risen to my feet and begun pacing the room. For a long time I tried to think of a way to cure myself of this love, but I was unsuccessful. I could only recall how beautiful she'd been. Scenes from our five years together floated before me. Ah, she'd said such and such that time; her face had looked like that; she'd done this with her eyes. Each memory was fuel for my regret. Most unforgettable of all were the days when she was fifteen or sixteen—I washed her body in the Western tub every night, and I played horse with her on my back crying, "giddap, giddap," as I crawled around the room. It was foolish of me to feel nostalgic about such stupid events, but if she came back to me, the first thing I'd do would be to play those games with her again. I'd put her on my back and crawl around the room. How happy I'd be if I could, I said to myself, fantasizing about it as though it were the greatest joy imaginable. In fact, I did more than fantasize. In the excess of my love, I got down on all fours and crawled around and around the room as though her body were resting firmly on my back even now. And then—I'm ashamed to write it—I went upstairs, took out her old clothes, piled them on my back, put her socks on my hands, and crawled around that room, too.

Those of you who have read this tale from the beginning will probably remember that I had a memory book called "Naomi Grows Up." Back in the days when I was bathing her, I'd recorded in detail how her limbs were growing every day. It was a sort of diary, in which I concentrated on Naomi's development from a girl into an adult. Remembering that I'd pasted in photographs of Naomi's various expressions and of every change in her form, I pulled the dusty, long-neglected volume from the bottom of the bookcase and leafed through the pages. They were photographs that I'd developed and printed myself; I could never let anyone else see them. Apparently I hadn't rinsed them thoroughly, because they were dotted with tiny freckles. Some of them were as indistinct as antique portraits; but this only served to increase the sense of nostalgia, and I felt as though I were reaching back ten years, twenty years, to distant dreams of my childhood. The photographs included almost all of her favorite costumes of the time—fanciful ones, cheery ones, extravagant ones, comical ones. There was a picture of her dressed in a man's velvet suit. On the next page, she stood like a statue, wrapped in cotton voile. On the next, she appeared in a glittering satin kimono and jacket, with a narrow sash high on her torso and a ribbon for a neckpiece. Then followed all sorts of expressions and movements and imitations of movie actresses—Mary Pickford's smile; Gloria Swanson's eyes; Pola Negri's wrath; Bebe Daniels' suave affectation. Whether she was indignant, smiling sweetly, terrified, or enraptured, her face and posture were different in each photograph, and each testified to how sensitive, skillful, and clever she was in these things.

What a mistake! I've let an extraordinary woman get away. Distraught, I stamped my feet in frustration. As I went on turning the pages of the diary, there were more photographs of every description. Gradually they came to dwell on minute details, and there were enlargements of certain parts: the shape of her nose; the shape of her eyes; the shape of her lips; the shape of a finger; the curve of her arm, her shoulder, her back, or her leg; her wrist; ankle; elbow; knee; even the sole of her foot—all treated as if they were parts of a Greek statue or a Buddhist image in Nara. Viewed this way, Naomi's body was a work of art, more perfect in my eyes than the Buddhas of Nara. As I gazed at the photographs, I even felt a deep, religious sense of gratitude well up in me. Why on earth had I taken such detailed photographs? Had I felt a premonition that one day they'd become sorrowful reminders?

My longing for Naomi continued to grow at an increasing rate. The day drew to a close, the evening star began to twinkle outside the window, and the air got chilly. I hadn't eaten or built a fire since eleven o'clock that morning, and I was too dispirited to switch on the lights. I wandered up to the second floor of the darkening house, then back down to the first; cried, "idiot!" and hit myself on the head; pressed my face against the wall of the hushed, deserted atelier and called, "Naomi, Naomi"; and finally, still calling her name over and over, I lay face down on the floor. Some way, some-how, I had to bring her back. I'd surrender to her un-conditionally. I'd yield to whatever she said or wanted. . . . What would she be doing now? With all that luggage, she'd probably gone by automobile from Tokyo Station. If so, five or six hours had elapsed since she'd reached the house in Asakusa. Would she have told the people at home the real reason she'd been thrown out? Or would she have made up some story, as usual hating to lose, and duped her brother and sister? She hated to be reminded that she was the daughter of a family that pursued its mean occupation in Senzoku; she treated them like members of some ignorant race and almost never visited them. What corrective measures would this ill-sorted family be devising now? Her brother and sister would naturally tell her to come apologize to me. She'd stand tough and say, "I won't apologize. Somebody bring in the baggage." And then, as if it hardly concerned her at all, she'd joke, talk big, spout English phrases, and show off her sophisticated clothes and accessories. She'd strut around like a princess visiting the slums. . . .

But whatever Naomi said, what happened had happened, and someone would have to come rushing over here. If she said, "I won't apologize," then her brother or sister would come instead. . . . Or could it be that no one in the family was concerned about her? Just as she'd been cool toward them, they'd long since ceased to take any responsibility for her. "We'll leave everything to you," they said when they gave her to me at the age of fifteen; their attitude then had been to let me do as I pleased with her. Would they abandon her again to do whatever she wanted? But they'd still come for her things, wouldn't they? "Send someone as soon as you get there; I'll give everything to him," I'd said; yet no one came. What did it mean? She'd taken a change of clothes and some of her other things, but she'd left behind the best of her wardrobe, which was more precious to her "than any-thing but life itself." She wouldn't stay cooped up all day in that messy house at Senzoku; she'd walk around every day, startling the neighbors with her showy fashions. She'd need her clothes more than ever; she couldn't bear to be without them. . . .

But no one came that night, wait as I might. I still hadn't

turned the lights on, though it had grown completely dark
outside. Fearing that people would think no one was home,
I rushed around the house turning on lights in every room
and checked to see that the nameplate hadn't fallen off the
gate. Then I pulled up a chair by the door to listen for footsteps outside. The hours passed—eight o'clock, then nine, ten,
eleven, and the day was gone—but no one came. As my heart
sank to the depths of pessimism, all sorts of conjectures
rambled through my mind. Maybe she hadn't sent anyone
because she didn't take the incident seriously—she thought
it'd all be settled in a few days. "Nothing to worry about,
he's in love with me and can't live a day without me. He'll
come for me." Maybe this was her tactic. She knew that
she'd grown too accustomed to luxury to live among those
people. And besides, there was no other man she could go
to who'd cherish her and give her a free rein, as I'd done.
Naomi was well aware of this. Bluff as she would, in her
heart she'd be counting on me to get her. Or maybe her
brother or sister would come tomorrow morning to mediate?
Their business kept them busy at night; maybe they couldn't
get away until morning. In any case, the fact that no one
came was a ray of hope. If there was no word tomorrow, I'd
go get her. It was no time to be stubborn or worry about what
people might think. It was stubbornness that got me into
this mess in the first place. Her family could laugh at me;
she could see through my weakness; I'd go and apologize
profusely, ask her brother and sister to put in a word for me,
and plead with her a million times to come back. Then she
could save face and return triumphantly.

I passed a sleepless night and waited until six o'clock the
next evening, but there was no word. Unable to stand it any
longer, I ran from the house and hurried to Asakusa. I
couldn't wait to see her. Everything would be all right if I
could see her face! "Consumed with love" describes me at

that moment: there was no room in my heart for anything but a desire to see her.

It must have been around seven o'clock when I reached the house in the labyrinthine alleys of Senzoku, behind the Hanayashiki Amusement Park. Self-conscious, I opened the door stealthily.

"I've come from Ōmori," I said softly, standing in the entryway. "Is Naomi here?"

"Oh, Mr. Kawai." The sister stuck out her head from the anteroom. She looked puzzled. "Naomi, you say? No, she's not here."

"That's odd. She must be here—she left last night saying that she was coming here. . . ."

21

A T   F I R S T   I suspected that the sister was following Naomi's instructions and hiding her. I tried several different appeals, but it really did seem that Naomi wasn't there.

"It's very strange. She had so much baggage, she couldn't
have gone anywhere else . . ."

"Baggage?"

"Yes, a basket, a suitcase, some bundles—she took quite
a lot with her. The fact is, we quarreled yesterday over some
silly thing."

"And when she left, she said she was coming here?"

"No, I said so. I told her to come straight to Asakusa and
send someone back to the house. I thought that if one of you
came, you'd understand."

"I see. . . . But she hasn't been here. Under the circumstances, she might come before long, of course, but . . ."

"I'm not so sure, if she left last night." The brother came
out as we were talking. "If you know someplace else, you

oughtta take a look there. If she isn't here by now, she probably isn't coming."

"And Naomi stays away from here, you know. Let's see, when was it? We haven't seen her in two months."

"Well, I'm sorry to put you to any trouble, but if she does come, please let me know right away, no matter what she says."

"Right. We don't have any plans for her, after all this time. If she comes, we'll let you know."

I sat down at the front door and sipped the coarse tea they gave me. I didn't know where to turn, but there'd be no point in unburdening myself to people who showed no concern when told that their sister had left home. I asked them again not to waste any time if she appeared. They should call me at the office if she came during the day. Recently I'd been missing work now and then; if I wasn't at the office, they should send a telegram to Ōmori. They shouldn't let her leave; I'd come for her immediately. Even after I'd repeated my requests at some length, I had the feeling that I couldn't count on these people, given their sloppy ways. To make doubly sure, I gave them my office telephone number and wrote out the address of the house at Ōmori. It wouldn't have surprised me if they hadn't known it before.

Now what shall I do? I thought. Where could she have gone? I felt like I was about to screw up my face like a baby set to cry—in fact, maybe I already had. Emerging from the alleys of Senzoku with nowhere to go, I wandered around the park at Asakusa and did some thinking. If she hadn't gone back to her family, then the situation was more serious than I'd expected.

"Kumagai's place—she's run away to his place," I thought. Then I recalled what she'd said the day before: "There're some things I'll need right away." Of course. She'd taken so much with her because she was planning to go to Kumagai's. The two of them had probably planned what they'd do when the time came. If so, then it was going to be difficult. First of all, I didn't know where Kumagai lived. I could probably find out, but surely he wouldn't be able to harbor her in his parents' house. He was a punk, but his parents were people of some importance. They wouldn't let their son get away with such misconduct. Had he left home, too, and gone into hiding with her? Maybe he'd run off with some of his parents' money, and the two of them were having a good time with it. If so, I'd have to make sure that his parents knew exactly what had happened. Then I could confer with them and get them to intervene. Even if Kumagai didn't listen to them, he and Naomi wouldn't be able to go on after they ran out of money. He'd go back home, and Naomi would come back to me. That's what would happen in the end, but what about my suffering in the meantime? Would it take a month? Two months? Three? What if it took six months? That'd be disastrous. As time passed it'd get harder for her to return; and who's to say she wouldn't get involved with a second man, and a third? This was no time to be dillydallying. Just being separated from her like this weakened the bond between us. She was getting farther away with every passing moment. Get to work! Don't let her get away! No matter what, I'll bring her back! Prayer in time of distress!—I'd never been very religious but, suddenly remembering where I was, I went into the Kannon Temple. With my whole heart, I prayed that I might learn as quickly as possible where Naomi was and that she might come back to me. Even tomorrow wouldn't be too soon.

After that, I wandered around some more, stopped at two or three bars, and got dead drunk. It was after midnight when I returned to Ōmori. Drunk as I was, though, I couldn't get Naomi out of my head. As the effects of the sake wore off, I began to brood again. How could I pin down her location? Had she really run off with Kumagai? It'd be rash to confer with his parents before I was sure; but there was no way to be sure without hiring a private investigator. I was at my wits' end, when suddenly I remembered Hamada. Of course, Hamada; I'd forgotten all about him. He'd take my side. He'd given me his address when we parted at the Matsuasa. I'd write him tomorrow. No, a letter would take too long. Should I send a telegram? That'd be a little too dramatic. They probably had a telephone—should I call and ask him to come? No, in the time it'd take for him to come, he could be looking for Kumagai. The most important thing now was to learn of Kumagai's movements. Hamada, with his connections, could bring me some information quickly. For the moment, he was the only one who'd understand my suffering and help me. Maybe it was another case of "prayer in time of distress," but I'd try it.

The next morning, I jumped out of bed at seven and ran to a nearby public telephone. Luckily, I was able to find Hamada's family in the directory.

"The young master?" said the maid who answered the phone. "I'm afraid he's still asleep . . ."

"I'm terribly sorry," I persisted, "but it's an emergency. Could I ask you to call him?"

After a few minutes, Hamada came to the phone. "Is that Mr. Kawai? From Ōmori?" he said in a groggy voice.

"That's right. I'm sorry for the trouble I caused you the last time we met, and it's terribly rude of me to be calling at this hour, but the truth is, Naomi has run away, and . . ."

In spite of myself, there was a sob in my voice when I said, "Naomi has run away." It was a cold, wintry morning; I'd come rushing outside with only a padded robe thrown over my night clothes. I was shivering as I held the receiver.

"Miss Naomi? She really did, then." He was disturbingly calm.

"Do you mean you already knew?"

"I met her last night."

"What? Naomi? You met Naomi last night?" I shuddered, trembling so violently that my teeth clattered against the mouthpiece.

"I went to a dance at the El Dorado last night. She was there. I didn't hear anything about what happened, but she was acting strangely, and I suspected something of the sort."

"Who was she with? Was it Kumagai?"

"Not only Kumagai; she was with five or six men, including a Westerner."

"A Westerner?"

"That's right. And she was wearing gorgeous Western clothes."

"But she didn't take any Western clothes with her when she left the house . . ."

"Be that as it may, she was in Western clothes. A splendid evening gown, at that."

I stood there blankly, totally baffled. I had no idea what to ask next.

22

"HELLO, hello. What's wrong, Mr. Kawai? Hello . . ."
Hamada was pressing me, I'd been silent for so long. "Hello,
hello . . ."

"Yes . . ."

"Mr. Kawai?"

"Yes . . ."

"What's wrong?"

"I don't know what to do."

"But there's no point in thinking about it on the telephone,
is there?"

"I know, but . . . Listen, Hamada, I'm at my wits' end.
I don't know where to turn. I'm suffering so much, I haven't
been able to sleep since she left." I put as much pathos into
my voice as I could, so as to elicit Hamada's sympathy.
"Hamada, there's no one else I can turn to. It's a terrible
imposition, but I . . . I just have to find out where Naomi
is. Whether she's at Kumagai's place, or with some other man.
I want to be sure. It's selfish of me to ask, but I wonder if

I could ask you to help find her. . . . You have the connections, and I thought that rather than my looking for her myself, . . ."

"Yes, I could probably find her quickly," Hamada said, as if there were nothing to it. "But Mr. Kawai, don't you have any idea where she might be?"

"I just assumed that she was with Kumagai. I wouldn't tell anyone but you, but the truth is that she's still seeing him on the sly. When I found out, we quarreled, and she ran off."

"I see."

"But according to what you've said, she was with a Westerner and a lot of other men, and she was wearing Western clothes. I don't know what to think. Maybe you could get a general idea of what's going on if you went to see Kumagai."

"Yes, all right," Hamada said, as if to put an end to my whining. "I'll see what I can find out."

"And could you do it quickly? It would be a great relief if you could let me know today, if that's possible."

"I see. Yes, I'll probably be able to find out within the day. Where can I reach you? Are you still at the company in Ōimachi?"

"No, I haven't been going to work at all since this happened. I've been trying to stay at home, just in case Naomi comes back. I know I'm being selfish, but it's awkward to use the telephone. It'd be most convenient if I could see you. Do you think you might come to Ōmori when you've learned something?"

"Yes, that'd be all right. I have nothing else to do anyway."

"Oh, thank you. I'd be so grateful if you would!" Now I'd have to wait for him to come, and each second would seem like an eternity. I was even more fidgety than before. "About

what time do you think you'll be coming, then?" I added,
"Do you think you'll have the answer by two or three o'clock?"

"Well, I think so, but I can't be certain about this until
I go and see for myself. I'll do the best I can, but it still
might be two or three days."

"Th-that's all right. Tomorrow, the day after tomorrow—
I'll wait right at home until you come."

"I understand. We'll talk about it more when I see you,
then. Good-bye."

"Hello, hello," I called frantically when it seemed he was
about to hang up. "Hello, . . . there's one more thing.
This will all depend on how things develop, but if you see
Naomi and have a chance to talk with her, there's something I'd like you to say to her. Please tell her that I don't
condemn her for what she did and that I know I share in
the blame for her behavior. I'll apologize humbly for my
mistakes, and I'll accept any conditions at all and let bygones
be bygones if she'll just come back. If she refuses, ask her
to see me just once. . . ."

After "I'll accept any conditions at all," I had wanted to
add, "If she tells me to grovel, I'll happily grovel. If she
tells me to press my forehead to the ground, I'll press my
forehead to the ground. I'll do anything to apologize." But
of course I couldn't say it.

". . . Please tell her, if you can, that I love her that much."

"I see. I'll be sure to tell her if I have the chance."

"And then, well, with that temper of hers, it could be that
she really wants to come back but she's being obstinate and
perverse about it. If that seems to be the case, tell her how
depressed I am. It'd be ideal if you could make her come back
here with you."

"I see, I see. I can't guarantee that much, but I'll do what
I can." Hamada sounded as though he'd had enough of my

importuning, but I went on talking until I'd used up all the five-sen coppers in my purse. It was probably the first time in my life that I'd spoken so eloquently and shamelessly in a tearful, quavering voice.

Far from being relieved when the call was over, I could hardly wait for Hamada to come. He said that he'd probably come today, but what should I do if he didn't?—or rather, what would become of me if he didn't come today? Aside from my yearning for Naomi, I had nothing to keep me occupied. I was incapable of doing anything. I'd have to stay in the house with folded hands, unable to sleep, eat, or go out, and wait for a perfect stranger to run around on my behalf and bring me his report. There's nothing so painful as doing nothing, and on top of that I was longing for Naomi so much I thought I'd die. Tormented by my desire, I'd entrusted my fate to another and had to wait, staring at the hands of the clock. The passage of time is astonishingly slow; even one minute seems infinitely long. Repeat that minute sixty times, and you finally have one hour. Repeat it one hundred and twenty times and finally you get two hours. If I waited three hours, I'd have to endure one hundred and eighty of these wearisome, inescapable minutes, one hundred and eighty tick-tock revolutions of the second hand! If it weren't just three hours, but four, or five, or half a day, one day, two days, three days—I thought I'd surely go mad from impatience and longing.

Nevertheless, I figured that Hamada wouldn't come until evening at the earliest, and prepared myself to wait; but around noon, four hours after I'd telephoned, the front doorbell rang loudly and I was surprised to hear Hamada's voice call, "Hello." I jumped up with joy and ran to open the door.

"Hello. I'll open it right away. It's locked," I said excitedly. I didn't think he'd be here so soon, I thought. Maybe he was able to see Naomi. Maybe when he met her, she understood right away, and he brought her with him. I felt an even greater surge of joy at this thought. My heart pounded in anticipation.

When the door was open, I looked around eagerly, thinking that she might be standing close behind Hamada, but there was no one else. Hamada stood there all by himself.

"Sorry about this morning. How about it?" I snapped. "Did you find out?"

Hamada was disturbingly cool as he gazed at me pityingly. "Yes, I found out, . . . but Mr. Kawai, there's no hope for her any more. You'd best give her up." He spoke emphatically and shook his head.

"Wh-wh-what do you mean?"

"It's far worse than you feared. For your own good, I think you ought to put Miss Naomi out of your mind now."

"Then, did you meet her? You talked to her, but it's hopeless?"

"No, I didn't meet her. I went to Kumagai and heard it all from him. It's too deplorable. I was shocked."

"But Hamada, where is Naomi? That's what I want to hear first."

"She's not in just one place; she's moving around."

"But there couldn't be that many places for her to stay."

"There's no telling how many male friends she may have, whom you don't know about. At first, though, on the day of your quarrel, she did go to Kumagai's. It would have been all right if she'd telephoned first and gone in secret, but she pulled right up to the front door in an automobile loaded down with baggage. The house was in an uproar, and everybody was asking, 'Who on earth is that?' Kumagai couldn't very well invite her in. Even he was nonplussed."

"Really? And then?"

"All they could do was hide her things in his room; then they left the house together and went to a disreputable inn.

To make matters worse, it was the something-or-other Pavilion here in Ōmori, near your house. He said it was the same inn they'd used that morning, the one where you'd seen them. What audacity!"

"They went there again the same day?"

"That's what he said. Kumagai sounded very pleased with himself, blabbering on recklessly, playing it up. . . . It wasn't very pleasant to listen to."

"They spent the night there together, did they?"

"No, in fact, they didn't. They stayed until evening, he said. Then, they took a walk together on the Ginza and parted at the Owarichō intersection."

"But that couldn't be right. Kumagai must be lying."

"No, listen to the rest. Kumagai felt sorry for her when they parted. He asked her, 'Where are you going to stay tonight?' And she said, 'I have lots of places to stay. I'm going to Yokohama now.' She didn't look unhappy at all. She marched right off toward Shimbashi Station."

"Who does she know in Yokohama?"

"That's the queer part. Kumagai thought she'd probably gone back to Ōmori. She might have a lot of friends, but surely there was no place she could stay in Yokohama. But then she called him the next evening and said, 'I'm at the El Dorado. Won't you come?' And when he went, there she was, wearing a dazzling evening gown, holding a peacock-feather fan, dripping with necklaces and bracelets, and making merry with a Westerner and a bunch of other men."

Hamada's account was like a jack-in-the-box—one startling fact after another came leaping out. In short, Naomi had spent the first night at the Westerner's house. His name was William McConnell, and he was the shameless, fastidious man in white makeup who'd come right up to Naomi without any introduction and forced her to dance with him the first time we went to the El Dorado. But what's even more startling (and this was Kumagai's observation) was that Naomi hadn't been particularly friendly with McConnell until the night she went to stay with him, though it does seem that she'd been secretly interested in him for some time. He had the kind of face that women like, and there was something smooth and actorly about him. The dance crowd called him "the wolf of the West." Naomi herself had said, "That Westerner has a good profile. He looks like John Barry, doesn't he?" (By "John Barry," she meant John Barrymore, the famous American actor, whom we'd seen in the movies.) She must have been interested in him. Maybe she'd even made eyes at him, and when he realized that she liked him, he'd probably flirted with her. With nothing more than that between them, she'd gone to his house uninvited. When she showed up, McConnell must have thought that a charming bird had flown in. "Won't you spend the night at my house?" he'd have said; and she'd have replied, "Yes, I don't mind if I do."

"But that's a little hard to believe—going to a man she didn't know and spending the night."

"But Mr. Kawai, it seems to me that Miss Naomi thinks nothing of that sort of thing. McConnell must have found it a little odd, too, because last night he asked Kumagai, 'Who on earth is this young lady?' "

"One might ask the same about a man who puts up a woman he knows nothing about."

"He not only put her up, he dressed her in Western clothes, bracelets, and necklaces. That's how outrageous he is. And after just one night, she was so familiar with him, she was calling him 'Willy.' "

"Do you suppose she had him buy the gown and the jewelry for her?"

"I hear that he bought part of her outfit and borrowed the rest from a Western woman he knows. Most likely it started with Miss Naomi cooing that she wanted to try wearing Western clothes. He probably agreed so he could get on her good side. The gown didn't look like something off the rack either; it fit her perfectly. She was wearing very high French heels; the toes were enameled and glittered with tiny gem-stones—probably rhinestones or something. She looked just like Cinderella."

My heart leaped at the thought of how beautiful Cinderella-Naomi must have been; but in the next moment I was appalled at her depravity, and an indescribable feeling of misery, regret, and mortification came over me. It'd been bad enough with Kumagai. Now she'd run off to a Westerner she knew nothing about, stayed for the night, and had him buy clothes for her. Was this any way for a woman to behave who'd had a husband until the day before? Was the Naomi I'd lived with all those years such a whore? Had I been living a foolish dream up to this moment? Was I finally seeing her true form? Hamada was right. However much I longed for her, I'd have to give her up. I'd been totally humiliated. My pride as a man had been dragged through the mud.

"Hamada, I know I'm being too persistent, but I want to be sure. Everything you've told me is true? Not just Kumagai, but you, too, will confirm it?"

Seeing the tears welling up in my eyes, Hamada nodded sympathetically. "I understand how you feel, and that makes it more difficult to say this; but I was there last night, too, and I think that what Kumagai says is probably true. There's a lot more I could tell you, but please try to believe me with-out hearing the rest. Please believe that I'm not just amusing myself by exaggerating the facts."

"Thank you. That's all I needed to hear. You don't have to . . ." I don't know what happened; but my words caught in my throat and huge tears suddenly began to fall from my eyes. This won't do, I thought. Abruptly I hugged Hamada tightly and pressed my face against his shoulder. Then I burst out crying and screamed, "Hamada! I . . . I've given her up! Now! Completely!"

"That's right! You've said the right thing!" Hamada's voice was thick, too. "To tell the truth, I came here today to give you my verdict. There's no hope for Miss Naomi now. Being the kind of person she is, she might show up here again as though nothing's happened, but the truth is that no one takes her seriously any more. According to Kumagai, they all treat her as a plaything, and they've given her an unspeakable nickname. There's no telling how often you've been disgraced behind your back."

Hamada had loved Naomi with the same passion that I felt and, like me, had been rejected by her. Now this youth's words, full of indignation and spoken with heartfelt compassion for me, had the effect of a sharp scalpel slicing off a lump of putrid flesh. They treated her as a plaything; they'd given her an unspeakable nickname—ironically, these terrifying disclosures breathed new life into me. My shoulders were light again, as though I'd been cured of the ague, and my tears stopped.

23

"MR. KAWAI, you shouldn't stay indoors. How about a walk?" Hamada said to cheer me up.

"All right, wait just a minute," I said. For two days I hadn't rinsed my mouth or shaved. I used the razor, washed my face, and, feeling completely refreshed, went outside with Hamada around two-thirty.

"This would be a good time to walk in the suburbs," Hamada said. I agreed. "Shall we go this way, then?" he asked, starting toward Ikegami. Feeling a sense of revulsion, I stood still.

"Not that way. That direction's taboo."

"Why?"

"The Daybreak Pavilion you were just talking about is in that direction."

"Oh, no! What shall we do, then? Shall we go straight down to the shore and walk toward Kawasaki?"

"Yes, all right. That'd be safest."

Hamada turned around and started toward the station, but

then I realized that this new direction might be dangerous, too. If Naomi was still going to the Daybreak Pavilion, then she might emerge with Kumagai just about now. Or she might be traveling between Tokyo and Yokohama with that dirty foreigner. In either case, stations on the National Electric Line were to be avoided. I went ahead of Hamada, saying casually, "I'm afraid I've put you to a lot of trouble today," and turned onto a side street so that we'd cross the tracks on a lane that ran through the ricefields.

"Not at all. I suspected that something like this would happen sooner or later."

"I must have looked comical, from your point of view."

"But I was absurd too, for a time. I have no business laughing at you. It's just that I felt terribly sorry for you, once I'd cooled off."

"It's all right for you; you're still young. But it's ridiculous for a man in his thirties to act like such an idiot. And if you hadn't told me, I might have gone right on."

When we came out into the fields, the late-autumn sky was high and crisply clear, as if to comfort me; but the rims of my eyes, still inflamed from crying, smarted in the wind. In the distance, the forbidden National Electric Line rumbled through the fields.

"Have you eaten lunch, Hamada?" I asked, after we'd walked for a while in silence.

"No, not yet. Have you?"

"I had some sake, but I've hardly eaten anything since the day before yesterday. I'm very hungry."

"I should think so. You ought to take better care of yourself, you know. You could easily become sick."

"Don't worry. I've seen the light, thanks to you. I'll take care of myself. Starting tomorrow, I'll be a new man. And I'll go back to work again."

"Yes, that'll take your mind off things. When I went

through this, I just wanted to forget. I devoted myself to music."

"It must be nice to be able to play music at times like this. I don't have any such talents; I can only work away steadily at the office. In any case, you must be hungry. Shall we get a bite to eat somewhere?"

We'd strolled as far as the Rokugō River while we talked, and before long we were in a Kawasaki beef restaurant with a boiling pot between us. We exchanged sake cups as we had at the Matsuasa.

"Here, have a cup, Hamada."

"I'll feel it if you make me drink so much on an empty stomach."

"Don't worry about that. Tonight my exorcism is complete. Help me celebrate. Tomorrow I'm going to stop drinking, so let's get drunk tonight and have a good talk."

"In that case, let me drink to your health."

By the time Hamada's face was flushed bright red and his pimples had begun to glisten like boiling beef, I was quite drunk and no longer knew whether I was happy or sad.

"By the way, Hamada, there's something I want to ask." Picking my moment carefully, I drew closer to him. "What's the terrible nickname that they call Naomi?"

"No, I can't tell you. It's too awful."

"It doesn't matter how awful it is. She's nothing to me any more, so there's no reason for you to hold back. Please tell me what they call her. I'll feel better if I know."

"Maybe you will, but I just can't say it. Please forgive me. Anyway, if you think about it you can probably imagine what it is. I could tell you how she got the nickname, though."

"Yes, please tell me."

"But Mr. Kawai . . . oh dear . . ." He scratched his head in embarrassment. "The derivation is pretty awful, too. You're not going to like what you hear."

"That's all right, that's all right. Please tell me! I just want to know some of her secrets. It's curiosity, plain and simple."

"All right, then, I'll tell you a little about her secret life. When you were in Kamakura last summer, how many men do you think Miss Naomi had?"

"I only know about you and Kumagai. Was there someone else?"

"Don't be startled, Mr. Kawai . . . Seki and Nakamura, too."

Drunk as I was, I felt as though a bolt of electricity had shot through my body. I gulped down five or six cups of sake before I said anything.

"You mean the whole group? Every one of them?"

"Yes. And where do you think they met?"

"At the Ōkubo villa?"

"At the nurseryman's cottage that you rented."

For a moment I couldn't say anything in response, I was so stunned. Finally I moaned, "That really is a surprise."

"The nurseryman's wife probably suffered the most at the time. She couldn't tell them to leave because she was indebted to Kumagai; but she must have worried what the neighbors were thinking when her own place had been turned into a brothel, with men coming and going all the time. And she was afraid of what would happen if you found out."

"Yes, of course. Now that you mention it, she was caught off balance when I asked her about Naomi. No wonder she was so jittery. And so the Ōmori house was your secret meeting place, the cottage was a brothel, and I knew nothing about it. I took a real beating, didn't I?"

"Mr. Kawai, let's not talk about Ōmori! I apologize for that."

"Don't worry. It's all in the past and no harm's done. But

it's exciting to be tricked so skillfully. Anybody would be impressed by such beautiful technique."

"It's like being thrown over the shoulder by a sumo wrestler, isn't it?"

"Exactly. Now, was Naomi manipulating all of them so that they didn't know about each other?"

"No, they knew. Sometimes two of them would even run into each other."

"Didn't they quarrel?"

"They were tacitly in league with each other. They shared her. That's where the awful nickname came from, and the nickname is what they called her behind her back. You were better off not knowing; but I knew, and it made me miserable. I wanted to rescue Miss Naomi somehow, but when I tried to give her some advice she got mad and made a fool of me. There was nothing I could do." Hamada's tone grew more sentimental as he remembered. "Mr. Kawai, I didn't tell you this much when I was with you at the Matsuasa, did I?"

"You said that Kumagai was the one who had a free hand with Naomi."

"Yes, I did say that. I wasn't lying, either. They were the closest, maybe because they're both so coarse. Kumagai's the ringleader. I said what I did because I thought that he was the worst influence on her; I just couldn't tell you the rest. I was still hoping that you wouldn't abandon her, that you'd lead her in the right direction."

"Far from leading her, I was dragged along myself."

"That's what happens to any man who comes up against Miss Naomi."

"The woman has a mysterious, magical power, hasn't she?"

"Yes, magical power is what it is! I felt it, and I realized that I should stay away from her, that I'd be in danger if I got close."

Naomi, Naomi—I don't know how many times the name

was repeated between us. It was the appetizer that accompanied our sake. We relished its smooth sound, licked it with our saliva, and raised it to our lips, as though it were a delicacy even tastier than beef.

"But it's all right, isn't it, to be taken in once by a woman like that?" I asked passionately.

"It certainly is! I owe my first taste of love to her. It didn't last long, but it was a beautiful dream. I have to be grateful for that."

"What do you think will become of her?"

"I suppose she'll just get worse. Kumagai says she won't be able to stay at McConnell's very long. She'll go somewhere else in two or three days; she might even go to his place, he says, because her things are there. But doesn't she have a family of her own?"

"They run a brothel in Asakusa. I've never told anyone before; I didn't think it'd be fair to her."

"I see. It's true, then; breeding determines all."

"According to Naomi, her family were low-ranking samurai living in a mansion at Shimonibanchō when she was born. Her grandmother was a modern sort who used to go to balls at the Rokumeikan, and it was this grandmother who gave her the name 'Naomi.' Who knows how much of that is true? Anyway, her upbringing was bad. I see that clearly now."

"This makes it all the more frightening. She was born with dissipation in her veins. It was fated that she'd turn out this way, despite your attempts to rescue her."

We went on chatting for about three hours. It was after seven o'clock when we left, but we hadn't run out of things to talk about.

"Hamada, are you going back by the National line?" I asked as we walked through Kawasaki.

"Well, it'd be too far to walk back now."

"That's true, but I'm going to take the Keihin electric line. If she's in Yokohama, the National line might be dangerous."

"I'll take the Keihin, too, then. But with Miss Naomi running around in every direction, you're bound to run into her sooner or later."

"I'll have to keep my wits about me when I go out, won't I?"

"No doubt she's spending a lot of time at dance halls, so Ginza is the most dangerous area."

"Ōmori's not much safer. It's on the way to Yokohama, the Kagetsuen, and the Daybreak Pavilion. . . . I may just get rid of that house and rent a room somewhere. I don't want to see her face until this cools down."

Hamada accompanied me on the Keihin line and we parted at Ōmori.

24

ANOTHER sad incident occurred while I was suffering from loneliness and disappointment in love. This was
nothing less than my mother's sudden death from a stroke.

A telegram saying that she was in critical condition came
in the morning, two days after I'd met Hamada. Receiving
it at the office, I dropped everything and hurried to Ueno
Station. I reached my home in the country at dusk, but my
mother had already lost consciousness and didn't recognize
me. She expired two or three hours later.

Since I'd lost my father when I was very young and
been raised single-handedly by my mother, this was the first
time I experienced the sadness of losing a parent. It was all
the worse because my mother and I had been closer than
most. I couldn't recall ever having disobeyed my mother or
having been scolded by her. I suppose that this was because
I respected her; but more important is that she was excep-
tionally thoughtful and kind. It often happens that when a
son grows up, leaves home, and goes to the city, his parents

worry about him and question his behavior. Sometimes the separation leads to estrangement. But even after I'd gone to Tokyo, my mother continued to trust me, understand my feelings, and wish me well. I had only two younger sisters. It must have made Mother lonely to let her only son go, but she prayed for my advancement and success without a single complaint. As a result, I felt the depth of her kindness more strongly away from her than I had at her knee. She'd always listened cheerfully to my selfish requests, especially when I'd married Naomi; and each time she had, I'd thought tearfully of her warmheartedness.

Having lost my mother so suddenly and unexpectedly, I felt as though I were in a dream within a dream, even as I sat in attendance beside her remains. Until yesterday, I'd been crazed, body and soul, with Naomi's charms. Today I was kneeling before the deceased and offering incense. There seemed to be no connection between these two worlds of mine. "Which is the real 'I'?" asked the voice that I heard when I examined myself, lost in tears of grief, sadness, and surprise. And from another direction I heard a whisper: "It's no accident that your mother died now. She's warning you; she's leaving you a lesson." This made me long for Mother all the more. I felt that I'd wronged her. Unable to hold back the tears of remorse and embarrassed to cry too much, I slipped out and climbed the hill behind the house. There, looking down on the woods, paths, and fields so full of childhood memories, I gave free vent to my tears.

This great sadness cleansed me of the foul elements that had accumulated in my heart and body. Without it, I would probably still have been suffering the pain of lost love, unable to forget that loathsome slut. Yes, Mother's death had not been meaningless. At least, I mustn't let it be meaningless. I thought at the time that I was tired of city air. People are always talking about "advancement and success," but going to Tokyo and living a vain, frivolous life wasn't "advancement"; it wasn't "success." A man from the country was best suited to the country. I'd withdraw to my hometown and get to know the land. Watching over my mother's grave and associating with the villagers, I'd become a farmer, like my ancestors. But when my uncle, sisters and other relatives heard how I felt, they said, "You're rushing things. It's only natural that you're discouraged now, but even the death of a mother is no reason for a man to bury his future. Everybody despairs when he loses a parent, but the sorrow lessens with time. It's fine if you want to come back, but take a while to think it over. For one thing, it wouldn't be fair to your company if you quit all of a sudden." I nearly said, "It's not just that. I haven't told anyone yet, but my wife ran away." But I didn't say it. I was ashamed in front of all of them, and the house was still in confusion. (I'd glossed over Naomi's absence by saying that she was sick.) When the seventh-day observances were over, I entrusted the other arrangements to my aunt and uncle (the ones who managed my property) and, accepting their advice, returned to Tokyo for the time being.

I went to work, but it was dull and joyless, and I wasn't as popular in the office as I had been. I'd been a hard worker of irreproachable conduct, nicknamed "the gentleman"; but now, because of Naomi, I'd made a mess of things. I'd lost the confidence of the managers and my co-workers. The worst of them jeered at me, saying my mother's death was just an excuse to take some time off. I got disgusted with it all and, when I went back to the country for one night on the twenty-seventh, I let slip to my uncle that I might quit the company soon. He didn't take me seriously, though; he just said, "There, there," and so I reluctantly went back to work the next day. At least I kept busy at the office, but I had nothing to do after work. Unable to decide whether to withdraw to the country or stick it out in Tokyo, I hadn't yet moved to a rented room. I went on spending the nights by myself in the empty house at Ōmori.

I went straight to Ōmori on the Keihin line after work, avoiding busy places for fear of meeting Naomi. After I'd eaten a simple dinner at a neighborhood restaurant, I was left with nothing to do. I'd go up to the bedroom and pull the quilts over myself, but I never fell asleep right away. I'd lie there with my eyes wide open for two or three hours. The bedroom was the attic room, of course; Naomi's things were still there, and the smell of five years of disorder, self-indulgence, and lust clung to the walls and posts. It was the smell of her skin. Always lazy, she'd rolled up her dirty clothes and tucked them away without washing them, and now their smell filled the poorly ventilated room. In the end, I couldn't stand it and began to use the sofa in the atelier; but I didn't sleep well there, either.

In early December, three weeks after Mother's death, I made up my mind to resign. It was decided that, for the company's convenience, I'd work to the end of the year. I arranged it by myself, without consulting anyone, and so they didn't know at home. I relaxed a little at the realization that I had to endure only one more month. In my spare time I read and took walks, but I was still careful to stay away from dangerous areas. One night I was so bored I walked as far as Shinagawa. I thought I'd kill time by watching a movie starring Matsunosuke, but when I entered the theater they were showing a Harold Lloyd comedy. The young American actresses on the screen brought back too many memories, and I had to leave. I mustn't see any more Western movies, I told myself.

It was a Sunday morning in the middle of December. I was in bed upstairs (I'd recently returned to the attic because the atelier was too cold), when I heard the sounds of someone moving around downstairs. That's odd, I thought; the door was locked. . . . Then I heard familiar footsteps coming straight up the stairs, and before I had time to be frightened a cheerful voice called out, "Hello." Throwing open the door, Naomi stood before me.

"Hello," she said again. She looked at me blankly.

"What do you want?" I said coolly, without getting up. She had a lot of nerve to come like this.

"Me? I came to get my things."

"You can take your things, but how did you get in?"

"Through the front door. I have a key."

"Leave the key when you go."

"All right."

I turned my back to her and said nothing. For a while she noisily wrapped bundles near my bed. Presently I heard the squeak of a sash being undone. She'd moved to a corner of the room where I could see her and, with her back to me, was changing into a fresh kimono. I'd noticed her clothes immediately when she came into the room. She was wearing a common silk garment I'd never seen before, and apparently she'd been wearing it for days, because the collar was dirty and the knees protruded. When she'd unwound her sash, she took off the dirty silk kimono and stood in an equally soiled muslin underrobe. She picked up a silk crepe underrobe that she'd taken out, draped it over her shoulders, twisted her body and let the muslin robe slide to the floormats like a discarded skin. Over the crepe robe, she put on one of her favorites, an Ōshima kimono with a tortoise-shell pattern, and wound a red-and-white checked undersash tightly around her torso. Just as I thought she was about to put on the outer sash, she turned toward me, sat on the floor, and began to change her socks.

The sight of her bare feet tempted me more than anything else. I tried not to look, but I couldn't help it. Of course she was doing this deliberately. Wiggling her feet, she watched my eyes closely. When she finished changing, however, she bundled up the clothes she'd taken off, said, "Bye," and dragged her bundles toward the door.

"Hey, aren't you going to leave the key?" It was the first thing I'd said.

"Oh, that's right." She took the key out of her handbag. "I'll put it here. But I can't possibly carry everything at once so I might be coming again."

"You don't need to; I'll send it all to Asakusa."

"But I don't want it sent to Asakusa. I'm making other arrangements."

"Where shall I send it, then?"

"I haven't decided exactly where, yet . . ."

"If nobody comes within the month, I'll send it to Asakusa anyway. You can't leave it here forever."

"All right, I'll come right back for it."

"Now listen carefully. Send someone with a car so he can carry it all at once. I don't want you to come yourself."

"All right." And she left.

I thought I had nothing to worry about, but several days later, at about nine o'clock in the evening, I was reading the evening paper in the atelier when I heard someone putting a key into the front door.

25

"WHO'S THERE?"

"It's me." The door flew open with a bang, and a large,
black shape like a bear burst into the room from the darkness outside. Whipping off a black garment and tossing it
aside, an unfamiliar young Western woman stood there in
a pale blue French crepe dress. The exposed arms and
shoulders were as white as a fox. Around her fleshy nape,
she wore a crystal necklace that glowed like a rainbow; and
beneath a black velvet hat pulled low over her eyes, the tips
of her nose and chin were visible, terrifyingly, miraculously
white. The raw vermilion of her lips stood out in contrast.

"Good evening," she said. When she took off her hat, the
first glimmer of recognition flashed across my mind. As I
studied the face, I finally realized that it was Naomi. I
know it sounds strange, but that's how much Naomi's appearance had changed. It was her face that deceived me
most. Through some magic, her face was utterly changed,
from the color of her skin and the expression of her eyes to

the profile and features themselves. Even after she'd removed her hat, I might still have thought that this woman was some unknown Westerner if I hadn't heard her voice. Then there was the terrifying whiteness of her skin. Every bit of rich flesh protruding from the dress was as white as the flesh of an apple. Naomi wasn't dark as Japanese women go, but she couldn't have been this white. When I looked at her arms, exposed almost to the shoulder, I simply couldn't believe that they were the arms of a Japanese. Once when I saw a brass band opera at the Imperial Theater, I was captivated by the whiteness of the Western actresses' young arms. Naomi's arms were just like those—in fact, they seemed even whiter.

Swaying in her soft blue dress, Naomi trotted unceremoniously toward me in high-heeled, patent leather shoes decorated with fake diamonds. (These are the Cinderella shoes that Hamada mentioned, I said to myself.) Looking strangely flirtatious, she kept one hand on her hip as she proudly sashayed up to me. I sat dumbfounded.

"I've come for my things, Jōji."

"Didn't I tell you to send someone and not to come yourself?"

"But there wasn't anybody to send."

Naomi was in constant motion during this exchange, though her face was grave. She tried standing with her legs pressed tightly together, then with one foot forward. She tapped the floorboards with her heels, and with each move her hands changed position. Her shoulders were drawn up, every muscle in her body was taut as wire, and all her motor nerves were in action. In response, my optic nerves tensed as I took in every movement and every inch of her body. When I examined her head, I could see why she looked so different. She'd cut the hair at her forehead to a length of two or three inches, aligned the tips perfectly and draped the hair like a shop curtain in bangs over her forehead, just as Chinese girls do. She wore the rest of her hair in a flat, round bun that covered her head from her crown to her earlobes, like the huge, floppy beret that the god Daikoku wears. This was a completely new hair style for her, and it changed the contours of her face almost beyond recognition. Continuing to study her face, I saw that the shape of her eyebrows was different, too. In their natural state, they were thick and broad and stood out in bold relief on her face; but tonight they formed thin, hazy arcs, around which showed a blue razor-trace. These devices I recognized immediately, but I couldn't figure out the magic behind the color of her eyes, lips, and skin. The eyebrows had something to do with the Western cast of her eyes, but there must have been some other trick as well. I guessed that the secret was in her eyelids and lashes, but I couldn't be certain exactly what the trick was. Her upper lip was divided in the middle, just like a cherry petal. The redness of her lips had a fresh, natural luster unlike that produced by ordinary lipstick. As for the whiteness of her complexion, it appeared to be the natural color of her skin; there was no trace of white makeup. And if she had used it, she had to have applied it to her entire body, because not only her face, but her shoulders, arms, and even the tips of her fingers were uniformly white. I had the feeling that this mysterious girl might be not Naomi herself, but Naomi's spirit, transformed somehow into an apparition of perfect beauty.

"You don't mind, do you, if I go upstairs for my things?" the apparition said. Judging from the voice, it was Naomi after all, not a ghost.

"All right. . . . I don't mind, but . . ." Clearly I was flustered. I added shrilly, "How did you open the door?"

"How? With a key."

"But you left your key here."

"Oh, I have lots of keys, not just one." A smile came sud-denly to her red lips, and she gave me a look that was both coquettish and derisive. "I didn't tell you before, but I made lots of keys, so it doesn't bother me if you take one of them."

"But it bothers me to have you coming so often."

"Don't worry. As soon as I've taken away all my things, I won't come even if you tell me to." Spinning around on her heels, she went clattering up the stairs and into the attic room.

How many minutes passed? Leaning back on the atelier sofa, I waited idly for her to come back down. Was it less than five minutes, or was it a half-hour, an hour? I have no sense of how much time passed in this interval. I was only conscious of Naomi's form lingering as a rapturous feeling of pleasure, like a memory of beautiful music—the high, pure song of a soprano, reverberating from some sacred realm outside this world. It was no longer a question of lust or love—what my heart felt was a boundless ecstasy that had nothing to do with these. I considered again and again. The Naomi of tonight was a precious object of yearning and adoration, utterly incompatible with Naomi the filthy harlot, the whorish Naomi, given crude nicknames by so many men. Before this new Naomi, a man like me could only kneel and offer worship. If her white fingertips had touched me even slightly, I'd have shuddered, not rejoiced. To what could I compare this feeling, so that my readers will understand? For example, a man comes to Tokyo from the countryside and, on the street, chances upon his daughter, who had run away from home when she was very young. The daughter, now a fine city woman, doesn't recognize the seedy farmer from the countryside as her father, although he recognizes her. But their social stations are so vastly different now that he can't go up to her. Astonished and overcome with em-barrassment, he steals away. Consider the mixture of loneliness and gratitude that he experiences at that moment. Or, a man who's been rejected by his fiancée is standing on the wharf at Yokohama five or ten years later, when an ocean liner docks and the returning passengers disembark. Unexpectedly, he sees her among them, apparently back from a trip overseas. But he lacks the courage to approach her— he's still a poor scholar, whereas she has lost all trace of her uncultured youth. She's become a fashionable lady accustomed to Parisian life and the luxuries of New York, and there's a gap of a thousand miles between them. Consider the self-scorn that the rejected scholar feels at that moment, mingled with the gratification he feels at her unexpected success.

These comparisons don't explain my feelings completely, but perhaps they give at least an idea. In any case, Naomi's flesh until now had been stained with indelible blots from the past. But when I saw Naomi tonight, the blots had been erased by her angelic white skin; what before had been disgusting even to think of was now turned on its head, and I felt that I was unworthy to be touched by her fingertips. Was this a dream? If not, where had Naomi learned such magic? Where had she mastered sorcery? She, who two or three days before had been wearing a cheap, soiled kimono?

I heard her come clattering energetically down the stairs; the fake diamonds on the toes of her shoes stopped in front of me.

"I'll be back in two or three days, Jōji," she said. Though she stood facing me, she maintained a distance of three feet between us and wouldn't let even the hem of her breezy dress touch me. "I just came for a few books this evening. I couldn't possibly carry all those big things on my back, especially dressed like this."

My nose detected a faint but familiar scent. Aah, that scent—it evoked in me thoughts of lands across the sea, of exquisite, exotic flower gardens. It was the scent of the dance teacher, Countess Shlemskaya. Naomi was wearing the same perfume.

Whatever Naomi said, I could only nod in response. Even after her form had vanished again into the darkness of night, my sharp sense of smell pursued her gradually fading fragrance as one pursues a phantom.

26

MY READERS are probably anticipating, from the progression of events so far, that Naomi and I soon got back together again, and that our reconciliation was not a miracle, but a natural development. This was, in fact, the end result; but it took more trouble to achieve than you might think. In the process I often made a fool of myself, and expended a good deal of futile effort.

It was no time at all before Naomi and I were again speaking amicably to each other. The reason is that she came to pick up something the next night, too, and the night after that, and every night thereafter. Each time she came, she went upstairs and returned with a bundle; but it was always just a token, some tiny thing that would fit into a small crepe wrapper.

"What did you come for tonight?" I'd ask.

"This? It's nothing, just a little thing," she'd answer vaguely. "I'm thirsty, could I have a cup of tea?" Then she'd sit down beside me and chat for twenty or thirty minutes.

"Are you staying somewhere near here?" I asked one evening as we faced each other across the table, drinking black tea.

"Why do you ask?"

"There's nothing wrong with asking, is there?"

"But why? What do you plan to do when you find out?"

"I don't plan to do anything, I'm just curious. Where is it? You can tell me, can't you?"

"No, I won't tell you."

"Why not?"

"I'm not obliged to satisfy your curiosity. If you want to know so badly, then follow me. You're good at playing private eye."

"I won't go that far. But I think you must be staying somewhere in this neighborhood."

"What makes you think so?"

"You come every night and take something with you, don't you?"

"Just because I come every night doesn't mean I live in the neighborhood, you know. There are such things as trains and cars."

"Then you go to the trouble of coming a long way?"

"Well . . . ," she said evasively. "Are you saying I shouldn't come every night?" Deftly she changed the subject.

"No, that's not what I mean. Besides, what can I do? Even when I tell you not to come, you come barging in anyway."

"That's true. If you tell me not to come, I'll just come more often. I'm perverse that way. . . . Are you afraid to have me come? Is that it?"

"Well, yes, a little."

She threw back her head so that her pure white chin thrust forward, opened her red mouth, and screamed with laughter. "Don't worry. I'll be good. What I'd really like is to forget all about our past and just be friends with you. All right? There's nothing wrong with that, is there?"

"I don't know; that sounds strange, too."

"What's strange about it? Why is it strange for people who used to be married to become friends? What an old-fashioned way to think. Really, I don't care even *this much* what happened in the past. I could still seduce you—right here—if I wanted to. It'd be simple. But I promise not to do anything like that. It'd be a pity to make you waver now, when you're so determined."

"You feel sorry for me. Is that why you're saying 'Let's be friends'?"

"No, that's not what I mean. You just have to be firm, so I won't pity you."

"That's what's so fishy about it. I am being firm, but I might start to waver if I spend time with you."

"You're so silly. Then you don't want to be friends?"

"Well, no, I guess I don't."

"In that case, I'll tempt you. I'll crush your determination." She grinned at me with a peculiar expression that was neither joking nor serious. "Which do you choose—to have a nice, clean relationship as friends, or to be seduced and get into trouble again? I'm blackmailing you tonight."

I wondered why on earth she was making this proposal. I felt certain she had some ulterior motive in coming to see me every evening. It wasn't just to tease me. First we'd be friends; then she'd win me over little by little until we became man and wife again without her having to surrender. . . . Was that what she had in mind? If this was her real intention, there was no need for such a complicated stratagem. I'd agree right away. I don't know when I became aware of it, but I knew that I wouldn't say no to any chance for us to be man and wife again.

"But Naomi, what's the point of our becoming just friends?"

I might have said to broach the subject, choosing my time carefully. "Wouldn't it be better if you went one step further and agreed to be my wife again?" But looking at Naomi tonight, I didn't think she'd respond well if I opened my heart and appealed to her this way. "Nothing doing," she'd say. "Just friends, or nothing." Once she saw through me, she'd press her luck and make fun of me. I wouldn't enjoy that kind of treatment; and anyway, if her real object was not to come back to me but to keep her freedom, trifle with a lot of other men, and add me to their number, then I'd have to be especially careful what I said. Since she wouldn't even tell me exactly where she was living, I had to assume that she still had a man. If I took her as my wife the way she was, I'd come to grief again.

Then an idea came to me. "All right, let's be friends. I don't want to be blackmailed." It was my turn to grin at her. If we were friends, I'd gradually learn what her real objective was. If there was any decency left in her, there'd be an opportunity later to open my heart and convince her that we should be together again. Then I could get her to be my wife under more favorable conditions—this is what I had up my sleeve.

"Do you agree, then?" she said, peering at me a little uncomfortably. "But we're just going to be friends, Jōji."

"Of course."

"No improper thoughts for either one of us."

"Of course not. I wouldn't have it any other way."

She laughed her usual snorting, nasal laugh.

After that, Naomi came even more frequently than before. As soon as I got home from work, she'd come flying in like a swallow. "Jōji, won't you take me to dinner tonight? You can do that much, can't you, since we're friends?" Then she'd gorge herself at a Western restaurant, at my expense. Or she'd come in late on a rainy night, knock on the bedroom door, and say, "Are you in bed? If you are, don't bother getting up. I came to spend the night." Then she'd go into the next room, lay out the bedding, and go to sleep. Sometimes when I got up in the morning I'd find her there, fast asleep. And every time she opened her mouth she'd say, "We're friends, remember."

At the time, it often seemed to me that she was a born prostitute. Though she was fickle by nature and thought nothing of baring her skin to any number of men, she also knew how to hide her flesh; she never let a man glimpse even the smallest part unnecessarily. To conceal the skin that is so readily available to all—this, if you ask me, is the harlot's instinctive desire for self-preservation. A harlot's skin is her most important attraction, her "merchandise." Sometimes she must guard it more fiercely than any virgin, lest the value of that main attraction diminish. Naomi knew exactly what she was doing. In front of me, her former husband, she kept herself under tight wraps. This is not to say that she was always modest and discreet. She deliberately changed clothes in my presence; while she was changing she'd let her under-robe slip with an "Oh!" and, putting her hands on her shoulders to cover herself, run into the next room. Or, returning from the bath, she'd sit in front of the mirror and begin to expose herself. Then, as if she'd just noticed me, she'd say, "Oh, Jōji! You shouldn't be here. Go away." When she wasn't displaying herself like this, the bits of her flesh that she did let me see now and then—the area around her neck, an elbow, a calf, or a heel—were the merest glimpses; but they were enough for me to see that her body was even glossier and more beautiful than before. In my imagination I often stripped the clothes from her body and gazed tirelessly at its contours.

"Jōji, what are you staring at?" she said once, as she changed clothes with her back to me.

"I'm looking at your figure. Somehow it's even younger and fresher than it used to be."

"Disgusting. You shouldn't look at a *lady's* body."

"Of course I can't see it, but I can tell from the kimono. Your hips always did stick out, but they've gotten plumper, haven't they?"

"They have; my hips are getting bigger. But my legs are perfectly straight and slim."

"Your legs always were straight. They used to come right together when you stood up. Do they still?"

"Yes, right together," she said, pulling the kimono around her and snapping to attention. "Look, they're right together."

I remembered a statue by Rodin that I'd seen in a photograph.

"Jōji, do you want to see my body?"

"If I did, would you show it to me?"

"I couldn't do that. We're just friends, aren't we? Now go away until I finish changing." She slammed the door as though she were flinging it against my back.

Naomi was always whetting my desire like this and luring me to the brink, but then she'd throw up a rigid barrier beyond which she wouldn't step. A glass wall stood between us: no matter how close I thought I'd gotten, there was no penetrating that final barrier. If I recklessly put out my hand, it would hit the wall; I might fret with impatience, but I couldn't touch her skin. Sometimes Naomi seemed about to remove the barricade. Ah, maybe it's all right now, I'd think; but when I drew closer, the wall was still there.

"Jōji, you've been a good boy," she'd say in mock seriousness. "I'll give you a kiss." Though I knew very well that she was taunting me, I'd respond when she offered her lips; but then she'd escape in the nick of time and blow a puff of air into my mouth from a distance of two or three inches.

"That's a friends' kiss," she would say with an ironic smile.

This peculiar greeting she called a "friends' kiss," in which I had to settle for her breath instead of her lips, got to be a habit with us. As she left she'd say, "Bye, I'll come again," and hold out her lips. I'd stick out my face and hold my mouth open, as though I were using an inhaler. She'd blow a puff of air into my mouth, and I'd gulp it down hungrily, with my eyes closed, letting it reach deep into my chest. Her breath was moist and warm and had a sweet, flowery fragrance that seemed incredible coming from a human being. (I realize now that she had secretly put perfume around her mouth to tempt me, but of course I didn't know about this trick at the time.) I often thought that perhaps even the internal organs of such an enchantress were different from those of other women, so that the air passing through her body to her mouth took on that bewitching fragrance.

I became increasingly distracted and confused; she could twist and wrench my mind any way she liked. By this time, I was no longer in a position to insist that we be officially married, or to say that I didn't want to be trifled with. Of course, if I'd really been so afraid of her enticements, I could just have avoided her, since I must have known from the beginning that it'd turn out this way; I was only fooling myself when I said that I was trying to ascertain her real motives, or waiting for the right opportunity. Though I said I was afraid of her temptations, the truth is that I looked forward to them. Yet these temptations never went beyond the silly game of friends that she kept playing. It was a scheme to tantalize me even more, I thought. She would tease me until I couldn't stand it any more, and then, when she thought the time was ripe, she'd rip off the mask of "friendship" and make the devilish advances of which she was so proud. She'll make her move soon, I thought; she's not a woman to hold back. If I went along with her scheme, fetched when she said "fetch," sat when she said "sit," and performed all the stunts just as she commanded, I'd finally get the prize. Every day I wriggled my nose in anticipation, but things weren't about to turn out as I expected. Will she finally take off the mask today? I thought. Will she make her move tomorrow? But when the day came, she always escaped by a hair.

Presently, I began to fret in earnest. I was constantly off guard, as if to say, "I can't wait like this any more. If you're going to tempt me, do it fast." I exposed my weak points. Finally *I* began to tempt *her*, but she refused to listen.

"Jōji! What are you doing? What about our promise? I didn't expect that," she'd scold, looking at me the way a mother looks at a naughty child.

"I don't care about our promise. I can't . . ."

"No! We're just friends!"

"Don't say that, Naomi . . . please . . ."

"What a pest! I said no! But I'll give you a kiss instead." She gave me her usual puff. "There, all right? You'll have to be satisfied with that. Even that much might be more than friends ought to do, but since it's you, I'll make a special exception."

This "special" caress did nothing to calm me down, however. On the contrary, it had an extraordinary power to stimulate me.

As each day ended unsuccessfully, I grew more and more exasperated. For some time after she'd gone sailing out like the wind, I'd be unable to do anything but get angry with myself and pace around the room like a caged animal, violently taking out my frustration on anything within reach.

I was tormented by frenzied attacks of what might be called male hysteria. Since she came every day, the attacks also came at the rate of one a day. To make matters worse, my hysteria was not of the usual sort—I didn't cheer up when the attack was over. On the contrary, when I'd settled down,

I would recall the tiniest parts of Naomi's anatomy even more clearly and tenaciously. It might be a glimpse of her foot, peeking out from the hem of her kimono as she changed; or her lips, only two or three inches away as she blew a kiss. They rose before my eyes in retrospect even more vividly than when they'd been shown to me in reality; and when I expanded my daydreams by following the lines of her lips or her feet, then other parts of her body—ones I hadn't seen in reality—came miraculously into view, like an image on a negative, until, suddenly, a figure resembling a marble statue of Venus appeared in the depths of my bewildered heart. My head was a stage wrapped in a curtain of black velvet, and on the stage stood a single actress, named Naomi. The spotlights poured illumination onto the stage from every direction and enveloped her swaying, white body in a powerful halo, setting her off from the pitch-darkness around her. As I concentrated my gaze, the light that blazed on her skin burned more and more brightly. At times it drew close enough to singe my eyebrows. Certain parts of her body were enlarged with the greatest clarity, like close-ups in a motion picture. In their terrifying capacity to arouse my carnal feelings, these images were no different from the real thing. All that was lacking was the ability to touch with my hand; in every other respect, the images were more full of life than the reality was. If I looked for too long, I began to feel dizzy; all the blood in my body rushed to my head; my pulse quickened. Then there'd be another attack of hysteria, and I'd kick the chair, yank down the curtains, smash vases.

My delusions grew more frenzied every day. I only had to close my eyes, and Naomi's image would appear. Often, remembering her fragrant breath, I'd look up at the sky, open my mouth, and take a gulp of air. Whenever I longed for her lips, whether I was walking down the street or closed up in my room, I'd look skyward and begin gulping. I saw

Naomi's red lips everywhere I looked, and every breath of air seemed to be Naomi's breath. Naomi was like an evil spirit that filled the space between heaven and earth, surrounding me, tormenting me, hearing my moans, but only laughing as she looked on.

"You're acting funny these days, Jōji. Is something wrong?" Naomi asked when she came one evening.

"You bet there's something wrong, the way you keep me dangling."

"Mmmm . . ."

"What do you mean, 'Mmmm'?"

"I, for one, plan to stick to our promise."

"For how long?"

"Forever."

"It's no joke. I'm going crazy."

"I'll give you a tip, then. You ought to try pouring cold water over your head."

"Listen, really, you . . ."

"There you go again! When you look at me like that, I just feel like teasing you more. Don't come so close. Stay farther away and don't let a finger touch me, if you please."

"All right, then, give me a friends' kiss."

"I will if you're good. But won't it make you feel crazy afterwards?"

"I don't care. I can't worry about those things any more."

27

T H A T evening Naomi seated me across the table so
that "not a finger would touch" her and, happily watching
the frustration in my face, chattered away late into the night.
The clock struck twelve.

"I'm going to spend the night, Jōji," she said in her usual
bantering tone.

"By all means. Tomorrow's Sunday and I'll be home all
day."

"But remember, just because I'm staying doesn't mean I'll
do what you want."

"That goes without saying. You're not a woman to do
what anyone else wants."

"You wish that I were, though, don't you?" She snickered.
"You go to bed first. Try not to talk in your sleep." Once I
was in my room upstairs, she went into the next room and
locked the door. Needless to say, I was so preoccupied with
the next room that I couldn't get to sleep. There'd been none
of this foolishness when we were married, I said to myself;

she was always here beside me. The thought filled me with chagrin. Beyond the wall, Naomi was busily—perhaps deliberately—making the house shake as she spread her quilts, took out the pillow, and got ready for bed. I could tell exactly when she undid her hair, when she took off her kimono, and when she put on her nightgown. Then she threw back the covers and fell onto the mattress with a thud.

"What a racket," I said, half to myself and half for her benefit.

"Are you still awake? Can't you get to sleep?" she replied immediately from beyond the wall.

"I'm going to have a hard time getting to sleep. There's a lot on my mind."

"I have a general idea what's on your mind, without you telling me," she chortled.

"It really is peculiar, though. There you are right on the other side of this wall, and I can't do anything."

"There's nothing peculiar about that. Isn't that how it was a long time ago, when I first came here? We slept just like this in those days."

She's right, I thought; there was such a time; we were both so pure then. . . . I was getting sentimental, but it did nothing to calm my passion. On the contrary, I could only think of the powerful bond that joined us to each other. I could never part with her, I felt.

"You were so artless in those days."

"I still am. You're the one who's artful."

"Say what you please; I'll chase you anywhere."

She chortled again.

"Hey!" I pounded on the wall.

"What are you doing? This house isn't out in the middle of a field, you know. Please try to be more quiet."

"This wall's in the way. I want to knock it down."

"What a lot of noise. The mice are on a rampage tonight."

"What do you expect? This mouse is hysterical."

"I don't like elderly mice."

"Go on, I'm not an old man. I'm only thirty-two."

"And I'm nineteen. When you're nineteen, thirty-two is elderly. Why don't you get another wife? I won't say anything. Maybe your hysteria would go away."

Whatever I said, Naomi just laughed it off contemptuously. Presently she said, "I'm going to sleep now," and began to produce fake snores. Soon it seemed that she'd really gone to sleep.

When I woke up the next morning, Naomi was sitting by my pillow in a revealing nightgown.

"Are you all right, Jōji? Last night was pretty bad, wasn't it?"

"These days I've been having attacks of hysteria like that. Were you frightened?"

"It was fun. I want to make you do it again."

"I'm all right now; I've recovered completely. Say, it's a beautiful day, isn't it?"

"It is. Why don't you get up? It's past ten. I was up an hour ago and went for a morning bath. I just got back."

I looked up at her from where I lay. A woman fresh from the bath—her true beauty comes not when she's just gotten out, but after fifteen or twenty minutes have passed. After a hot bath, the skin of even the most beautiful woman will look blotchy for a time, and the tips of her fingers will be red and swollen; but when her body has cooled to its proper temperature, her skin will begin to take on the translucent quality of hardening wax. Naomi, having been exposed to the outside wind on her way back from the bath, was now at the most beautiful moment. Her delicate skin, though still moist, was a pure, vivid white, and around her breasts, hidden under the collar of her kimono, was a shadow like lavender watercolors. Her face was glossy, as though a membrane of gelatin had been stretched across it. Only her eyebrows were still wet. Above them, on her forehead, the cloudless winter sky was reflected in pale blue through the window.

"Why should you want to take a bath so early in the morning?"

"That's none of your business. Oh, it felt so good."

She patted around her nose with both hands. Suddenly she thrust her face down in front of my eyes.

"Look! Do I have a mustache?"

"Yes."

"While I was out, I should've gone to the barbershop for a shave."

"But you don't like to shave, do you? Didn't you say that Western women never shave their faces?"

"It's different now. In America they all shave their faces these days. Look at my eyebrows. American women all shave them like this."

"Is that why your face has looked so different recently?— why the shape of your eyebrows has changed?"

"That's right. But it's a little late for you to be noticing now." She looked preoccupied. "Jōji, are you really over your hysteria?" she asked abruptly.

"Yes, why?"

"If so, I want to ask a favor. It's too much trouble to go to the barber now. Would you shave my face for me?"

"You're only saying that to give me another attack of hysteria, aren't you?"

"No, I'm making a serious request. You could do that much for me, couldn't you? Of course it'd be awful if you had another attack and I got cut."

"Why don't you shave yourself? I'll lend you a safety razor."

"That wouldn't work. It's not just my face. I'm going to shave the back of my neck down to my shoulders too."

"Why shave there?"

"Oh, you know. When I wear an evening gown my shoulders are exposed." She uncovered her shoulders just a little. "Here, I'm going to shave this far. I can't do it myself." Hastily, she covered her shoulders again. Though I knew it was just a trick, I found the temptation hard to resist. She didn't want to shave her face; she'd gone to the bath just to set me up. I understood this perfectly well, but shaving her skin would be a totally new challenge. Today I'd be able to look at her skin up close; I'd be able to touch it. The thought took away my courage to refuse.

While I warmed water in the gas heater, transferred it to a metal washbasin, and changed the blade in the Gillette, Naomi moved the table close to the window, stood a small mirror on it, sat down on her knees with her bottom between her feet, and wrapped a large white towel around her collar. Going around behind her, I moistened the bar of Colgate soap and was about to start shaving when she said, "Jōji, I don't mind if you shave me, but there's one condition."

"A condition?"

"That's right. Nothing especially difficult."

"What is it?"

"I don't want you to use this as an excuse to pinch me all over with your fingers. You have to shave me without touching my skin."

"But . . ."

"No 'buts.' You don't have to touch me. You can apply the soap with a brush, and you'll be using a Gillette razor. In a barbershop, the assistants don't touch you if they're any good."

"I don't like being lumped together with barbers' assistants."

"None of your cheek! I know how much you want to shave me. But if you'd rather not, I won't force you."

"It's not that I don't want to. Let me shave you, please.

We've gone to all this trouble to get ready." There was nothing else I could say as I gazed at Naomi's hairline, exposed where she'd pulled back the collar of her robe.

"Do you accept my condition, then?"

"Yes."

"Absolutely no touching."

"I won't touch."

"If you touch me even a little, I'll call it off right there. Now, put your left hand on your lap."

I did as I was told. Then I began to shave around her mouth, using only my right hand.

With her eyes fixed on the mirror, she let me shave her. Spellbound, she seemed to be savoring the pleasurable sensation of the razor's caress. I could hear her steady, drowsy breathing, and I could see the carotid artery pulsing beneath her chin. I was close enough to her face now to be pricked by her eyelashes. The morning light shone brightly in the dry air beyond the window; it was bright enough for me to count the pores in her skin, one by one. I'd never before scrutinized, in such a bright place, at such leisure, and so minutely, the features of the woman I loved. Seen this way, her beauty had the grandeur of a giant. It forced itself upon me with volume and substance. The fearfully long slits of her eyes; the nose, as prominent as a splendid building; the two lines rising sharply between her nose and mouth; and beneath the lines, the richly, deeply chiseled, red lips. This was the miraculous matter known as "Naomi's face," the matter that was the cause of my lust. It was strange and wonderful to consider. Unconsciously, I took up the brush and desperately raised a lather on the surface of the matter. It moved only quietly, unresistingly and with a soft resilience, however much I churned the brush around.

The razor in my hand crawled down the gently sloping skin

like a silver insect, from the nape to the shoulders. Her full back, as white as milk, rose high and broad into view. She'd seen her own face, but did she know that her back was so beautiful? Probably not. I knew better than anyone else; I'd washed this back every day in the bath. Then, too, just as now, I'd raised a lather with the soap. This back was a landmark of my love. My hands, my fingers had frolicked joyfully in this chillingly beautiful snow; they'd trod here freely and happily. Perhaps some trace remained even now. . . .

"Jōji, your hand's shaking. Get a grip on yourself." Naomi's voice came out of the blue. I realized that my head was ringing, my mouth was parched, and my body was trembling. "I've gone mad," I thought. As I fought it back with all my strength, my face went hot, then cold.

But Naomi's mischief didn't end there. When I'd finished shaving her shoulders, she rolled up her sleeve, lifted her elbow, and said, "Now under the arms."

"What? Under the arms?"

"That's right. One has to shave under the arms when one wears Western clothes. It's rude if it shows, isn't it?"

"You're cruel!"

"Why am I cruel? What a funny man. Make it fast—I'm feeling cold after my bath."

In that instant, I threw the razor aside and sprang at her elbow. I should say, I snapped at her elbow. She firmly repulsed me with the elbow, as if she'd been expecting this. But my fingers touched somewhere—they slid on the soap. With all her strength, she pushed me again toward the wall.

"What are you doing!" she cried sharply as she stood up. I looked at her face. Maybe it was because all the color had drained from mine: her face, too, was ghastly pale.

"Naomi! Naomi! Don't tease me any more! I'll do anything you tell me!" I had no idea what I was saying. I just jabbered on frantically, as though delirious with fever. Naomi stood there like a post, silent, unblinking, staring at me in total astonishment.

I threw myself on my knees at her feet.

"Why don't you answer? Say something! If you won't, then kill me!"

"Lunatic!"

"Is it wrong to be a lunatic?"

"Who wants to associate with a lunatic?"

"Then let me be your horse. Ride on my back as you used to. At least do that much!" I got down on all fours.

For a moment, Naomi seemed to think that I really had gone mad—for that moment, her face was gray, and there was something close to terror in her eyes as they remained fixed on me. But then, with a bold, audacious look, she leaped savagely onto my back.

"Satisfied?" She spoke like a man.

"Yes, that's good."

"Will you do whatever I say?"

"I will."

"Will you give me as much money as I need?"

"I will."

"Will you let me do whatever I want, and stop poking your nose into every little thing?"

"I will."

"Will you stop calling me 'Naomi' and call me 'Miss Naomi' instead?"

"Yes."

"For sure?"

"Yes, for sure."

"All right. I'll treat you like a human, not a horse. Poor thing."

Soon Naomi and I were covered with soap. . . .

. . .

". . . Now we're finally man and wife. I won't let you run away again," I said.

"Did it bother you that much, to have me run away?"

"Oh, it did. For a while I thought you weren't going to come back."

"Now do you see how frightening I can be?"

"Only too well."

"Then you won't forget what you said a little while ago, will you? You'll let me do whatever I want. You can say 'man and wife,' but I won't stand for a rigid, strait-laced marriage. I'd run away again."

"It's 'Miss Naomi' from now on."

"Will you let me go dancing?"

"Yes."

"And can I have lots of friends? You won't complain the way you did before?"

"No, I won't."

"I'm not seeing Ma-chan any more, though."

"You've broken with Kumagai?"

"I have. That hateful person. From now on, I'm going to spend my time with Westerners. They're more fun than Japanese."

"That fellow in Yokohama, named McConnell?"

"I have lots of Western friends. And there's nothing sinister about McConnell, you know."

"Well, I wonder . . ."

"That's what's wrong with you. You're so suspicious. If I say it's so, just believe me. All right? Now! Do you believe me or not?"

"I believe you!"

"There's something else. What do you plan to do after you leave the company?"

"I was going to go back to the country if you abandoned me, but I won't now. I'll dispose of my property in the country and bring it here in cash."

"How much will it come to?"

"I can muster up about two or three hundred thousand."

"Is that all?"

"That's enough for the two of us, isn't it?"

"Can we live in luxury and take it easy?"

"Well, we can't just take it easy. You can, but I plan to open an office and work independently."

"I don't want you putting all that money into your work. You'll have to set aside enough to keep me in luxury. All right?"

"Yes, all right."

"Will you set aside half, then? If it's three hundred thousand, then one hundred and fifty thousand; and if it's two hundred thousand, then one hundred thousand?"

"You're not leaving anything to chance, are you?"

"Naturally. I'm setting the conditions first. All right? Do you agree? Or are you unwilling to go that far to have me for your wife?"

"Of course I'm willing."

"If you're unwilling, just say so. It's not too late yet."

"I agree, I agree."

"There's one more thing. We can't go on living in a house like this. I want to move to a big, modern house."

"Yes, we will, of course."

"I want to live in a Western house on a street where Westerners live, a house with a beautiful bedroom and dining room, a cook, a houseboy . . ."

"Do you suppose there are houses like that in Tokyo?"

"Not in Tokyo; in Yokohama. There's one for rent on the Bluff in Yokohama. I went to see it the other day."

That's when I realized that she'd devised a careful scheme. From the beginning, she'd made careful plans and lured me on.

28

T H R E E or four years have passed since then.

. . .

We moved to Yokohama and rented the Western house
that Naomi had already found on the Bluff; but soon, growing more and more acccustomed to luxury, she said the
house was cramped, and so we bought a house in Hommoku,
furniture and all, that had been occupied by a Swiss family.
Subsequently, everything on the Bluff was lost to fire in the
great earthquake, but much of Hommoku was spared. Aside
from some cracks in the walls, our house suffered hardly any
damage at all. There's no telling in what disguise good for-
tune will come. We're still living in the same house today.

As I'd planned, I resigned from the company in Ōimachi,
disposed of my property in the country, and, with several
former classmates, formed a limited partnership for the manu-
facture and sale of electrical machinery. I don't need to go
to the office every day; my friends do most of the actual work,

in return for my having made the biggest investment. But for some reason, Naomi doesn't like to have me in the house all the time, and consequently I make the rounds reluctantly once a day. I leave Yokohama for Tokyo at around eleven o'clock in the morning, show my face for two or three hours at the office in Kyōbashi, and return home at about four o'clock.

I used to be a very hard worker and an early riser, but these days I never get up before nine-thirty or ten o'clock. As soon as I'm up, I tiptoe in my nightclothes to the door of Naomi's bedroom and knock quietly. Being even more of a sleepyhead than I am, she'll sometimes be half-asleep at that hour and reply with a faint "hmm," and sometimes she'll be sound asleep. If there's a reply, I go in and say good morning; if not, I turn away from the door and go straight to the office.

It was Naomi's idea to sleep in separate rooms. A lady's boudoir is sacred, she said; even a husband mustn't invade it without permission. She took the biggest room for herself and assigned me the small room next to it. Actually, the two rooms don't adjoin directly. Between them are a lady's bath and toilet, through which one has to pass to go from one room to the other.

Naomi stays in bed drowsily until after eleven o'clock, smoking or reading the newspaper. Her cigarette is Dimitrino slims; her newspaper, the *Miyako*. She also reads magazines like *Classic* and *Vogue*. Actually, she doesn't read them; she studies the photographs of Western designs and fashions. Her room, open to the east and south, gets very bright early in the morning. The Hommoku coast lies right below her veranda. Naomi's bed is placed at the center of her room, which is large enough to hold as many as twenty mats, if arranged in the Japanese style. It isn't your ordinary, cheap bed: originally from an embassy in Tokyo, it's fitted with a canopy and white gossamer curtains. Naomi seems to sleep more soundly since we bought it; she stays in bed even longer than she used to.

Before she washes her face in the morning, she takes black tea and milk in bed while the amah prepares her bath. She rises, goes straight to the bath, then lies down again for a while and has a massage. After that she does her hair, polishes her nails, works on her face with scores of lotions and implements, and ponders which kimono to wear. It's about one-thirty by the time she reaches the dining room.

After lunch, she has virtually nothing to do until evening. She always does something in the evening, whether she's invited out, invites someone in, or goes to a hotel dance. When the time comes, she makes herself up again and changes her kimono. It's especially serious when there's a ball. She goes into the bath and, getting the amah to help, applies white makeup to her entire body.

Naomi's friends have changed frequently. Hamada and Kumagai stopped coming altogether. McConnell seemed to be her favorite for a while, but he was soon replaced by a man named Dugan. After Dugan came a friend named Eustace. This person was even more disagreeable than McConnell. He was very good at ingratiating himself with Naomi. Once I got so angry I slugged him at a ball. That started an uproar; Naomi sided with Eustace and shouted, "Lunatic!" at me. I went berserk and chased Eustace. They all held me back, yelling, "George! George!" (My name is Jōji, but Westerners call me "George.") Eustace stopped coming to the house after that; but Naomi imposed a new condition on me, and I had to submit to it.

Needless to say, there have been new friends since Eustace, but I've grown so docile that it surprises even me. It seems that once a person has a terrifying experience, the experience becomes an obsession that never goes away. I'm still unable to forget the time Naomi left me. Her words echo in my ears: "Now do you see how frightening I can be?" I've known all along that she's fickle and selfish; if those faults were removed, she would lose her value. The more I think of her as fickle and selfish, the more adorable she becomes, and the more deeply I am ensnared by her. I realize now that I can only lose by getting angry.

There's nothing to be done when one loses confidence in one's self. In my subordinate position, I'm no match for Naomi at English. No doubt she's gotten better as she uses it. She seems strangely Western as she goes around spouting English and making herself agreeable to the ladies and gentlemen at a party. Often I can't make out what she's saying. Her pronunciation has always been good. Sometimes she calls me "George."

The record of our marriage ends here. If you think that my account is foolish, please go ahead and laugh. If you think that there's a moral in it, then, please let it serve as a lesson. For myself, it makes no difference what you think of me; I'm in love with Naomi.

Naomi is twenty-three this year and I am thirty-six.

Junichirō Tanizaki was born in 1886 in Tokyo, where his family owned a printing establishment. He studied Japanese literature at Tokyo Imperial University, and his first published work, a one-act play, appeared in 1910 in a literary magazine he helped to found.

Tanizaki lived in the cosmopolitan Tokyo area until the earthquake of 1923, when he moved to the gentler and more cultivated Kyoto-Osaka region, the scene of his great novel *The Makioka Sisters* (1943–48). There he became absorbed in the Japanese past, and abandoned his superficial westernization. His most important novels were written after 1923; among them are *Naomi* (A Fool's Love) (1924), *Some Prefer Nettles* (1929), *Manji* (1930), *Arrowroot* (1931), *Ashikari* (1932), *A Portrait of Shunkin* (1933), *The Secret History of the Lord of Musashi* (1935), modern versions of *The Tale of Genji* (1941, 1954, and 1965), *The Makioka Sisters, Captain Shigemoto's Mother* (1949), *The Key* (1956), and *Diary of a Mad Old Man* (1961). By 1930 he had gained such renown that an edition of his "Complete Works" was published. He received the Imperial Prize in Literature in 1949 and died in 1965.

A NOTE ABOUT THE TRANSLATOR

Anthony H. Chambers was born in Pasadena, California. He received his B.A. from Pomona College, his M.A. from Stanford University, and his Ph.D. in Japanese literature from The University of Michigan. He is Associate Professor in the Department of Asian Languages and Literatures at Wesleyan University.